Lara Temple was three years old when she begged her mother to take the dictation of her first adventure story. Since then she has led a double life—by day she is a high-tech investment professional, who has lived and worked on three continents, but when darkness falls she loses herself in history and romance...at least on the page. Luckily her husband and her two beautiful and very energetic children help her weave it all together.

Discover more at millsandboon.co.uk.

THE EARL
SHE SHOULD
NEVER DESIRE

Lara Temple

MILLS & BOON

First Published in Great Britain 2022
by Mills & Boon, an imprint of HarperCollins*Publishers* Ltd,
1 London Bridge Street, London, SE1 9GF

www.harpercollins.co.uk

HarperCollins*Publishers*
1st Floor, Watermarque Building,
Ringsend Road, Dublin 4, Ireland

The Earl She Should Never Desire © 2022 Ilana Treston

ISBN: 978-0-263-30165-6

04/22

MIX
Paper from
responsible sources
FSC® C007454

This book is produced from independently certified FSC™ paper
to ensure responsible forest management.
For more information visit www.harpercollins.co.uk/green.

Printed and Bound in Spain using 100% Renewable Electricity
at CPI Black Print, Barcelona

To my dear friends Nina and Neta.

I've always been in awe of your adventurous spirits and giving souls; now even more so as you bravely battle breast cancer.

How lucky I am to have you in my life.

Chapter One

'Lord, what fools these mortals be.'
—A Midsummer Night's Dream,
William Shakespeare

Birmingham—May 1818

Lily smoothed out Annie's letter and went to the window to read it again by the light of the fading sun. She could light a candle, but it was a week yet before she received her wages and she preferred to be careful. Luckily her sister's large looping handwriting was a model of legibility.

Unlike her own.

Lily murmured the words aloud as she read. It was foolish, but it made Annie seem closer.

"'Lord Sherbourne is so much more pleasant than any of the men Mama and Papa tried to secure for me the previous two Seasons. He doesn't make me feel uncomfortable. He is amusing and

kind and never seems quite serious about any-
thing. And he is very handsome which is nice..."'

Kind. Nice. Handsome.

High praise indeed for a marriage of convenience. But Lily didn't want her sister to make
a marriage of convenience. The undisputed diamond of the last three Seasons deserved more
than *kind* and *nice* and not feeling uncomfortable
with the man with whom she must spend the rest
of her life.

Still, it could have been much worse.

She turned over the sheet and continued reading.

*"'Could you come to town, Lily dear? I know it
is foolish, but I'm feeling rather alone. This is such
a big step and Mama and Papa are all caught up
in Settlements and Festivities and there's no one to
talk to. Piers is down from Oxford, but it isn't the
same. Please, Lily. I need you. Your loving sister."'*

I need you.

Annie rarely played that card. She was too responsible.

Lily glanced about the tiny parlour she shared
with Eleanor, another veteran's widow. Spring had
finally arrived, but it was chilly here on the top
floor of Mrs Spratt's Boarding House for Young
Women. And damp.

It would be nice to be pampered and cosset-
ted in a house full of servants and crackling fire-

places. She could explore London as she had with Tim the one time he'd been on leave during his last year of the war. Or rather as she had on her own as Tim had been rather busy with his cronies enjoying a whole different aspect of London.

There had been awful parts to that year, but she'd come to love her time in London.

She raised her head. The last three stairs creaked like an off-key organ grinder. One day they would collapse entirely and either she or Eleanor would find themselves on a pile of debris in the Ames's back parlour.

Eleanor entered the room and heaved a sigh of relief as she sank into a chair by the empty fireplace, tossing her limp straw bonnet on to the table with weary disgust.

'They were protesting outside Birkin's so I had to walk all the way around by Needles Alley. I really must remember to have my boots resoled. I don't know what's worse—the cold or the ache.'

Lily handed her a blanket one of the soldiers' wives had knitted last winter and went to pour tea from the kettle hanging on the hob. It wasn't very hot, but then the room wasn't much warmer than outside and Eleanor took it gratefully and nodded at the sheet of paper Lily had set aside.

'A letter?'

'From my sister. She is to be married.'

'Oh, how wonderful. Has the star of the Season finally fallen in love?'

Lily considered the letter.

'Well, it doesn't sound like love. Affection, more like.'

'Even better. Love is all too often a prelude to disappointment. Look at us.'

Lily smiled.

'Point taken. She hopes I shall join her in London for a period. Now that term is over I might go.'

'Oh, you lucky beast! London! I haven't been there since I was a child. There was a trip to Astley's to see the horses and I remember a man fell into the Thames. It was very exciting.'

Lily laughed. 'Watching a man drown? This is a side of you I haven't encountered yet.'

'He didn't. It was low tide and he fell face down in the mud. It took five men to drag him up to the road. They were all drunk and singing and kept slipping and tripping over each other. It was better than Astley's. Oh, I do envy you. I love working at Hope House, but sometimes I wish I could...' She rubbed her knee absently. 'I don't even know what any longer. Travel, I suppose. Or not. Something...different.'

'I know.'

They both fell silent for a moment, then Lily shook herself.

'Will you manage on your own?'

'Goodness, Lily. Of course not. I shall shatter to smithereens the moment you and your portmanteau are out the door.'

Lily smiled.

'I know I'm being silly. I'm merely… I'm quite certain my mother would rather I not come.'

'Devil take her, then. You have allowed that shrew to chase you out of your home twice before—do not let her stop you from spending some time with your sister before she weds.'

'To be fair she didn't chase me away the first time, I eloped. And the second time…'

'…she made your life so miserable you leapt at my suggestion to join me as a teacher at Hope House with the alacrity of a horse bolting from a burning barn.'

'I leapt at the suggestion because I wished to be doing something useful, not wasting away in Kent while my mother pricked at me with her needle-sharp tongue. Teaching veterans and their children to read and write and do sums is by far the most useful thing I have done with my life.'

'Yes, yes, but I won't allow you to turn the conversation. Your mother is a shrew, but you are no longer dependent on her. You are not going for her, but for Annie.'

'And Piers will be there, too.'

'Well, then, that's settled. I know how much you miss your brother and sister, mooning over their ridiculously short letters as if they were *billets-doux*. You go spend your time with them and ignore your nasty mama. That's what I do with my father. The moment the sermons begin I paste a smile on my face and nod every ten breaths while I dream of knights and corsairs. Works like a charm. How shall you reach London?'

Lily reviewed her savings and her budget for the month. And her wardrobe. She looked down at her serviceable boots. They were perfect for her work in Birmingham, but for London...

Eleanor made a strange sound, between a sigh and a curse.

'Oh, please don't start *thinking*, Lily Walsh. Just go. Annie needs you. And just think—London! This requires a toast. Where is that bottle of claret Mr Featherstone gifted us for Christmas?'

'London,' Lily repeated obediently as Eleanor rooted around the cupboard for the bottle and glasses and again the image of walking through the Park and visiting Somerset House and... 'I shall go. Devil take my mother.'

'By all accounts he probably will.' Eleanor laughed and raised a glass with a sensible finger of claret in a salute. 'Go live a little, Lily Walsh.'

Chapter Two

London

London was clearly extending her a warning.

Lily bent her battered umbrella into the wind and turned up Brook Street. How on earth would she know which house was Number Twenty-Three? Half of them had no numbers at all.

Thunder roared at her and carriages sped past, wheels throwing up mud and worse. She ought to have hailed a hackney cab, but she'd been stubborn and now she would arrive looking like a drowned rat, if she arrived at all. Her boots were soaked and her portmanteau hung painfully on her arm. She'd packed too much which was foolish because by the look of the women she'd seen at the posting inn, her clothes were a decade out of fashion at least...

She stopped before a narrow house in dark brick. Number Twenty-Three. It was just like the others on either side: respectable, with a bay window and two storeys above, all shielded by heavy curtains. Somehow she'd expected her mother to have insisted on something grander.

Lily stood for a moment, her heart thumping.

'Watch yourself, miss.'

A man pushing a wheelbarrow covered in barrels was trying to get by on the narrow pavement and she rushed up the stairs. There was no turning back now.

The maid who opened the door stared at Lily, her round, freckled face framed by a linen cap.

'Miss Lily!'

'Hello, Ailish.' Lily smiled at Annie's maid. She'd turned from a girl to a young woman since Lily had seen her in Kent two years ago. Ailish visibly shook herself, her gaze moving down and up.

'Why, you're soaked through, Miss Lily! Oh, dear, oh, dear, you'll catch your death. Come through to the back parlour, there's a fire on and we'll soon have you dry. You leave that right here and I'll have Henry Footman see to it.'

Lily set her ragged portmanteau down with a sigh and followed the little whirlwind down the narrow corridor by the stairs. The house was no grander inside than out, but she supposed houses leased for the Season rarely were. Certainly not on her parents' budget, whatever her mother's pretensions.

'Is my sister home?'

'Well, of course, miss. It is not gone ten o'clock. They're all abed. They were at Lady Cratthock's ball yesterday and only back past midnight, Mr Devenish and Mr Piers not being one for late nights.'

'I don't remember Anne being one for late nights either,' Lily said as she struggled out of her sodden coat.

'Well, needs must,' Ailish replied philosophically.

'Lily.'

Lily turned at the familiar voice, her empty stomach clenching. Her mother had a lovely voice, deep and musical. It took Lily years to realise what was wrong with it. The same thing that was wrong with her mother—it lacked warmth.

'Hello, Mama.'

Mrs Devenish signalled to Ailish who hurried out with Lily's belongings.

'Didn't you receive my letter, Lily?'

Lily concentrated on undoing the wet tangle of her bonnet ribbons, but it had snagged a lock of her reddish-brown hair and refused to give.

'No, Mama. I haven't received a letter from you since last August.'

'Well. Goodness. What a pity. We weren't expecting…'

'I sent a letter saying I was coming a week ago, Mama. I know you had it because Annie mentioned you'd received it in *her* letter confirming my arrival.'

'Well, yes, but that is it, you see. What with all the preparations for the wedding we have been at sixes and sevens. This really is not a good time for you to visit. We shan't have any time to entertain you.'

'I don't require entertaining, Mama. I came because Annie…' Lily finally managed to tug open the ribbons and took a deep breath. Best not lay it at Annie's door. '…because Annie is to be married and I wished to spend some time with her before she is swept away by her new husband.'

Mrs Devenish went to the table and fiddled with the pink and mauve flower arrangement.

'Nevertheless…'

Whatever further objections her mother was about to raise were left unsaid as the door flew open and Annie rushed straight into Lily's arms, which opened of their own accord at the sight of her sister.

'Lily! Oh, how wonderful you are here. I missed you so!'

'Anne. A little more decorum, if you please.'

Annie withdrew abruptly at their mother's admonition, but she took Lily's hand and drew her towards the fire.

'Your gloves are wet! Take them off and come warm yourself. Was the coach awful? I kept thinking while we were at the ball you were already aboard the mail and crammed in on all sides by people reeking of cabbage and onions while I was dancing and sipping champagne… Well, lemonade, really, but still I felt hideously guilty all of a sudden. Do tell me it wasn't horrid.'

Lily laughed and lied as she peeled off her gloves.

'It wasn't in the least horrid. I slept much of the way.'

Annie smiled, but shook her head.

'I'd wager you didn't. You must be exhausted. Ailish is putting your room in order and will bring some cocoa and then you shall sleep and if the weather permits this afternoon you shall come with me and Lord Sherbourne for a turn in the park. I want you to meet him right away.'

Mrs Devenish had been watching them with a look they knew well and had both learned to ignore, but now she intervened.

'I doubt Lord Sherbourne would care to take up two passengers in his curricle, my dear Anne. Those fashionable men's sporting vehicles are not built for excessive weight.'

Annie's hand tightened on Lily's.

'No, Mama. Why don't we go upstairs so you may change, Lily?'

Lily followed her upstairs, thankful to leave their mother's baleful glance behind. She'd not expected to be welcomed and she'd long ago denied her mother the power to hurt her, but the sullen resentment was already wearing at her, pushing her back into her memories of unhappier times.

That comment about her weight had worn thin long ago, along with her. Years of following the drum and war and loss and counting pennies had done what her mother's insults had failed to do. She would never be reed thin like Annie, who was very much like Piers in both looks and build, but those same years of being surrounded by soldiers had taught her that many men didn't agree at all with her mother. They'd seemed to appreciate her generous hips and breasts and had no compunction telling Tim so. At first she'd worried he might take offence at their comments, but he always seemed pleased her attributes were appreciated.

The guest room connected to Anne's was narrow but pleasant and out of the corner of the wet window Lily made out the tips of dark green trees which was more than she could see from the murky panes of her window in Birmingham. The rain had stopped and as she wiped the condensed moisture from the pane with her sleeve, the sun heated up the edges of the clouds and then burst through with a patch of freshly pressed blue.

Lily smiled. She was exhausted and ached inside and out, but the sun was coming out and she was so happy to see Annie.

'I'm so happy I came, Annie. I missed you awfully.'

Annie hugged her from behind and started unfastening Lily's dress, as Lily had used to do to her when they were girls.

'I don't care what Mama says, Lily. Marcus… Lord Sherbourne…won't care about his silly curricle and appearances. He isn't like that at all which sometimes makes Mama quite cross though she hides it with that laugh of hers, you know, the one full of air. I cannot wait to hear what you think of him.'

'I am certain I shall like him if you do, love.'

'I hope so. He can be quite charming, but sometimes… Anyway, Piers thinks he's a capital fellow. They've been talking in Latin or Greek or something. You know how people tend to set poor Piers aside because he has no polite conversation and he slips off into some corner, but Marcus brought him out of himself immediately. It was the first thing I noticed about him when we met last year when Piers was down after Hilary term.'

Clever man, thought Lily. He must have realised compliments would get him nowhere with

Annie. The surest way to her heart was through Piers.

'That is an excellent sign indeed. How long has Piers been here this time?'

'He is attending a series of lectures in town for his fellowship and he comes and goes between here and Oxford. It has been grand having him here though he hates all the to do that Mama adores and he tries to evade all the balls and what not. It is apparently a great honour to be allowed to take part of these lectures and he's as happy as a pig in swill. Not even Mama's hints can get him down. Oh, I'm so happy you're here. I missed you so.'

There was a crack in her voice as she wrapped her arms around Lily.

She hugged her back, holding Annie in silence until her sister's body eased a little. Lily had almost forgotten Annie was two inches taller than she. She'd always felt larger, and it was rather strange to be enveloped in a hug by one's younger sister.

She was also thinner than Lily remembered. Her ribs were firm under Lily's hand and the point of her hip bone pressed into Lily's waist.

A shaft of worry coursed through her, but she reminded herself she'd also been a bundle of nerves before she'd eloped with Tim. Though that had been a little different. They'd both been penniless and on their way to join his regiment in Portugal, against the express wishes of their families, not to marry a wealthy member of the social establishment who could provide Annie and her family with every comfort and advantage.

Finally, Annie pulled away and tugged out her handkerchief from her sleeve and blew her nose.

'What did you mean Mama's hints to Piers?' Lily asked. 'Surely she cannot want him to marry so young. He is barely nineteen.'

'Oh, not marry. Find a position. She has been pressing him to go with Marcus to meet people at the Foreign Office. She used to hint to Marcus as well, but somehow she doesn't any more. But Marcus likes Piers so perhaps she thinks Piers can convince him even if she cannot.'

'Lord Sherbourne is in the Foreign Office?'

Annie frowned.

'Well, he is something there, though I don't quite know what. Piers's friend's elder brother is under-under-secretary there or some such thing and says Marcus is very well regarded there. Perhaps Marcus held an appointment there before he inherited the title? The title is a very old one and he's very wealthy so he has no need to support himself, you see.'

Oh, yes. She saw. No wonder Mama was *aux anges*.

'I do know he is very well travelled,' Annie

continued, 'He seems to know all the foreigners in town. His mama came from some Italian nobility or something.'

Annie fell silent as Ailish entered with a tray of cocoa and a plate of bread and butter. Lily's mouth watered and she swallowed and thanked Ailish.

When the maid left Annie said a little brusquely, 'Now you eat and rest and then you shall come driving with us.'

Lily laughed and shook her head.

'I shall meet your nice, kind lord, but I shan't go driving, Annie. My wardrobe isn't up to London standards.'

'Hmmm. Well, we shall have to do something about that—'

'Annie,' Lily interrupted. 'I am fine as I am. I did not come here to gad about, but to spend time with you.'

'Well, there is nothing we can do about it today, in any case. But at the very least you will meet him when he comes to collect me. I think you shall like him. Most people do once they drum up the courage to approach him. He is very… What did Piers call him? *Laissez-faire*. That's it.'

Chapter Three

'Lily, this is Lord Sherbourne. Marcus, this is my darling sister, Mrs Lily Walsh.'

Lily looked at the man standing with her parents by the drawing room windows and couldn't help searching the room for another person before returning her gaze to her sister's fiancé.

This was Lord Sherbourne?

Kind? Nice? *Laissez-faire?*

In her mind she'd constructed a softer version of her father—a tall man with light brown hair and a slightly round but still handsome face, sleepy blue eyes and a pleasant smile.

She could not have been further from the mark. The only aspect she'd approached getting right was his height. Otherwise this man would make a fine model for a villain of the Gothic novels Eleanor delighted in. Not the ugly, twisted kind, but the handsome Count who appears too good to be true and then is discovered to be precisely that.

Hair dark as pitch and deep-set eyes were strik-ing enough, but his face was beautifully built—lean, sharply carved, and with two deep lines bracketing a rather hard mouth. As he turned a lit-tle she saw his eyes were a strange golden amber, or that might be a trick of the afternoon sun cut-ting in from the west. Tigerish eyes. Even more perfect for one of Eleanor's villainous counts.

Nice?

And then he smiled and moved towards her, a subtle sliding motion that went well with her tiger image. Or was it a panther? Both.

'Mrs Walsh. Finally, we meet. Your sister speaks of you often.'

Lily glanced at her sister. 'You cannot be that short of topics to discuss, surely.'

She'd meant it lightly, but regretted the words the moment they were out. Mama hated her sad attempts at humour and she could see the twitch of annoyance on her mother's face. But Annie's betrothed laughed, perhaps out of politeness.

'Not at all. I happen to find fascinating people fascinating.'

Lily's eyes widened at this compliment to both her and Annie in one short sentence. She had no idea if he was either nice or kind, but she rather thought he *was* quite clever.

The smile receded a little in his gaze, giving way to a considering look. Probably assessing her viability as his future sister-in-law. That line of thought would not end well. She wanted to move away a little and held her hands still against the need to fidget.

Then he turned and smiled at Annie. 'Anne tells me you won't be joining us for a drive this afternoon, but perhaps tomorrow?'

'Oh, Lily isn't here to gallivant about, Lord Sherbourne,' Mrs Devenish intervened. 'She is merely here to spend time with Annie before she must return to Bi…her home. She is a widow, as you know.'

Lord Sherbourne bowed slightly and directed a most charming smile at her mother.

'I am aware of that, Mrs Devenish. But surely after five years even the strictest sticklers won't condemn Mrs Walsh for joining her family in their activities while in town. In fact, they might find it rather peculiar if she does not.'

Ho! Lily had to press her lips together to stop her smile. That cut her mother off at the knees.

Not that she wanted to join her family in their activities, but it was rather pleasant to see her mother routed, especially as it was done in such a pleasant, almost teasing tone. Amazingly her mother did not seem to mind. She was actually smiling.

'And tomorrow's excursion is quite unobjectionable,' Lord Sherbourne continued. 'Merely a visit to the museum. I promised Piers a private viewing of the new Assyrian exhibition before it opens to the public next week.'

Gratification and dismay warred their way across her mother's face, but she had her own weapons and she didn't hesitate to use them.

'That would be quite the thing. One needn't dress in the first stare of fashion for the museum.' Her gaze moved pointedly over Lily's dark grey merino wool dress and Lord Sherbourne's followed suit, his long lashes lowering. It really was like being watched by a prowling cat.

'Naturally not. As long as we are rather better dressed than some of the exhibits. I never understood the insistence of the ancients on wearing bedsheets. They might be cool in hotter climes, but only imagine the scandal if someone steps on your train.'

Annie giggled and Mrs Devenish flushed lightly and something resembling a titter escaped her. Lily smiled as well at the image of a host of denuded Romans grabbing desperately for their slipping togas. At least until she caught Lord Sherbourne's gaze. Suddenly her fertile imagination placed him right in the middle of the Roman Forum where he was doing nothing to hold up the sheet slipping from a pair of very broad shoulders.

The image was gone as swiftly as it came and she turned away, clearing her throat.

Mrs Devenish swept forward and took Lily's arm. 'Come along, my dearest Lily. Let us see if you have anything in your portmanteau suitable for such a delightful excursion. Annie, you two had best be off to the Park before the weather turns yet again. I would hate for your lovely new promenade dress to be ruined.'

Chapter Four

My dearest Lily.

Marcus had rarely heard a less endearing endearment.

He guided his team through Hyde Park Gate into the park. The gravel roads were still a little soggy at the edges, but the horses were happy for the change of surface and twitched their tails in enthusiasm.

Anne had not said much since they left Brook Street. He could feel the force of her thoughts and consternation. She was always like this after her mother revealed her unpleasant side. It was one of the reasons he'd chosen to offer for her. His theory about people was that they either resembled their mothers or were reactions to them. Anne was clearly in the latter camp.

He'd thought the elder sister would be in the 'resembling' camp and that Anne's adoration of her older sister was merely for a lack of better options, but even in that brief introduction he could tell she too was very different from Mrs Devenish and just as different from Annie as well. He wasn't at all certain how she fit into the Devenish family mould.

'I wish Lily would have come,' Anne said with uncharacteristic abruptness. 'I should have insisted.'

'Perhaps. Though that might have set up your mother's back and made it even harder for your sister in the end.'

She looked up at him, her lovely face framed by one of Madame Fanchot's creations of pale pink satin and white ribbons.

'True. I wish they could rub along better. It is so…distressing.'

'If they haven't before, they are unlikely to change now. Try not to worry about it. Your sister certainly didn't seem overly upset by your mother's charming comments. I almost felt sorry for your mother. It must be frustrating to take such care dipping her arrows in poison only for them to bounce off your sister's thick hide.'

She giggled.

'It wasn't always thus. Lily used to snap at her and there were battles royal, but that was before she married Tim when she was seventeen and left with him.'

'Seventeen!' The report he'd commissioned on the Devenishes hadn't mentioned ages. 'That's barely old enough to wipe one's nose, let along elope and follow the soldiers' drum into war.'

'Well, I was twelve at the time, so she seemed much older. And many women marry at seventeen.'

There was a touch of defiance there. He'd already noted that Anne was very protective of her rebellious sister's image. He liked that about her as well. Loyalty was useful.

'Perhaps they do, but they shouldn't. Of my four sisters, only one married before the age of twenty and she is by far the most miserable.'

'Oh.'

He sighed. Perhaps marital disappointment was not the best topic to introduce, for either of them.

'Tell me some more about her,' he invited, 'so I don't say anything foolish to her tomorrow.'

Anne straightened, her face brightening.

Good. That should keep her occupied for the remainder of the drive. Thank God she was so easy to appease. Top of his list of characteristics he did *not* wish his future wife to possess was sulking. Followed by resentfulness *à la* Mrs Devenish and the propensity to become bored and needy. He might have to marry, but he was damned if he would saddle himself with a clinging ivy complete with vicious thorns.

He listened idly to Anne's recounting of her sister's life and character. It was a tale that told as much about Anne as it did about her sister. Anne's confidence in her sister's love had begun early and held firm in the face of their mother's not very maternal regard. The rituals of motherhood had somehow revolved around the three siblings rather than the parents—bedtime stories, sickbed vigils, lessons, long walks in the Kent woods complete with a fortress built of branches and blankets.

It sounded like an idyllic childhood, but for the fact that Mr and Mrs Devenish were notably absent from her account. Marcus rather thought that might have been a very good thing. For Anne at least. If her sister was her elder by five years, her experience was probably quite different. There would have been no siblings to hide away with or act as shields.

'Is she envious of you?' he asked when Anne fell silent.

'Lily? Of *me*?'

The incredulity sounded rather overdone and he pushed back at a rippling of impatience. There were a couple of characteristics on his *Not Wife Material* list that Anne unfortunately was blessed with. Saintliness and naiveté were not as bad as resentment and viciousness, but sometimes they could be just as annoying.

'Why not? You are younger, prettier, the diamond of the last three Seasons with half a dozen offers under your belt and your parents' favourite child. Most women in London are envious of you. Why not her?'

She flushed bright red and he regretted his bluntness. It was not his object to make her, or him, uncomfortable. Quite the opposite.

'You're wrong about her.' Her voice shook a little, her fingers tightening on her reticule. 'She isn't envious because she does not wish to be me. If anything, it is the other way around. Lily may have had a hard life, but at least she has *lived*…' Her gaze shot to his and was immediately withdrawn. She stared at the ribbons of her reticule, running them through her fingers again and again.

Well, well, where had that come from?

He was saved from responding by the plop of several fat raindrops. He hadn't even noticed the clouds were gathering again.

'We'd best turn back before your beautiful promenade dress is ruined.'

She tugged the ribbons harder and he wished he hadn't used her mother's phrase. He was becoming sloppy in his old age. He sighed and guided his team towards the road. The sooner they were married and Anne settled into her new role at Sherbourne Hall, the better. He was growing tired of playing society games.

He didn't believe in heaven, but if by some chance it existed and his mother was watching, he very much hoped she appreciated his sense of filial duty.

Chapter Five

‘It's not polite to stare,’ said the half-dressed woman in a deep voice, not looking up from her game of knucklebones.

Lily managed not to squeak, barely. She'd been so caught up in her thoughts she hadn't heard anyone approach. One would think someone as large as Lord Sherbourne would make more noise.

‘I wasn't staring. I was admiring.’

‘Hmmm. I can see why. Very nice.’ He came to stand beside her, inspecting the marble statue of the kneeling young woman with her hand outstretched in mid-play, her expression far away from the mundane child's game she was playing.

‘Admiring the *craftsmanship*,’ she emphasised, but now she couldn't help but fix her gaze on the one exposed breast and the delicate folds encompassing the lithe body. Trust a man to ruin her enjoyment of a perfectly lovely piece of art with lewd comments. Not that it had been lewd, precisely. But somehow…

'The face doesn't match the body,' he stated and leaned towards the statue, bringing him a little too close and she caught his scent—warm but distant, like sunshine warming the cool pine forests up in the mountains of Spain. She wanted to move away but that would be impolite.

'What do you mean?' she asked, politely.

'Her face is very…strict. There's no character to it. All the character is in her body. Here.'

He took her gloved hand and raised it so that it blocked out the head. She stood there, her hand and his together.

If he'd meant for her to inspect the now headless statue, it wasn't working. She'd always thought her hands were unfashionably large, but his hand made hers look like a child's. It was disorienting.

'Now look only at her face.' He moved her hand lower. 'Can you see it?'

She blinked several times, clearing her own head, and tried to focus.

The statue.

She frowned. It was true. The face looked as though it had been plucked from a painting on a Grecian urn. It was formed of simple classical lines, a thin straight nose and closely crimped hair. A typical representation of Greek female beauty.

It was quite… Well, it should have been lovely, but it was…soulless.

She gave a huff of disappointment. When she'd first noticed the statue she'd thought it was different and wonderful, but now…

'What a pity.' She sighed. 'It is brilliantly done, but there is more expression in her hands than in her face. It should be as lovely and lost and dreamy as her body, but it isn't. I wonder why. He was such a skilled artist.'

Lord Sherbourne let go of her hand and walked full circle around the statue before stopping to prop himself on a pedestal holding the head of a disapproving Roman general. His stance was relaxed, one leg swinging lightly, but his face was intent, his dark hero's looks more pronounced than when he smiled.

'Perhaps he was afraid.' His gaze flickered to her and then back to the statue.

'Of what?'

'Of putting a face to the dream. He might have ended up like Pygmalion. Dreams are all well and good when kept in their corners. They tend to wreak havoc if you let them take centre stage.'

His words struck her as far more intimate than his near comment about the statue's state of undress.

'I think dreams don't like being kept in corners, Lord Sherbourne. They tend to rebel.'

He shifted a little on the pedestal and she had to fight an urge to tell him to get off it before he knocked over the priceless marble head.

'Rebellions rarely end well, Mrs Walsh.'

Ow. That struck a little too close to the bone.

'True. But most dreamers believe they will be the exception to that rule. Or perhaps like Pygmalion he *did* create that perfect statue, but then he could not bear to part with it so he made another to fulfil his commission.'

'Heavens, Mrs Walsh. You're a secret romantic.'

'You were the one who started talking about dreams and mismatched heads,' she said a little crossly. 'I was merely trying to think of a rational explanation.'

'Greek romanticism and Roman rationality. All that in such a small package. It must be crowded in there.'

She couldn't help laughing.

'It isn't polite to poke fun at my lack of inches.'

'Oh, you don't appear to lack anything. Anne said you always had this tendency to wander off. Did you find the party I assembled boring?'

Lily struggled to adjust from his ambiguous comment to his question.

'No, no, not at all. They are all very…pleasant. But looking at art when one is in a crowd and everyone telling you what they think isn't the same. Sometimes I prefer to look without thinking.'

He didn't answer. His silence was almost worse than his comments. She put on her polite smile. She really ought to return to the others. It wasn't at all proper to be standing with her sister's fiancé admiring a semi-nude statue.

'But you are quite right, Lord Sherbourne. I ought to return before Mama notices I am missing.'

He didn't smile back, just nodded slowly.

'Yes. Back into our corners.'

'Your corner is far more commodious than mine.' She couldn't help the little snap in her voice. There was something rumbling under Annie's *nice* and *kind* lord and Lily was beginning to think he wasn't quite trustworthy.

'I don't know if that is accurate, Lily Walsh, but we shan't debate it. Come. Back to the family fold for you.'

'I can find my own way.'

He shrugged.

'Very well. You go first.'

She went. Her nerves were twanging like a cat dancing on a broken violin.

She'd been enjoying herself thoroughly until he'd ruined it.

Marcus knew he ought to return to the others as well, but he was in no hurry. He glanced down at the glassy-eyed Roman general sharing his pedestal.

'She's a strange bird, isn't she, Augustus?'

Augustus ignored him and continued glaring at the bare-breasted knucklebone player with disdain. Or was it lust? It couldn't be easy facing that whimsical young woman all these years while she clearly found a child's game far more entertaining.

'Well, I think she is,' Marcus answered his own question, patting Augustus on his marble curls. 'Not what I was expecting. I miscalculated with the eligible men Anne asked me to gather for her. She clearly finds them as exciting as damp toast. One would think it is enough that I am about to save the Devenish family from financial ruin without being asked to play matchmaker, too. Ah, well. The sacrifices one makes for one's future family.'

He pushed to his feet and went over to inspect the statue more closely.

The woman's right hand was missing a finger and this flaw only made her look more poignant. It was really a pity about the face. He tried to imagine Lily Walsh's theoretical first statue that the sculptor had kept to himself, but nothing came. All he could see was this formulaic prettiness.

It reminded him a little of Anne.

He sighed and turned away, meeting Augustus's glassy gaze. Now the Roman looked mocking rather than annoyed. Marcus could almost hear his taunt:

Forty years of this at the very least, Marcus. That's what you signed up for. If you don't cock up your toes sooner.

'You're a damned pessimist, Augustus.'

Chapter Six

Marcus rapped on the side of the hackney cab and it drew to a halt.

'Change of plans, sir?'

'I'm not certain. Actually, yes, I'll alight here.'

'Here, sir? I picked you up not a dozen yards back!'

'Here.' He handed the driver double his fare and jumped down.

It was early, but Cheapside was already crowded with tradespeople and customers. There was no reason for him to have noticed a particular woman emerge from a narrow lane in Cheapside and slip into the mass of humanity pressing along the pavements. Especially not dressed in a drab grey pelisse and with her face hidden by an even drabber bonnet.

Yet he had.

'Very curious,' he murmured and followed at a discreet distance.

* * *

Lily didn't see him until he stopped right in front of her. Her heart flew into her throat, cutting off her breath. Even though there were dozens of people pressing past them like water round a boulder, for one panicked moment she felt utterly exposed.

'Lord Sherbourne! What on earth are you doing here?'

'Following you, Lily Walsh. I think the far more appropriate question is what were you doing down Carter's Lane?'

She glanced back towards the small lane with its hidden square. It was unnerving to think he had been following her. His eyes were narrowed against the glare of the early sun and she wished she had worn the crepe mourning veil she sometimes employed when she went about her business in Birmingham. She cleared her throat.

'If you must know, I was visiting friends.'

'You have friends at Hope House?'

She masked her surprise that he knew of the institution that provided shelter and services to veterans of the long years of war against Napoleon. She raised her chin, a rather futile gesture when one was being looked down upon from such heights.

'There is surely nothing wrong with that, Lord Sherbourne?'

'Nothing at all. Someone from your time in Spain?'

She really ought to lie. It was so much simpler than explaining and risking him telling her parents. But he was watching her with that same non-judgmental curiosity he'd shown at the museum and somehow lying…

'I am a teacher at the Birmingham branch of Hope House. When I knew I was coming to town I wrote to the proprietresses in London and they invited me to visit.'

A man with a wheelbarrow was pressing through the jostling crowd and Lord Sherbourne took her arm and drew her into the entrance of a dank, narrow passageway. She pulled her arm away, but he merely crossed his arms and leaned against the wall.

'Careful. Your poor coat,' she said involuntarily and he gave a faint laugh and shook his head, but didn't move from his lounging position.

'Does Anne know of this?'

'Anne and Piers do, but my parents don't, so please don't mention it. For Anne's sake.'

'What has it to do with Anne?'

'I shall be safely back in Birmingham soon, but Anne shall have to hear our parents moan about the shame of it all and be reminded half a dozen times a day not to mention it to anyone.'

'Poor Anne. Does she always bear the brunt of your misdemeanours?'

'Always. I'm a sad burden to her.'

'Strange. I rather had the impression she loved you dearly. She's rather convinced you love her as well.'

Lily's eyes burned with a suddenness that shocked her. 'Of course I do.' Her voice sounded as rough as the paving beneath her boots and she cleared her throat. 'We were always close.'

'Until you eloped.'

She nodded slowly, wondering what he was aiming for. A warning?

'She was only twelve at the time. I know she was upset that I abandoned her. But I wrote to her often.'

'And Piers was ten, wasn't he?'

'Yes… Is there an object to this catechism, Lord Sherbourne? I really ought to be returning home before…'

'Before the rest of the house wakes and you are missed. Good point. Come.'

'I can find my own way…'

He took her arm. 'We are heading in the same direction, are we not? Think of the savings on the hackney fare.'

She snorted. He likely hadn't thought about saving on anything in his life.

The press of people on Cheapside had quadrupled since her early morning arrival, but the crowd gave the tall, well-dressed man beside her a wide berth and she wasn't at all surprised to see that the moment he raised his hand two hackney cabs drew to a stop. He chose the first, tossed a coin to the second and handed her up with the same unconscious ease as he showed in their drawing room.

The world was his oyster, she thought with growing resentment and stared out the grimy window at the crowds and noise.

'Are you sulking, Lily Walsh?'

Something went pop inside her. Right in the middle of her chest. A little box flipping open. Out came the djinn. It had been too, too long since she'd been angry.

'You are annoying as all hell, Lord Sherbourne. If you choose to call wishing to shove you out of this hackney cab sulking, you are more than welcome to.'

He crossed his arms again and grinned at her descent into profanity. 'I'm a bit large for a fair shoving match, but you can have a go if it will soothe that temper of yours.'

'I don't *have* a temper.'

His brows rose. 'Is that what you tell yourself? And here I thought you were a refreshingly honest person. Life is full of disappointments.'

'I don't *lose* my temper,' she amended. Now

her voice sounded sulky even to her own ears. She added, 'You've ruined a perfectly lovely morning.'

A growl of thunder overhead was followed by flat plops of water on the thin wood of the hackney roof. Lord Sherbourne burst into laughter.

'And *you've* made it rain. We ought to market you to the Levant as a rainmaker. You'll fetch a good price.'

Her anger crumbled. He was impossible. 'They'd be disappointed. I'll have you know I very rarely sulk.'

'So I bring out the worst in you, Lily Walsh?'

'I'm afraid you do. But now I'm warned I shall watch myself.'

'That would be a pity.' He turned away, frowning at the passing streets. It was such a sharp transition she wondered if he had remembered something he had to do. She'd probably interrupted his plans in Cheapside. Whatever they had been.

'I'm sorry you had to interrupt your plans on my account, Lord Sherbourne.'

He turned back at her perfunctory statement.

'I was already done, in any case.'

'So early?'

'I'm an early riser.' He smiled, a different smile. As if he knew what she was thinking, what she wanted to ask… She ought not to prod, but she did anyway.

'I didn't know anyone in the *ton* rose before noon at the earliest.'

'We're all sad fribbles, aren't we?'

His tone was sorrowful and she realised she'd not only sounded sulky again, but he'd sidestepped her line of enquiry. She now had to ask a direct question or let it slide. His smile widened a little. He knew she was struggling, damn him.

But what would she do if she asked and he told her the truth? He wasn't yet accountable to Annie, betrothal or not. If he had been visiting a mistress or…or a brothel, that was his prerogative.

Still, it would hurt Annie. But as he'd said, life was full of disappointments.

He reached into his coat and pulled out a package wrapped in brown paper and untied the string to reveal a long wooden box inlaid with mother-of-pearl flowers.

'Open it.'

She took it without thinking. It was warm and for some reason that made her want to hand it right back to him.

'I didn't mean…'

'It's meant for Anne. Look inside.'

She didn't want to, but she had no choice now. She undid the metal clasp and raised the lid. A small silver locket inlaid with tiny pearls surrounding a single amethyst lay on a bed of claret-coloured silk. The box was almost more elaborate than the locket.

'It was my mother's, given to her by the previous Lady Sherbourne. She kept miniatures of her children inside. Unfortunately, my mother died four years ago, but she had always meant to give it to her daughter-in-law when I wed. There's an excellent jeweller up the road here. I had it cleaned and the clasp fixed.'

She touched her finger to the shining clasp and withdrew her hand abruptly. It felt warm as well. Or perhaps she was. One day the miniatures of Anne's children with this man would be placed inside this silvery capsule of life.

Shame and embarrassment and something else were all tangling inside her. The swaying of the hackney wasn't helping. She swallowed.

'It's beautiful. She will love it.'

'Not too simple?'

She could feel the pressure of his gaze on her profile, but didn't look up from the locket.

'No. Simple but beautiful. And even more so for its history. Annie will treasure it.'

'It is rather early as our wedding is not for another two months, but I like to be prepared.'

His voice was curt now. Her suspicion had probably offended him.

'I'm sorry, Lord Sherbourne. I have been impolite and you have been very gracious...'

'You haven't been impolite. You were annoyed, rightly so, at my interference with your morning plans. But in my defence I didn't have much choice once I realised it was you wandering around Cheapside.'

'I dare say you didn't. But I *can* fend for myself, you know. Birmingham is rougher yet than London and I go about there on my own.'

She closed the box regretfully and handed it back to him. He returned it to his coat pocket and continued playing with the wrapping paper.

'Can we reach a compromise?'

'About what?'

'About your activities in London.'

She sighed. 'What manner of compromise?'

'If you must go about on your own to such places, take a footman.'

'I'm afraid that won't work. I told you I don't wish my parents…'

'Then send me word and I'll supply the footman. Mine are more reliable than your parents' in any case.'

'I don't quite think that is proper either, Lord Sherbourne.'

'It is very proper. Don't argue about everything. This is a compromise.'

'Now who's becoming all huffy?'

Annoyance lost the battle to laughter in his

eyes. He shook his head. 'Anne did not tell me the whole of it. And you think *I'm* annoying.'

'Well, you are.'

'Allow me to return the compliment.'

'Fine.'

'Fine.'

She turned back to her window. She hoped he would be quiet for the rest of the drive. Though she doubted it. He seemed to enjoy the sound of his voice. She wasn't surprised when he broke first.

'Don't tell her about the locket. It is meant as a wedding gift.'

'I'm not an idiot, Lord Sherbourne.'

'Pity. You'd be far more comfortable if you were.'

'It isn't my object to be *comfortable*.'

He laughed again. 'You say that word as though it's covered in slimy slugs. Comfortable is a wonderful thing to be. It has ever been my object to be as comfortable as I possibly can.'

'And Anne is part of your *object* to be comfortable.'

He canted his head, considering. 'I suppose she is.'

He looked away again, his sharp-cut profile softened for a moment by a flash of the sun between two buildings. She had an absurd compulsion to trace that line just as she'd wanted to trace the folds of the statue's marble skirt, could almost feel the press of firm bone under his skin…the sudden softness of his lower lip…

Lily!

She turned away abruptly, breathing through her tingling lips. She very much hoped she was becoming ill because otherwise she had no excuse for such treacherous thoughts.

The hackney slowed as they turned on to Brook Street and she barely waited for it to stop before she jumped off and hurried up the stairs.

Marcus watched the door close behind his future sister-in-law.

Anne had *definitely* not told him the whole of it.

Or rather, Anne's adoration of her older sister clearly blinded her to her imperfections. Unfortunately, those imperfections were by far the most interesting parts of Mrs Lily Walsh.

He gave the driver his direction and settled back, his hand going to the box in his pocket. He ought not to have shown it to Anne's sister, but she'd clearly thought he was on his way back from some debauchery. Not that it was any concern of his if she wished to think the worst of him and he doubted she would have tattled to her sister. It wasn't her style. But she would likely worry and that might upset Anne and there was nothing wrong with showing her the locket.

Yet now he wished he hadn't. The moment he'd told her to open the box he'd wanted to stop her. Foolish. There was nothing mystical about it.

Though her reaction had definitely been disproportionate to the simple piece of jewellery. She'd glowed. Even in profile, with her long lashes shielding those all-too-seeing grey eyes, she'd seemed to shine with…something.

Something unsettling.

In fact, that best described the effect she seemed to have on her family as well. In the week since she'd arrived all members of the Devenish household had become a tad more themselves, for good and for ill. As if a watchmaker had given their keys an added little twist. He wasn't at all certain he liked the results.

Well, at least she would soon be on her way, back to teaching veterans and their children at the Birmingham branch of Hope House. No wonder her parents rarely spoke of her. Doing so might lead to questions they preferred not to answer.

Anne had only mentioned she was a schoolmistress and he'd imagined her working at some insular girls' school where the greatest challenges were confiscating unseemly novels hidden under the girls' beds and preventing flirting with the dancing master.

Hope House was as far from that tableau as they were from the Antipodes. It provided help and succour for veterans struggling to recover from the effects of war, be they effects on body, mind, or purse. He was good friends with the former officers who had established Hope House after the war and he knew it was not an easy place to visit, let alone work in.

Men who were maimed in body and soul resided there and still others came daily, often with wives and children, to receive food and work, and education to help them find their feet in a world that was struggling to accommodate them. Working there would not be for the faint of heart. He could well see why Lily Walsh would prefer to keep her parents in ignorance.

'We're here, sir,' the driver said, clicking his tongue at the horse as a large carriage squeezed by.

Marcus looked up in surprise. He hadn't even noticed they'd reached Sherbourne House. He paid his fare and jumped down, his hand closed tight on the jewellery case. He would put it in the safe and forget about it for a while.

He'd never realised becoming betrothed would bring with it so many unwelcome complications. He rather suspected this was only the beginning.

Chapter Seven

'No, Lily! You didn't,' Piers groaned, tugging at his already disordered hair.

Lily waved a white rook under his nose with a complete lack of sportsmanship.

'Look on and weep, my lad. You shall soon be naught but mulch beneath the hooves of my charger! Revenge is sweet indeed.'

Mrs Devenish shushed them from where she was playing a sedate game of cards with Mr Devenish. Neither of her children took heed of her comment other than Mr Devenish, who sighed and glanced longingly at the bookshelves before his wife recalled his attention to their game.

Marcus stretched out his legs and tried to concentrate on Anne's commentary on a play she'd attended. She was working away on a needlepoint of a garland of roses which would one day likely bloom into a lovely cushion or screen.

He shifted uncomfortably on the lumpy sofa.

The furniture in the stuffy little drawing room definitely showed the effect of being leased Season after Season to hopeful families. The room's only character was in its inhabitants. For better and for worse.

It had certainly become a little less gloomy since the elder sister arrived. Anne was relaxed and smiled more often. He liked her better like this.

The same was true of her brother, Piers. Marcus liked the boy—he was as kind as Anne and passionate about his studies, but there was also something a little lost about him. As if he was afraid to poke his nose out for air. It probably didn't help that Mrs Devenish was often impatient with her son's indecision. She tried to hide it under smiling 'encouragement', but Piers must feel her comments like acid-tipped thorns prodding him in the back.

Since Lily Walsh had arrived he, too, had bloomed. Now when Marcus visited Brook Street he'd often find the boy in some corner of the drawing room with his older sister, talking a mile a minute about his studies while Lily Walsh listened, chin on her hand and a smile lighting her face while the boy basked in her glow.

No wonder Mrs Devenish and her daughter rubbed each other the wrong way. He knew envy when he saw it. Lily Walsh might have an improving effect on her siblings and Mr Devenish, but Mrs Devenish was a whole different, and rather malodorous, kettle of fish.

'I'm still one game up on you,' Piers pointed out and Lily tossed the rook up and caught it, balancing it on the tip of her finger.

'I let you win the first game.'

'Did not! I won fair and square. You never even noticed my feint with the bishop.'

'Not notice him hiding behind the queen's skirts? I most certainly did. But I told myself, let the poor lad win a little. If I keep taking the shirt from his back, he'll slip into a decline and start writing sonnets, the poor fellow.'

'Lily! You're awful. And I would never, ever write a sonnet. I have some dignity.'

'How about limericks? Here's one for you:
There once was a boy who played chess,
who made of his pawns quite a mess.
He lost to his sister,
who said, "Look here, mister.
You've really no chance of success."'

'That's the worst limerick I've ever heard,' Piers scoffed. 'Try this on for size:
There once was a woman named Lily,
who was known far and wide as quite silly.
When she came to call,
'twas a warning to all,
to take to the hills willy-nilly.'

'Oh, Piers, you beast! That was far better than mine. You win that round.' Lily's laugh was warm and tumbling and musical and for no reason at all the hair on Marcus's nape rose.

'They're impossible when they're playing chess,' Anne said softly, looking up from her needlepoint with a smile. He forced his attention back to her. Anne looked like a painting of a young matron in her parlour. She would be just like this as a mother—calm, indulgent, but not blind.

The perfect choice.

He rose, a little too abruptly. Anne glanced up in surprise and the players stopped playing.

'Is anything wrong?' Anne asked, her voice as soft as a dandelion's fluff settling on his sleeve.

'Nothing. I merely forgot the time. I'm afraid I must leave now or be late for a meeting. My apologies. I shall call for you tomorrow to accompany you to Lady Sefton's ball.'

He bade them all farewell and left.

He was halfway to St James's before his breathing settled again.

'What did you say to chase him away, Anne Devenish?'

'Nothing,' Anne replied, more distraught now than at Lord Sherbourne's departure. 'Truly nothing unexceptional, Mama. It must be as he had said. He recalled a meeting.'

'He is a busy man, my dear,' Mr Devenish intervened. 'I hear he is often in discussions with Castlereagh and Wellington. They are preparing for the Congress about France this autumn, you know.'

This reminder of Lord Sherbourne's importance soothed Mrs Devenish a little. 'I dare say. How lovely that will be for you, Anne. To travel to France in the autumn. I hear the summers there are quite unbearable.'

'Oh, but I shan't be going with him, Mama. He shall be far too busy to attend to me.'

'He said so?' Mrs Devenish's outrage had a resurgence and poor Anne's curls set to bobbing as she shook her head.

'Oh, no. Not like that. Merely...he said that I shall be more comfortable becoming acquainted with Sherbourne Hall than in Aix-la-Chapelle.'

'Where on earth is Aix-la-Chapelle?'

'It is a city in Prussia, Mama,' Lily replied. 'It was part of France before that and part of the Holy Roman Empire before that.'

'Well, I can see why all that hopping about won't do for Lady Sherbourne.' Mrs Devenish's feathers settled a mite. 'Still, it is rather poor form of him to wed you and immediately hare off to the Continent.'

'We could always delay the wedding until his

return.' Anne's voice was tentative, but Mrs Devenish's reply wasn't.

'Absolutely not! Why, a thousand mishaps may befall him amid those Russians.'

'Prussians,' Piers corrected and was silenced with a glance.

'There shall be no talk of delays. A good wife waits for her husband. And rather than you remain alone I shall come and stay with you at Sherbourne until his return.'

Annie's eyes widened. She was too honest to hide her chagrin. Lily wondered what Lord Sherbourne would say to that.

'I think Annie had best wait until she discusses such matters with Lord Sherbourne. Don't you agree, Annie?'

'Yes. Oh, yes,' Annie sent Lily a grateful smile. She stood before her mother could continue her advance. 'Did we not say you would come with me to Madame Fanchot, Lily? I wished to see her about my costume for the masquerade ball.'

Chapter Eight

Anne sank into the hackney cab with a groan.

'I don't *want* her to come to Sherbourne. But how can I prevent her?'

'The beauty of being married is that you have someone else to blame. Tell Lord Sherbourne you don't wish her to come. He strikes me as a very slippery and resourceful man. He will arrange it.'

'Oh, I could never ask him such a disloyal thing. He shall think me quite unprincipled.'

Lily curbed her impatience.

'Sometimes you must be unprincipled to protect your principles, Annie. One of the reasons you accepted Lord Sherbourne's proposal was because you were tired of living under Mama's thumb, correct? And because you recognised he would never allow her to play him as she does Papa or Piers. Well, take full advantage of that to lay down the new rules of your life. I have little doubt Lord Sherbourne won't be in the least surprised by your request.'

Annie drew a deep breath and let it out slowly. 'Yes. You are right on all counts. I shall speak with Marcus. He will know what to do.'

Lily clasped her hands together. She ought to be happy Anne had such faith in her future husband. She *was* happy. It was merely…

'Anne. *Do* you wish to delay the wedding?'

'Of course not. Why would I? Oh, good, we've arrived. Come along. You shall adore my costume.'

Annie made a beautiful shepherdess. Though none of the shepherdesses Lily had ever seen wore such confections of billowing white and pink.

'Well? Isn't it lovely?' Annie asked, twirling and setting her many flounces and the ribbons on her tall wooden staff fluttering. 'It is horribly dear, but Mama insisted.'

'You are lovely. It is almost a pity you must wear a mask.'

'Oh, I love the idea of a mask and no one knowing you.' Before Lily could reply to that comment Annie hurried on. 'I asked Madame Fanchot if she could prepare a costume for you as well…'

'No, Annie. It is one thing having Ailish adjust your old gowns for my use, but another thing entirely to commission a new dress. Mama will make us all suffer for it.'

'But that is precisely it, Madame Fanchot very kindly said that she has some costumes sitting by that haven't been collected and she thinks one might suit you very well. It appears now I am to be Lady Sherbourne there is nothing tradespeople aren't willing to offer us for the taking.'

Lily had never heard that note of cynicism in her sister's voice and Annie herself seemed shocked. She clapped a hand over her mouth and looked about the empty dressing room.

'That was awful of me,' she whispered. 'I think I must be rather tired. And Mama…'

'I know, sweetheart. She's enough to try a saint and though you do try to be one sometimes, you aren't, nor should you be. You are allowed to be angry, you know. And hurt.'

Annie shook her head. 'Not around her. It is too…wearing.'

Lily wished she knew what Annie truly felt about her upcoming nuptials. She was clearly fond of Lord Sherbourne and he of her, but Lily had seen her deep in love four years ago when Anne almost married the son of their neighbours, John Smithson. She and John had always been touching or holding hands when they thought themselves unobserved and then they would jump apart and blush only to slip back together at the first opportunity.

They'd been so dear together and Lily had always thought that though their parents decided against the match, in time he and Anne would find each other again and follow through on their youthful love. She'd known that Anne had not corresponded with John, but through local gossip they'd occasionally heard of his being sent to one diplomatic outpost or another and Lily had watched her sister for remnants of that youthful love and seen nothing but Annie, placid and accepting.

But then she herself had regarded Tim with wide-eyed adoration at seventeen and that had not ended well at all. Young love was all well and good for poems, but it weathered ill when faced with the adversity of real life.

She shivered. Tim wasn't to blame for their marriage's failure. They'd managed well enough in the difficult circumstances of the war. The cracks had begun when Emma was born, but it was only when Emma died of the fever that their little idyll had been stripped of its varnish and exposed the rotten beams beneath.

Tim had cared for Emma, but just as he recovered from the horrors of each battle with impressive aplomb, his let-live attitude helped him move on from his daughter's death. He would reassure her that there would be other children, preferably when the wars were over.

Perhaps if he hadn't expected Lily to do the same she might have had an easier time of it, but his impatience with her need to mourn only drove the wedge deeper between them after Emma's death. They'd stayed together, but gone their separate ways in mind and mostly in body.

Lily had mourned alone, holding her pain inside just as she'd carried her babe inside. For a while she'd even hated Tim for his ability to move on, but that, too, had faded. Without Emma as a shield between them, she'd realised quite a few unpleasant truths that year. Tim was a lovely, charming man, with more enthusiasm than substance. He was rather like her father before he'd been trodden down into glumness by her mother. Her love had been a youthful fantasy built on a delusion.

Annie's love for John Smithson had possibly been the same. This alliance with Lord Sherbourne was probably far better suited to provide her what she needed in life. And if it was not deep and hot, at least it would be warm and steady.

Lily pressed her hands together. Her palms were tingling and raw as they always were before an episode, but she didn't feel the awful rushing in her ears that usually followed. Only a dull, thumping ache at her centre. It echoed in emptiness, a gong calling no one to dinner.

The seamstress entered and for a few moments the only sounds were those of rustling silk and humming as last adjustments were measured and pins slipped in place. Then the woman helped Annie undress and was off again, costume held up by the shoulders like the queen's train. Once she was gone Annie stood and stared at herself for a long moment in the tall thin mirror in the corner, but Lily wasn't certain she saw herself at all. Lily came to stand beside her and took her hand.

'Is it only Mama that is on your mind, love? Or is there something else worrying you? Is it the wedding?'

Annie gave a quick smile and moved away from the mirror and from Lily.

'I am very lucky. Lord Sherbourne is by far the nicest of the men who showed any interest in me these past three Seasons. He doesn't make me feel…uncomfortable.'

That was one hell of a criterion for marriage, Lily thought, but kept her peace.

'And he is good to me and kind and he wants children as much as I do. I think we shall manage very well together.' Annie's voice strengthened as she spoke. She glanced at Lily. 'I don't believe in anything else, Lily. What I had with John was a…a child's first glow of love. Life isn't like that.'

'I don't think it is that simple, Annie.'

'Those were *your* words, Lily.'

Lily flushed hot and hard. Had she said that? 'I didn't mean you were a child. You were seventeen. I meant you were young.'

'I was. Now I'm not.'

'Twenty-one isn't precisely old.'

'It feels so sometimes. I'm so tired of parties and At Homes and going about town. It's been three years, Lily. I want quiet. I want my own home and…'

She was braiding the ribbons on her staff, but she cast a quick glance up at Lily.

'You want children,' Lily supplied, keeping her voice very bland and level. She didn't want Annie to feel constrained from discussing something so important to her. No matter how hard it hit.

'Yes,' Annie said with relief. 'I can't explain it. I see children and I want to hug them. I love going to the park and watching them play by the lake. I imagine myself there, watching over them and loving them and having them love me. It's a different kind of love than what I had with John. It is the kind that lasts.'

Lily nodded, keeping herself still inside as she went to warm her hands by the small fireplace at the end of the dressing room. The rain hadn't stopped for two days and everything felt damp and chill.

Yes, that kind of love lasted. Well beyond the little grave in the Spanish mountains where she'd laid Emma to rest. Lily only had two years with her daughter, but Emma would be with her until her death, locked for ever in her two-year-old form, with her curly brown hair and deep grey eyes and a laugh that could make Lily smile no matter how dark the day or night.

Lily might not want to go down that path ever again, but Annie deserved that love. Those bonds. That joy. As she'd proved, even a deficient husband could supply the necessary for that purpose and Lord Sherbourne was certainly not deficient.

Annie joined her by the fire, her arm against Lily's as if apologising for pulling away earlier. After a moment she cast a quick glance towards the door and continued, 'Not that being a mother is a guarantee of being loved. Sometimes I feel dreadfully guilty I don't feel that manner of bond with Mama.'

Lily hooked her arm through her sister's and squeezed it. 'It isn't for you to feel guilty for something Mama could never provide and therefore isn't likely to receive in return, Annie. But I am certain *you* would be loved because you would love your children with all your heart.'

Annie sniffed. 'Yes. I think Lord Sherbourne would, too. Love his children, that is. That is what made me decide. I looked at him with Piers and I realised—he has that rare quality that can be there for another and yet remain whole. We needn't love each other to be comfortable, as long as we love our children. There's a comfort in that, in a way. Mama and Papa were a love match and look where they are now. Perhaps it is healthier to have no expectations.'

Annie's voice was low and rushed and Lily nodded, but she couldn't answer. She might have lost her own illusions, but she hated that Annie had lost hers.

'I wish I hadn't said a thing about John back then. He was nothing like Tim. I feel terribly guilty.'

Annie unhooked her arm from Lily's and went back to take her shepherdess's staff from the table, untangling the braided ribbons and straightening them between her fingers.

'That is foolish, Lily. I was hurt at the time, but I understood why you were wary. I thought you and Tim were perfect together, too, and it was sad to learn that it had not been a happy match by the end. But it was our parents and John's that came between us, not you. And we were neither of us daring enough to elope as you did. I dare say they were right. I was quite certain that once John became established at the Foreign Office he would seek me out. But clearly I was merely a passing fancy and we are both better off for having been denied the chance to ruin our lives. Do you think this shade of blue too dark beside the pink?'

They fell silent as the door opened and Madame Fanchot, a tall, handsome woman of about forty years of age, entered. Annie smiled and held out the ribbon.

'Do you not think a lighter shade would look better?'

Madame Fanchot inclined her head. 'I do believe you are correct, Mademoiselle Devenish. Come and see my collection and we shall choose.'

The sewing room was a bustle of activity. Three women were at work and their chatter stilled for a moment at their entrance. The room was warm and well lit, nothing like the sewing shops Lily was accustomed to in Birmingham, with their dim, narrow rooms and girls squinting over their needles in the half dark and wearing fingerless gloves to warm their hands. Apparently privilege begat privilege.

'What of this?' Madame Fanchot asked, holding a lovely blue ribbon on her calloused palm. It had a hint of lavender in it. Annie exclaimed in delight.

'How lovely! What shade is that?'

'This blue is called forget-me-not, Mademoiselle Devenish.'

Chapter Nine

'Are you certain women are allowed to attend the Academy's lectures, Piers?'

Lily stepped out of the hackney and followed her brother into a wide courtyard surrounded on all sides by dark brick buildings with white-rimmed windows.

'Quite certain. Several women were in attendance last week, though most were older and none as pretty as you.'

'Piers!' She laughed. 'Are you practising your town polish on me?'

'I'd rather practise on you than on Annie's friends. They all titter and smirk. Thank goodness she hasn't changed too much.'

'Annie is more likely to change those around her than change herself. She has a strong core. So do you, little Brother.'

He flushed and added a little gruffly, 'I'm glad you're here, Lily. If it weren't for Annie, I would have hared back to Oxford already. I can't seem to breathe right in that house. She's so lucky Marcus wants to marry her.'

Lily's hackles rose. She lowered them. 'I think he's lucky Annie wants to marry *him*.'

'Well, of course, but you know what I mean. He is far older than her and very, well, experienced. He could have married anyone, but he chose Annie.'

Lily smoothed her hackles once more. She loved Piers, but he was a tad old for hero worship.

'That is even a greater indication of Annie's worth. If he could marry anyone and he chose her, that means our sister is truly exceptional.'

Her brother grinned and guided her through a tall wooden door with glass panes decorated with coats of arms.

'You're still doing it, Lily-pad. We're old enough to fight our own battles, you know.'

'And you're too old to be preening Lord Sherbourne's feathers for him. He appears perfectly capable of doing so himself.'

'You don't like him,' Piers said, surprised.

'It isn't that I don't like him, I merely…'

Merely what? She could hardly say she mistrusted him. She had no good reason to do so. He'd been nothing but pleasant to her. If he was annoying and intrusive at times, well, so were most people she'd met since she'd arrived in London a fortnight ago.

Perhaps it was jealousy? She'd come to London hoping to spend time with Lily and yet somehow Lord Sherbourne was always underfoot. She'd hoped to have a little longer before she must share the closest person in the world to her.

He often joined them when they went for an afternoon walk in the park, or fell in with Annie's insistence that Lily join them on their drives, despite Mama's opinions about men's sporting curricles. He accompanied them on an excursion to Kew Gardens and made regular appearances at Brook Street. The only place he did not join them was at the balls her mother delighted in.

Lily watched him for signs of something other than Annie's *kind* and *nice*, and though her instincts told her there was a great deal happening under his urbane surface, none of it justified alarm.

He was always considerate of Annie and her family and if occasionally it felt as though he was laughing at all of them… Well, that might be her imagination and it certainly never felt malicious. More…indulgent. The way an adult might observe a sweet yet awkward child. Imagined or real, Lily found it, and him, increasingly aggravating.

'I think you will come to like him when you know him better. He really is a capital fellow,' Piers said as she remained silent. 'Now come along, we're early yet, but there are usually some chaps attending and always much to talk about. It's nothing like those stupid balls.'

He led her down a long wide corridor that was fusty with the smell of old books and lined with dour portraits of bewigged and paunchy men. As they passed through a double door at the end into the lecture hall she did indeed note a couple of bonnets among the crowd. A group of half a dozen men hailed and approached Piers. They were all rather young and two of them even blushed as Piers made the introductions. Lily felt very matronly.

At the first opportunity she slipped away to inspect some drawings on the far wall, leaving the young men to enjoy their company unhindered by Big Sister's shadow.

'Were the striplings being tedious?'

She squeezed her eyes shut briefly before she turned. Perhaps if Piers hadn't championed him only a few moments earlier she might even have been a little pleased to see him. As it was, she was feeling a trifle predisposed against him.

'Lord Sherbourne.' She smiled politely.

'Mrs Walsh.'

They stood for a moment in silence. It was most definitely *not* her imagination. The bastard was laughing at her.

'How *delightful* to see you here, Lord Sherbourne.'

His brows flicked and the lines beside his mouth deepened. They weren't quite dimples, but she'd noticed they sometimes were just as telling.

'May I return the compliment, Mrs Walsh? An unforeseen delight. My favourite kind. I did not know Piers had an interest in the impact of the rise of the Austro-Hungarian Empire on Continental politics.'

Her mood lifted. 'Is that what the lecture is about? He said the topic was the Phoenician influences on Etruscan pottery.'

'That is the day after tomorrow.'

'Oh, Piers.'

'Don't be hard on him. If I remember correctly the option was to pay a visit to Lady Ombersley with Anne and your parents. Isn't that why you are here as well?'

She tried not to smile. 'Guilty. Well, at least now I might remain awake for the talk. Unless the lecturer is soporific.'

'I'm afraid he might be. No offence, Dom.'

'Idiot,' said a voice behind her and she turned. Either her reflexes were useless, or Lord Sherbourne and his friends practised sneaking up on people.

For a moment she just stared. Lord Sherbourne was a handsome man, but this one snatched the breath from her lungs for a moment.

He was perfect. He was almost Lord Sherbourne's height, but though his face was also sharply hewn, it did not have Lord Sherbourne's harsh look in repose. His eyes were a deep stormy blue, his hair dark brown and touched with mahogany where the gas lights struck it.

She doubted this man would put anyone to sleep during a lecture, unless it was into a dream state. In fact, she was surprised there was not a whole horde of women filling the hall, happy for a chance to sit and stare at him for an hour or so. Or perhaps that was precisely what many of the young men were here to do.

'Mrs Walsh, may I introduce Lord Wrexham?'

The cynical bite in Lord Sherbourne's voice recalled her from her momentary reverie. She had been far too close to staring at his friend with her jaw down to her knees.

'Mrs Walsh. I hope I don't put you to sleep.' Lord Wrexham bowed politely, but he sounded bored himself, his gaze cataloguing her and moving on.

What does one say to that? she wondered. At least Lord Sherbourne had decent manners.

'Dom, this is Miss Devenish's sister,' Lord Sherbourne added, his tone lowering a little, rather the same way she spoke to her students when their thoughts wandered in class. It worked. Lord Wrexham's gaze narrowed and returned to her.

'Ah. I see. And is your reputedly beautiful betrothed attending as well, Marc?'

'I'm afraid not. Mrs Walsh was dragged here by her brother who thinks he is about to hear Frasier discussing the Etruscans.'

Lord Wrexham grinned.

Now she knew what a wickedly charming grin looked like. She rather thought she mistrusted this man even more than she did Lord Sherbourne.

'Well, at least that sets expectations low. Frasier could make birds fall asleep mid-flight.'

'That is quite a talent,' she replied, rather offended on this poor Mr Frasier's behalf. 'Imagine the savings in shot during grouse season.'

Lord Wrexham's gaze snapped back to her and the lines bracketing Lord Sherbourne's mouth quivered and deepened and the hint of a dimple appeared as well.

He had a *dimple*.

It was too annoying.

Lord Wrexham had no dimples to soften his now wolfish grin.

'An excellent point. I shall keep that in mind when next I'm hunting, Mrs Walsh.'

'You plan to bore your prey into submission?'

'I hope not, but it occurs to me you are right that boredom can be very disarming. It is hard to be on alert when one is struggling to keep one's eyes open. But hopefully I shall not put that theorem to the test this afternoon. Are you interested in politics or are you one of those lecture prowlers who gripes when they find themselves on the opposite side of an opinion?'

'The latter. I plan to frown throughout the first quarter-hour and tut at least three or four times when you present your conclusions. I might even give a telling sigh of pitying disdain that you have so clearly missed the most obvious inferences.'

'Oh, please do. In fact, I'd love to hear your version of the pitying sigh. I've been collecting them.'

She shook her head. 'Not until you've earned it. I'm not so easy with my favours.'

'My dear Mrs Walsh, I am now sorely tempted to give you reason to flaunt your full repertoire of superior disdain.' His grin retreated into a smile and something rather less prickly appeared in his gaze.

She'd won this round and he didn't even know it, she thought. Men were just schoolboys after all.

'Don't you need to go review your notes or something, Dominic?' Lord Sherbourne suggested, but Lord Wrexham tapped his head.

'I have everything I need up here, Marc. Next time bring your beautiful bride-to-be as well so I can finally meet her.' He winked at Lily. 'I think he's afraid I shall tell her the truth about him.'

More likely afraid that she'd become enamoured of his pretty friend, Lily thought. Instead she said, 'Is it that bad?'

'Not enough to outweigh a coronet and a fortune.'

Lily waited apprehensively for Lord Sherbourne to respond to this rather blunt statement. He didn't appear annoyed. If anything, his lazy, sardonic amusement returned.

'Very little does. It is an excellent way to make friends.'

'Oh, stuff it, Marc.' Wrexham's smile turned boyish again. 'I don't know why the devil this old fellow puts up with me, Mrs Walsh.'

'Perhaps because you don't put him to sleep?' she ventured and he laughed.

'Lord Wrexham?' a weedy young man interrupted tremulously. 'Are you ready to begin?'

Lord Wrexham gave an excellent example of a pitying sigh and followed the young man towards the lectern. Lily made to move towards Piers, but Lord Sherbourne took her arm and guided her towards the last row of seats.

'But I should sit with Piers,' she objected.

'Nonsense. You'll ruin it for those poor boys. Half of them are here to gawp at Dom and they can't do that with a clear conscience while Big Sister is planted in their midst. Besides, the last row is the only one where the padding on these archaic chairs hasn't been flattened into granite.'

She sighed but went with him, rather glad not to be engulfed by noisy young men.

'Will we hear your friend from up here?'

'You actually plan to listen to him?'

'Well, I certainly didn't come here to gawp at a pretty face. I can go to a museum for that. Is that what you came for?'

He laughed. 'I didn't, but now I can. And you'll be able to hear him even better up here than down there with all those idiots whispering comments to each other. Acoustics. That's the science of...'

'I know what acoustics are, Lord Sherbourne,' she replied a little more tartly than necessary, but his initial and very ambiguous comment had unsettled her. He hadn't meant *her*. Her looks were passable, but she doubted someone like Lord Sherbourne would consider hers 'a pretty face'.

'Of course you do. Apologies for my presumption, ma'am.'

'Hush. Your friend is speaking.'

He laughed, but fell silent, stretching his long legs under the seat in front of him. He'd been right about the acoustics. His friend's deep voice swept up the stairs and was held firmly by the wooden walls behind them with an effect that would definitely have been soporific in the best possible way if only the topic had not interested her so much.

He opened with a tale of a family torn apart by the collapse of the Holy Roman Empire and on that foundation he set out the cynical political machinations that had shaped so much of Europe by creating the Austro-Hungarian Empire.

She could *see* it. From the feudal poverty of the villages to the glistening, debauched grandeur of Viennese wealth. He spoke of Bismarck and Nesselrode as if he'd clinked glasses of Austrian wine and Russian vodka with them and been privy to their thoughts and schemes.

Having been indirectly caught in the fire of an ambitious emperor and his wars, she found the mélange of ambition and pettiness of those all-powerful individuals so captivating that at one point she realised she was literally poised at the edge of her seat. She slid back into a more lady-like posture and hoped Lord Sherbourne hadn't noticed her childish gaucheness. She threw him a quick glance. He didn't turn, but there was the faintest hint of that dimple.

She focused her attention once again on the lecture. She didn't care if Annie's lord thought her foolish. This was by far the most enjoyable excursion she'd had in London other than her visit to Hope House. Lord Wrexham might be an ill-tempered cynic and a wretch, but he was not merely a pretty face.

When it was over Piers bounded up the stairs towards them.

'Hello, sir!' he hailed Lord Sherbourne almost shyly before turning to Lily. 'I'm so sorry, Sis. I

must have confused the days. Were you terribly
bored? I admit this fellow speaks well, but all this
political faffing about had my head spinning and
I'm afraid I might have dozed a little. I'll make
it up to you. We'll return for Frasier's lecture…'

'I'm certain your sister would love to hear Frasier hold forth on his Etruscan finds, but I'm afraid
she and Annie and your parents are already spoken for that afternoon.'

'Oh, no! What a pity. Well, perhaps we can
catch him next week, then.'

Lily almost contradicted Lord Sherbourne's
presumptuous claim, but somehow the bird-fell-
ing Frasier was a less attractive proposition after
today's fascinating talk. Still, she raised one brow
at her mocking saviour.

'Perhaps. At what hour is the…ah…excursion,
Lord Sherbourne?'

'Your visit to Sherbourne House? At four, I'm
afraid. You're more than welcome to come, Piers,
but knowing that Frasier was set to speak at the
same hour, I rather thought you would prefer the
lecture to a collection of tedious adults admiring
wallpaper patterns and Chinese urns and what
not.'

'Is that what awaits us?' she asked politely.

'I'm afraid so.'

'I dashed well would prefer the Etruscans to

that,' Piers replied with a comic grimace. 'Sorry, Sis. Next week then, Lily?'

'If I am still in town, of course, Piers.'

'Oh, but you cannot leave London so soon!' Piers objected. 'You've barely been here at all. I thought you meant to stay until the wedding.'

'I shall return for that, I promise.'

Piers shrugged. 'I see. Well, I'd best escort you home. I've agreed to meet the fellows at Boodle's afterwards.'

'I can make my own way home, Piers. You go with them.'

'I said I'll escort you home,' Piers's tone turned mulish and Lord Sherbourne spoke before Lily could.

'You go along with them, Piers. I shall see your sister home safely.'

Piers murmured a half-hearted thanks and ran back down the stairs to his friends.

Lily stood for a moment, holding her ache inside.

'Surely you are not teaching in the summer months, Mrs Walsh?'

She shook her head at Lord Sherbourne's question, but her thoughts were with Piers. She hadn't realised she still had the ability to hurt him.

'Or is there something or someone in Birmingham you must return to?' Lord Sherbourne's voice was curt, almost disdainful. That brought her back to the moment and she frowned at him.

'My reasons are my own, Lord Sherbourne.'

'And they outweigh the welfare of your brother and sister? They clearly wish you to stay. Anne didn't mention you were attached.'

'Attached? You make me sound like a bandbox tied to the mail coach. And I don't appreciate you passing judgment on my relations with my siblings. They are also none of your concern.'

Lily wished she'd bitten her tongue. She ought to be happy he was concerned for Annie and Piers' welfare. It wasn't his fault he'd stepped on her guilty toes.

Lord Sherbourne didn't respond. He was looking down the aisle towards his friend who was surrounded by eager crowd of young men and a few classic tut-tutters who were clearly waiting to illustrate to Lord Wrexham precisely where he had gone astray in his thinking.

'Does he need rescuing; do you think?' she asked Lord Sherbourne, trying to reinfuse the situation with some of his previous light-heartedness. At first she thought he had not understood her. He looked down at her with a rather hard, distracted look. Then it was gone, though his smile wasn't as easy-going as before.

'No. Dom is a master at rescuing himself. Come, I shall see you home.'

'There's no need…'

'I told Piers I would see you home.'

Goodness, he could be stubborn. *And* ill-tempered. It was almost comforting to know he was not as perfect as Anne believed him. There wasn't a tinge of humour about his face now.

She didn't want to be treated like an ageing aunt in need of escort lest she wander down Piccadilly in search of a straying cat. But neither did she wish to antagonise this version of Lord Sherbourne.

And to think he'd accused *her* of sulking.

They walked in silence out into an early summer storm. As an attendant opened the door to the courtyard a burst of squalling wind attacked her and she grabbed her bonnet before it took flight. The attendant was surprised into letting go the door and it slammed shut in his face. Rain flung itself at the stained glass and dared them to try such effrontery again.

'I dare say you'll blame me for this as well,' Lily said, tying the ribbons of her bonnet more securely.

'It's tempting, Lily Walsh.' Lord Sherbourne's tiger eyes lightened with the sudden flare of laughter she found so disconcerting. This time it knocked a burden from her shoulders and she almost physically sighed. She wasn't comfortable with his anger, which was foolish.

She smiled back. 'Well, wherever lies the blame, we'd best brave the storm.'

'I have a better idea. Come this way.'

She came. 'Let me guess. You know a secret tunnel under the City like the catacombs of Paris.'

'You have been to Paris?'

'Unfortunately not. But I love reading about different places. I wish I could have seen them.'

'I don't know if the reality would match your fantasies.'

'They never do. But I don't mind. There is room for both.'

'You are a very peculiar woman, Lily Walsh.'

'I dare say you are saving all your gallantry for Annie. Commendable.'

He paused and glanced at her, but the anger that had unsettled her was nowhere in sight.

'You've a sly way with criticism, too. Do you wish for gallantry?'

'Goodness, no. I never know what to say and I hate being flustered. Luckily I am very rarely the recipient of gallantry.'

'Luckily?'

'Luckily,' she repeated. Firmly.

He opened a door for her and they passed through a corridor so narrow she thought any moment he would have to walk sideways. It led into a covered alley and though the rain seemed to be pummelling the wooden covering and ran down a gutter on one side, only a few drops seeped through their shelter. Halfway down this urban tunnel her body recognised a scent before she did. Her stomach grumbled hopefully.

'Is that…baking bread?'

'Yes, we are now passing behind a bakery.'

'It smells delicious.'

'It is. They bake for some of the clubs on St James's. Their master baker hails from France and once baked bread for Marshal Ney. Wait here a moment.'

To her surprise he opened a door and a whirl of warmth attacked her, picking up her skirts. They flopped back down as the door closed behind him. Lily stared at the door.

Had he just left her here?

She looked back at the covered tunnel and then ahead. She'd not even noticed, but people were passing back and forth between buildings and a woman carrying a large basket overflowing with leeks squeezed by her, the sharp green scent adding to her grumbling stomach. She not the slightest idea where she was—whether he'd turned east or west or whether they were even still in London.

Of course we are, Lily Walsh. Don't be fanciful.

She winced a little at this reappearance of her mother's voice in her head. When the door reopened she gave a sigh of relief as Lord Sherbourne ducked under the low lintel. One of the dark blue sleeves of his coat was dusted with flour.

'Here.'

He held out a round loaf of bread as big as two fists and a cracked crown that was steaming gently. Her mouth watered.

'What about you?'

'I was hoping you would share.'

She laughed, the antagonism she'd been clinging to going up in a puff of yeasty steam. She ought to be happy Annie's lord was so very clever about people.

'Annie is right. You shall make an excellent father.'

Oh, blast, she ought to watch her tongue. She'd not imagined he was the kind of man to blush, but he did. She concentrated on breaking the loaf in half, breathing in the wondrous scent of wheaten bread with…

'Oh, how wonderful. Rye. Here.' She handed him his half and he took it and they continued down the tunnel, eating their bounty.

'Eleanor, my friend in Birmingham, loves to bake,' she said between bites. 'We both learned in Portugal and Spain, but I was never any good. It takes patience and precision. I am not good at either. I wish I was so I could create such wonders, too. Thank you, Lord Sherbourne.'

'You knew each other from Spain?'

'Yes, our husbands were in the same battalion. Hers was killed in Toulouse. Not that it makes much difference in the end, but there is something more poignant about losing someone after the war was already over. If only they'd received word of the abdication earlier, he might have been spared. But it wasn't a happy marriage, so perhaps in a way it is better. Goodness, that sounded brutal.'

'Honest.'

'Honesty is often an excuse to say things one oughtn't.'

'True. Your mother excels at that.'

She looked up at him, surprised again.

'*That* was honest.'

'Oughtn't I to have said it?' he asked with a show of feigned concern and she laughed.

'I'm glad you did. Sometimes I think Annie and Piers and I are the only ones who see that side of her. Everyone back in Kent and here in town thinks she is charming.'

'Because her type knows how to charm. That is their primary tool of survival.'

Her type. Yes, she did have a type. Lily hadn't known that until she'd married Tim and seen the world a little. There were others like her mother.

'Her type is most dangerous when they know they've been rumbled,' he continued.

'Rumbled?'

'Uncovered. When someone sees their faults.

That's when they are dangerous, because you are contradicting the face they present to the world and that puts them in danger. Look, it's stopped raining.'

They'd reached the dripping end of the tunnel and though the clouds still sagged low over the buildings, they were holding themselves together for the moment. She noted it absently, her mind working over what he'd said.

'You speak as if you know this type well.'

'The world is full of them and they tend to gravitate towards positions of power. Or towards people in positions of power. It is best to mark them out early. They require handling.'

She nodded. He did indeed handle her mother. She wished she knew how to do so even half as well. Clever Annie for finding such a useful man. Lily felt a surge of envy, though she wasn't certain at what.

They continued for a while in what she thought was a westerly direction. There were no hackney cabs, only carts here. She was a little curious to know where they were, but not very. And she certainly wasn't in a hurry. The alternative was being in Brook Street.

'I probably handle her all wrong.' The words came out a little gruff and challenging and she squeezed her eyes shut for a moment in embarrassment.

'We're at our worst with people we care about. Besides, I doubt there is anything you could do to handle her right at this point.'

She took both blows in silence. He stopped suddenly, touching her sleeve, and she stopped as well, waiting for a third.

'*That* was too honest. Annie was right about you as well; you are easy to talk with. I apologise.'

She shook her head. This third blow felt even more powerful than the previous two, which didn't make sense. She would *not* cry.

'You're quite right, though.' She cleared her throat and continued, 'And it is good to hear it spoken aloud. I know it is the truth and I am mostly reconciled to it, but sometimes I forget.'

A hackney rumbled towards them and he raised his hand. They were inside just in time to avoid the clouds losing their battle with gravity. It smelled of mould and damp and she raised her gloves to breathe in the remnants of his gift of bread.

'I won't ever know how to find that wondrous bakery again. I used to know Lisbon like this when we lived there. Down to the bakeries and the best fishmongers and the tiny little shop where a deaf man fixed boot heels and nothing else.'

He didn't answer, but she knew he was listening. Soon she recognised the streets and then they were on Brook Street and slowing before Number Twenty-Three. Only a few weeks ago she'd stood before that door with her portmanteau in the pouring rain. It felt so much longer.

For a moment she almost imagined that woman was someone else entirely and would come walking by, the sagging grey and blue portmanteau dragging down her left shoulder. Except she would not stop and they would continue on entirely different paths.

'Thank you, Lord Sherbourne.'

He nodded but didn't speak as he helped her down and she hurried up the stairs and inside.

Dom was standing by the doorway of the Institute when Marcus stepped out of the hackney, still in conversation with one of his admirers. The rain had stopped again and he felt the need to walk. He took Dom by the elbow and pulled him away.

'Where did you disappear to?' Dom asked as he strode through a puddle. Dom had always been hell on his boots.

'I saw Anne's sister home while her brother went off to debate Ovid and Homer with the striplings.'

'Lucky you. Well, did she tut at my performance? Or sigh?'

'Only in pleasure. You have made another conquest, Dom. Just remember she is to be my sister-in-law and stay away from her, will you?'

'But I liked her. She's amusing. Clever little

thing. And those eyes. I could easily take a nice cool swim in them. I like widows.'

'Not this widow. Don't make me break your pretty nose.'

'You would? To protect your beloved's sister? How romantic you've become in your old age, Marc. Did she really sigh?'

Marcus wished he hadn't mentioned that. Dom was unpredictable at best and had an imagination that could be both useful and downright dangerous. He should not have planted that image in his friend's mind. Or in his.

'She was fascinated by your lecture, that is all. Don't get cocky. You spoke particularly well today.'

'I was on my mettle after her armour-piercing arrows. Damned if I was going to be listed in the same genus as *frasieris soporifus*. Is her sister very like her?'

'Not in the least.'

'Oh. Pity.'

Marcus ignored that and concentrated on crossing Albemarle Street without sinking into a malodorous puddle. The water sparkled up at him, the reflection of the scudding clouds broken for a moment by a breeze carrying a faint smell of hay under the less appealing scents of London, like a traveller from some far-off village, eager to explore.

A perfect summer day by London standards.

He wished with a sudden unaccustomed urgency that he were far away.

Not for a while.

In two months precisely to the day he would be wed in St George's in Hanover Square. Then he and his bride would remove to Sherbourne Hall in Hampshire for the required week and then he would be free to return to his concerns and in the autumn he would be on his way to the Congress of the five nations in Aix-la-Chapelle and everything in this new chapter in his life would fall into place.

'Will she and that little sprig of a brother of hers be attending Frasier's talk?' Dom asked.

'No. The Devenish family is invited to Sherbourne House that afternoon.'

'Good lord. To do what?'

'I don't know. To discuss wall hangings. It is an opportunity to introduce them to some of the less sociable among the Sherbourne clan.'

'I thought you hated having people invade your house.'

'Since it will soon be their house as well, I might as well accustom myself.'

Dom whistled below his breath. 'You're in a temper.'

'I am not in a temper.'

'Of course not. Did the sharp-tongued widow give you a thrashing as well? Are you certain you wish to marry into that family? I like a good dose of spice myself, but I thought you wanted a quiet life.'

'I told you Anne is nothing like her.'

'So you did. Well, I shall come and see for myself.'

'You're not invited.'

'Not invite your best friend? I hope I am at least invited to your wedding?'

'I'll consider it. Since when are you my best friend, anyway?'

'Not in a temper. Not at all. All honey and sugar here. I did tell you this whole betrothal business was a mistake, didn't I?'

'If I'd listened to your advice I would have been dead long ago. Several times over. Anne will be the perfect wife.'

'Ah. Absolutes. You *never* use them. You live by Kant's dictum: *"Out of the crooked timber of humanity, no straight thing was ever made."'*

'Don't try to be clever, it doesn't suit you. You know what I meant.'

'Certainly. That you trawled the tepid waters of the *ton* and she was the least un-tempting.'

'If you're in this mood, you'll be useless at the meeting. Go home.'

'Don't have one. Don't want one.'

'Good, because at this rate you are highly unlikely to find one.'

'Besides, I know I can always depend on my *best* friend for succour in times of need.'

Marcus sighed. They'd reached Sherbourne House and they both stopped at the bottom of the three wide marble steps. Dom made a strange motion with his hands.

'Sorry, Marc. I just don't like it.'

'You're going to have to grow up and accept it, Dominic. You may not want a quiet life, but I do. I enjoy what we do for Oswald and Castlereagh, but now we're no longer living on the knife's edge I need something more in my life.'

'Children.' Wrexham spat the word out.

'Yes. Even without the promise my mother wrung from me I would probably marry. Unlike you I was raised in a big noisy house and I miss that. And for that I need a wife. Besides, I'm tired of mistresses.'

'Good lord, Marcus. You're making me feel three score years at least.'

Marcus smiled.

'You shall have to adjust. Especially if you want to be invited to Sherbourne. I won't have you upsetting Anne.'

'I wouldn't say any of this to her.'

'You were rather free with your comments to Lily...to her sister.'

'Well, that sweetheart can give as good as she gets.'

Marcus held back a comment on Wrexham's endearment.

'How the devil do you know that? You only just met her.'

'The devil always knows his own, doesn't he? Are you certain you won't let me indulge in a little flirtation? It will keep me out of trouble.'

'Your definition of keeping out of trouble leaves a lot to be desired. The answer is no. Besides, she might already be involved with someone in Birmingham.'

'Did you just invent that to keep me off the scent?'

Marcus shook his head. Rising to Wrexham's bait would only encourage him. Better to change the subject.

'And don't forget you agreed to come to Sefton's ball with me, so don't make plans.'

'Oh, hell, must I?'

'Yes. I've managed to avoid most balls thus far in my courtship, but Sefton himself insisted I attend now that I've started showing my face at society events and he and Lady Sefton are too pleasant to turn down. But I'm damned if I'm going without someone at my back. Consider this your penance for being such an idiot.'

'Damn cruel choice of penance. Very well. But remember, all good things come at a price. I'll expect you to have my back at some society do when next I need it.'

He stalked off and after a moment Marcus ascended the stairs. Juan was waiting in the hallway and took his hat and cane. Ombra poked his shaggy head out of the open door of the study and trotted over with a panting grin. Marcus scratched the dog's head.

'We shall be having guests the day after tomorrow, Juan. Afternoon.'

Juan's round face turned even rounder. 'Did you say afternoon, *señor*?'

'I'm afraid so. The future Lady Sherbourne and her family and a few others. Cousin Godfrey and his wife, I think. And cousins Anthea and Matilda. Lord Bartleby and his wife, too.'

Juan made a croaking sound and Marcus sighed.

'I know. But I need some unobjectionable people for the occasion. Devenishes meet Endicotts. Damnable, but there it is.'

'Food?'

'Yes, light. None of your delicacies.'

It was Juan's turn to sigh and Marcus relented.

'Actually, you could serve some tapas along with the sandwiches and cakes. One of our guests spent some years in Spain.'

'One of your soldier friends?' Juan asked suspiciously. 'They do not always appreciate my cooking. In Spain they dream of steak and beer, the philistines.'

'Well, she was married to a soldier, but I think she might be a willing audience for your cooking. If not, you and I and Ombra will do it justice once we clear the decks.'

When he was alone he went to his desk and unsealed the documents sent for his review. Ombra settled in his usual position beneath the desk, curving his lanky body around Marcus's boots and after some settling he gave a contented huff and closed his eyes. Marcus leaned down to stroke his dog's head for a moment.

'You have the right of it, boy. A quiet life. What is wrong with that? I've earned it.'

Ombra gave another satisfied huff, leaning his head into the scratching. Marcus kept at it, his gaze moving about the familiar room. His favourite place in Sherbourne House. He probably spent more time here than in his bedroom.

He would have to make it clear, in the gentlest possible way, that Anne was to regard this room as taboo. He could always use his work with the Foreign Office as an excuse. As for the rest of the house... He would soon have to resign himself to changes. In less than two months some rooms in this house would begin to fill with sewing tables and embroidered screens and fashion magazines and young women visiting his... He drew a long breath and forced the words into his mind. His wife.

Anne Devenish would be living here, with him—the woman he had selected to be the mother of the children he wanted.

At least there was that. There would be sons and daughters. He wondered if they would have his colouring or Anne's or something in between. He picked up one of the sharpened pencils from the silver tray and tried to imagine them, idly sketching on the paper that always lay ready on his blotter.

A little girl with a pert nose dusted with freckles…

He let his mind empty as he drew, his imagination filling in the shape and colours of her world. She was seated at the little desks he and his nephews and nieces had used in the nursery at Sherbourne Hall, all the way at the edge, her face shining with curiosity, her wavy hair tumbling down her back. Then she turned and smiled up at him with dark grey eyes.

He dropped the pencil. Beneath the desk Ombra gave a startled woof.

'Did I kick you? Sorry, old boy.' Marcus reached down and stroked the dog. His hand was shaking.

He set the pencil aside, dropped the sketch into the cane basket by the desk and pulled a sealed case of documents towards him.

Five minutes later he set aside the page he'd been trying to read and took the discarded sketch from the basket, shoving it instead into the bottom drawer of his desk with a curse.

He was not superstitious, but somehow…

'Dom is right, Ombra. I'm getting old. Hallucinations and sentimentality. What next?'

Chapter Ten

'I *hate* balls.'

Annie fluttered her fan before her face to shield her giggle.

'They aren't that bad, Lily. It is merely that you don't know anyone yet.'

'I don't *wish* to know anyone. I only came to London because you asked. If I had known it included being trussed up in your refurbished gowns and forced to discuss fashion and the weather with a brigade of Mama's friends while drinking sickly-sweet ratafia, I would have fled for the hills.'

'Hush. And I'm sorry we hadn't time to order you new gowns, but Ailish has done wonders with mine. It looks far better on you than it did on me.'

Lily gave up. Anne actually believed this patent untruth. She smiled at her sister.

'Well, I'm glad I am with you anyway. I've missed you these past couple of years, Annie.'

Annie plied her fan faster. 'So have I. Couldn't you come work in London instead? You said they had another institution here in town. I would love to have you close. Especially…'

She trailed off.

Annie was doing that more and more often, Lily noted, opening doors to glimpses of the future, only to shut them again. Before Lily could respond Annie shook her head.

'I truly do love that shade of rose pink on you, Lily, and I think my pale primrose evening gown with the square bodice shall also suit you to perfection.' She smiled that soft smile of hers at nothing in particular, her perfect skin softened by the light of chandeliers and her creamy dress accentuating her slim height.

Lily looked down at her own gown. Annie was right that the dusky rose colour was pretty. She particularly loved the silvery stars embroidered along the low-cut bodice and along the single flounce. For the first time in years she was wearing a colour distinguishable from that of a dank winter evening.

Ailish was just as talented with a brush and pins and had set Lily's thick hair in a fashionable arrangement that perched on the crown of her head like an animal, secured with pearl-encrusted pins and trailing wavy tendrils that tickled her cheeks as she fanned herself. It felt strange and she kept expecting the pins to fly in every direction and the precarious creation to topple over her shoulders or transform into snakes and start waving about like Medusa.

How did that not happen more often?

But altogether she had to admit she did look... rather fine. As they'd passed a gilt-framed mirror by the receiving line she'd caught a glimpse of her and Annie side by side and had to look again. Annie was stunning as always, a true princess in looks and carriage. But Lily thought she herself looked...different. More like young Lily who had once dared to live grandly and dream even more grandly.

It was unsettling.

'Oh, look, Lily. Marcus has arrived. Goodness, Lord Wrexham is with him.'

Lily turned as Annie raised her fan a little and smiled. Lord Sherbourne had just entered the ballroom with his friend and the two of them were drawing a great deal of attention from both sexes.

'We have never been formally introduced. Lord Wrexham is the Duke of Rutherford's eldest son and is not quite...well, he rarely attends balls,' Annie whispered. 'Marcus hasn't either, until recently, at least.'

She didn't add—since he'd become engaged. That would be vanity and Annie's mind just didn't work that way. It was one of her more aggravating characteristics. She was about to mention to Annie that she'd already met Lord Wrexham, but Lord Sherbourne and his companion were already heading in their direction. Lily noted a peculiar tension to Lord Sherbourne, as if the two men had been arguing. When Marcus introduced him, Lord Wrexham bowed over Annie's hand.

'So you're the beauty that has turned Marcus from the path of good and right.'

Annie blinked and Marcus sighed. 'Ignore him. He hates balls almost as much as I do.'

'Then why come?' Lily asked before she could think better of it. Lord Wrexham turned to her with a shrug.

'Marcus forced me. Misery likes company.'

'I didn't force you, I asked you.'

'Well, you never ask for anything, so that's tantamount to forcing. What the devil do we do now we're here? Must I talk to people?'

Lily unfurled her fan to hide her smile. She hadn't been certain she'd liked him when they'd met at the lecture hall, but he was rather growing on her.

Annie was still looking a little shocked, her gaze searching Marcus's face for clues on how to handle his irascible friend.

'Yes, you must,' Marcus said in his usual languid drawl. Whatever had caused that initial tension, it was tucked away now. 'And dance, too, Dom. You promised.'

'I did not promise to dance. I would definitely have remembered that, drunk or sober. Unless it's a waltz. That's the only dance worth dancing.'

'You enjoy waltzing, Lord Wrexham?' Annie swept into that opening, ever hopeful. His smile turned a little wolfish.

'I enjoy anything that reminds me of more pleasurable activities.'

'Try not to be too much of an idiot, Dom.' Lord Sherbourne's warning was rather weakened by his sudden grin.

'Just for that I'm going to steal your bride-to-be for a waltz, Marc.'

'I'm afraid this dance is promised to Lord Sherbourne—' Annie said, but Lord Wrexham rode right over that polite distinction.

'All the better. That will add some spice. Marcus can dance with Madame Tut-and-Sigh.' His gaze swept over Lily and the wolfish smile deepened and something very like a warning entered his gaze and dripped from his voice. 'You and I shall share the next waltz, Mrs Lily Walsh. How is that for a Solomonic resolution, Marc? *Adieu.*'

Lily and Marcus stood for a moment in silence, watching the couple move towards the dance floor. She rather hoped Lord Sherbourne would ignore his friend's suggestion.

'Well, Lily Walsh, it seems you have no choice. You *can* waltz, yes?'

'Yes, but...'

'Well, then. Let us go to it.'

He sounded as reluctant as she and there was no amusement in evidence either in his tone or his face. He looked tired and rather grim and once on the dance floor they moved in silence to the rhythm of the dance.

Was he upset about Lord Wrexham and Annie? About being forced to dance with Anne's unfashionable sister? Neither seemed to account for his unusual behaviour.

She ought to have felt insulted, but she felt worried instead. She wished she had the courage to ask him what was bothering him. No, she wished he would smile and say something annoying. She needed to find her balance again.

She'd never known anyone who upset her quite as much as this man and she was beginning to hate this feeling. Just moments ago she'd felt hopeful and confident and pretty and now she felt...

She had no notion what she felt except that it was uncomfortable. Her lungs were tight and her palms tingled like they did before an episode, except she wasn't cold and there wasn't that horrid rushing sound in her ears. If anything, she felt a crackling heat lick against her insides and, instead of the urge to push everyone away and slink into a

corner, she wished he would say something, anything, to break this tension.

She felt as though she'd done something terribly wrong though she didn't know what.

She felt…

Everything.

His hand on her waist, from the heel of his
palm to the pressure of his fingers through the
silky soft fabric. She could almost swear he was…
vibrating. Or she was. As if they were dancing on
a tuning fork.

He was far too close, too. She wanted to look
up, but was afraid to, so she stared at the pearl
pin hiding among the milky folds of his cravat. It
brought back the memory of the tiny pearls on his
mother's locket laying on her palm in the hackney
cab, a token of a bond through time.

Sensations piled one on top of another: his
fingertips on her hand through her thin gloves,
her own hand resting on his shoulder, warm and
safe… And then her mind took her hand and
slipped it under the dark wool and soft linen of
his clothes, touching the warm skin beneath…

Only an awful, dreadful, *traitorous* person
would be so aware of the man who was to be
Annie's husband. She gritted her teeth, trying to
think of anything else, but she couldn't stop it.

Sense was doing its best to catch up with sensation, like a messenger running after an advancing

army, helplessly waving an order to retreat: *Don't go there!* But her troops were in full forward motion, leaving the messenger behind.

One shouldn't want to move closer, lean her cheek against the dark fabric of his coat, soak up his warmth and heartbeat. One shouldn't have to fight against the urge to look at him. And one definitely shouldn't imagine stopping right here in the middle of Lady Sefton's ballroom, standing on tiptoe and touching her mouth to his to see if her worst fears were correct and it would feel horribly right.

Oh, no.

The two words rang inside her like a bell underwater—muted but reverberating. She didn't want this part of her to wake. It had sunk to the bottom of some muddy lake even before Tim died. It should stay there where it and she were safe.

The very last place it should choose to revive itself was in the middle of a fashionable ballroom—and the very, very last person who should revive it was Annie's Lord Sherbourne.

She lost her step and his hand tightened on hers, his other palm moving against her waist, steadying her and bringing her a little closer. Above the cloying scent of perfumes and the acrid smell of heated bodies and souring wine she caught the same cool oak and pine forest that followed him about. As if he'd just this moment transported himself from the foothills of the Pyrenees.

She reached deep down into whatever reservoirs of strength she had left. She would stop this right here, right now. Face it and then wrench it out like a rotten tooth. She had dealt with far worse and she would deal with this, too.

Annie would never, ever know.

One of them had to say *something*.

Marcus hoped Lily would, because his mind was a blasted blank. At least he was trying to keep it blank. He'd been raw all day, that strange episode in his study following him about like Ombra. He'd tried to tell himself it was pure nerves, a natural resistance to his sensible decision to marry. A reaction to Dom's words which he knew were aligned with at least one of his conflicting inner voices. He'd known these months leading up to the *fait accompli* of marriage would be challenging. He hadn't figured on them being purgatorial.

And he certainly hadn't considered…

He didn't want to consider.

This strange curiosity about Lily Walsh was just that. She was a curious little thing. If he could put things in their right place, she could eventually become a good friend.

The fist tightened around his chest again as it had when he'd realised he had to dance with her.

A good friend.

What a liar he'd become.

One didn't have hallucinations that one's imaginary daughter far too closely resembled a good friend. One didn't have one's whole body lurch into alertness because of a good friend's laugh. One didn't rush into a bustling bakery to procure a loaf of bread because a good friend had a smile that always seemed to drag his to the surface. And one certainly didn't lose his grip on his temper's reins because a good friend wanted to leave London, possibly because said good friend had someone waiting for them in Birmingham.

A shaft of fear shot through him as sharp as any he'd felt when his life was in the balance.

Even during the war, he'd been able to plan ahead, envisage threats, prepare for them. That was why he'd survived and thrived. He'd been afraid but prepared.

Now he was afraid and damnably unprepared.

He tried to push it away, but the realisation was white-hot and burned through his defences.

He'd made a horrible mistake.

It was a terrifyingly depressing realisation and the worst possible place to realise it—in the very middle of the battlefield.

He wanted to push Lily away and walk out of this ballroom-turned-purgatory so he could rebuild his defences and get perspective on his new worst enemy.

No, he wanted to pull her closer, lean in to catch the scent that had been teasing him since he'd been fool enough to stop and follow her in Cheapside. Orange blossoms. Damn her.

What was *wrong* with him? He'd found the perfect bride. Why on earth was his idiot mind and body fixating on the sister?

This was not supposed to happen.

It *wouldn't* happen.

His mother had warned him he ought to be watchful of the Sherbourne rebellious streak. He'd thought he'd long outgrown it, but apparently it was alive and well and convincing his weakening mind and body that Lily Walsh was just what it fancied right now.

Well, there would be none of that.

'What will it be—the weather or gossip?' he demanded, a little too loudly.

Her lashes flickered up, her eyes silvery with tiny gold reflections from the chandelier above them. A hundred little pinpricks danced along his nape.

'I beg your pardon?' Her voice was misty and the pinpricks showered down his spine. He clung to the saddle and soldiered on.

'And so you should beg my pardon for snubbing my perfectly respectable conversational opening.

You ought at least to have tried the winning combination of simpering and saying, *Whichever you prefer, Lord Sherbourne*. That should do for the next few turns.'

Her distant expression faded as she burst into laughter. He wished he hadn't goaded it out of her. The flames he'd been beating back roared up from the chasm. The last time she'd laughed like that it had only been the hairs on his nape that rose to attention. This time his body didn't give a damn about decency and propriety and honour. Every cell turned its whole and avid attention on Lily like his dog did when Marcus took an India rubber ball out of the drawer. He could see it in Ombra's eyes—the whole world narrowed into one object: ball. Want. Now. *Mine*.

His body was no better. Right now that was the sum total of its comprehension: Lily. Want. Now. *Mine*.

God, he was in trouble.

He'd never dreamed a waltz could be so hellish.

Chapter Eleven

'One day your portrait shall hang here, Anne dear. It simply must be by Lawrence, even if he does insist on drawing those scandalous actresses.'

Mrs Devenish's voice rang with anticipated triumph and for one anxious moment, Lily worried her mother might actually inform Lord Sherbourne which of the many portraits gracing the long gallery at Sherbourne House must be removed to accommodate her daughter's future likeness.

When her prey did not look up from his discussion with Mr Devenish and Lord Bartleby, Mrs Devenish tried another tack.

'Why isn't there a portrait of you here, Lord Sherbourne?'

The three men paused their discussion and Lord Sherbourne smiled at her mother's question. But it was an absent smile. The same Lily had seen him don at the ball yesterday and since their arrival this afternoon. Like their host, it was polite and accommodating and not really there.

Anne had noticed it as well and was doing her best to keep their mother entertained and away from His Lordship. But Mrs Devenish was made of sterner stuff.

'Perhaps you should have a portrait done together,' Mrs Devenish persevered.

'Mama!' Annie whispered with unaccustomed heat. To Lily's relief Lord Wrexham strode over from his discussion with Piers and began flirting with Mrs Devenish, standing just so that his large form blocked her mother's line of vision with Lord Sherbourne. Lily liked Lord Wrexham all the better for this gesture of concern.

She took advantage of her mother's distraction to slip through the double doors that stood ajar and into the library they had visited earlier. She needed quiet and that wasn't likely to be found among the party assembled by Lord Sherbourne, which was composed of several prosy members of the Endicott family. Though to be fair to them they appeared to regard Anne with universal approbation, Lady Bartleby commenting several times in a high grating voice that 'the child is quite, quite lovely'.

Lily wished she'd pleaded a headache and stayed in Brook Street, but that would have been cowardly and worried Annie. So she'd come, determined not to fall into her foolish, maudlin thoughts. She'd even hoped they'd been an aberration, driven by wearing a wholly inappropriate pink ball gown.

It had been a foolish hope.

So, since denial was not working, she tried rationalisation. It went something along these lines: if Lord Sherbourne hadn't been Annie's, this unwanted attraction wouldn't have horrified her so.

After all, he was undeniably attractive. He could also, sometimes, be amusing and charming. And kind.

In addition, this weakness of hers was undoubtedly exacerbated by being back in the family fold after two years of blessed freedom. She'd known it would be difficult. Perhaps this was some form of rebellion? Perhaps she was trying to create an insurmountable barrier between her and her family so she could scurry back to the safety of Birmingham?

If any of this was true, she concluded, frowning at nothing in particular, it was a damned foolish way to go about it. And embarrassing. And painful.

The library was cooler than the picture gallery where the curtains had been drawn back to allow the damp sunshine to show the portraits to advantage. Here was the scent of lemon oil and books and of the full-blown pink and white roses in a lacquered vase on a large round mahogany table. A lovely room. One day all this would be Annie's.

It was all so normal, yet with every passing moment ticked out by the standing grandfather clock by the door it felt more and more like a nightmare. She stopped before a small print of a seascape with a stone castle on an island. She wished she were there. It looked faraway and quiet and...

'Not interested in portraits of the Endicotts? I can't blame you. They're pretty enough, but a bland, upright lot. It was his mother's Italian family that brought some life into the mix, thank God.' Lord Wrexham was standing in the doorway and Lily smiled politely, wishing he would leave.

'I am more interested in these prints at the moment, Lord Wrexham. I prefer landscapes to portraits in any case.'

'Ah, I suspected you had misanthropic tendencies as well.'

She didn't give him the satisfaction of asking *As well as what?*

'Hardly. It is merely that I always wished to travel and would look for paintings of foreign lands in the periodicals and imagine myself there and in the midst of adventure.'

'Ah. A dreamer. I hear you did indeed travel, though under less than ideal circumstances.'

Had Lord Sherbourne told him? She hadn't thought anyone cared enough to gossip about her.

'I did see quite a bit of Portugal and Spain. When it wasn't horrible it was very beautiful. And very different from England.'

'Certainly that. I never knew dust could have so many different flavours.'

She laughed and he shut the door and moved closer, his eyes narrowing.

'You have the laugh of a Venetian courtesan.'

Her jaw dropped and she snapped it shut. 'Have you actually heard a Venetian...uh...courtesan laugh?'

'Several. Like Marcus, I have Italian roots. It was another thing that drew us together at school and I later travelled there extensively. Though to be fair, none of said courtesans had a laugh as seductive as yours. I shall have to embellish my fantasies with it.'

She really ought to remonstrate with him. If anyone overheard... But she was a widow and widows didn't have to make-believe they were ignorant prudes.

'No one has ever told me I have a seductive laugh. Embellish away.'

It was his turn to laugh and the tension he seemed to carry about him like an over-tight coat unravelled a little. His smile was real and very charming.

'I like you. Does your sister also have hidden depths? I'd like to think so for Marc's sake.'

'My sister is a truly wonderful person. She is kind and caring and considerate.'

'I was afraid of that.'

Her amusement fled in an instant and guilt and fear were back.

'I won't have you speaking against her.' She lowered her voice into a hiss. 'Any man would count himself lucky to secure her as his wife.'

He raised his hands, but the laughter was gone from his face as well. 'But you see Marcus isn't any man. He's my friend. It's my role to worry, just as it is your role to worry about your sister's happiness.'

She wanted to be angry with him, but all she felt was the persistent ache pulsing away somewhere below her sternum and between her eyes. Life pounding away at her.

'I would rather we not discuss them, Lord Wrexham.'

He moved towards her, his mouth twisting a little. 'Fair enough. Believe it or not, I didn't mean to upset you. I rather like you.'

'I don't think I can say the same at the moment, Lord Wrexham.'

'Dominic.'

'No.'

He laughed, a softer, almost sweet laugh, and held out his hand. *'Pax?'*

'Then don't poke fun at my sister.'

'Word of honour.'

'Huh.'

'I do take that seriously.'

'Very well.'

She held out her hand and he took it, smiling down at her.

'You're a very unique young woman, do you know that?'

'Everyone is unique. By definition.'

He burst out laughing and stroked her cheek with his fingertips before bending to brush it lightly with his mouth.

'Mmm…you smell of orange blossoms. Lovely.'

Shock held her still for a moment, curiosity held her still a little longer. His closeness felt pleasant, comforting. His mouth was soft against her skin, unthreatening. The invitation was open and all she had to do was turn her head an inch to accept it.

Why not? It had been a long time since she'd kissed a man or been kissed. She'd missed that part of her life with Tim.

'Forward or back?' he murmured, nuzzling the corner of her mouth.

She sighed. 'Back, I'm afraid.'

He gave a huff of laughter and drew away. 'Pity. I rather like you.'

'You are nicer than you appear, too.'

'But?'

'No "but". Just that.'

He smiled, his eyes accepting her rebuff without rancour. A rare gift. He took her hand in a rather formal clasp, as if they had only now been introduced.

'You're a strange bird, Lily Walsh. My favourite kind.' He leaned forward, her hand still in his, and deposited an almost brotherly peck on her temple.

Neither saw the door open.

'Dom, have you seen…?' The languid drawl was cut as by the greased blade of a guillotine. 'Hell and damnation!'

Wrexham's instincts were spectacular. He was halfway across the library before the echo of Marcus's curse faded. Marcus took a step towards him and stopped.

'This is my *home*, Dominic.'

She'd never heard that voice before. Never even known Lord Sherbourne had the capacity for that tone. Ice-cold fury.

Wrexham shook his head. 'My mistake. Sorry, Marcus. I'll leave.'

Lily woke from her surprise. 'For heaven's sake, there's no need for such dramatics. Nothing happened.'

The blazing hazel eyes turned on her and she

raised her hands, palms out, warding off the force of that glare.

'Really, Lord Sherbourne,' she said more softly. 'I'm not a child.'

'You're...my guest.'

'Well, yes, but Lord Wrexham was merely flirting a little because he's bored and upset about something. I didn't take it seriously.'

'Ow,' Wrexham said from his corner.

'Be silent, Dom,' Marcus shot at him. 'You put your paws on any of my guests again and I'll steal Pegasus from you and gift him to Metternich.'

'Fair enough. Sorry, Marc. Apologies, Lily... Mrs Walsh. I'll...uh, go join the others.'

The door shut very softly behind him.

Lily debated slipping out as well, but Marcus had moved towards the door and was glaring at it. She had not the faintest idea what he was thinking, but they were certainly not charitable thoughts.

'I've never seen you lose your temper before.'

He didn't answer and didn't move away from the door either. He was likely formulating a lecture.

She rushed ahead. 'If you're worried I shall disgrace you and Annie, I assure you I am not in the habit of allowing strangers...well...to do anything inappropriate.'

'Then why Dominic?' His words were each

snapped out and they stung like pebbles being flicked at her.

'Because he wasn't serious and I was…' She owed him some truth. It wasn't fair to allow his friend to bear all the blame. 'I was feeling low and needed cheering up. It was foolish.'

'Why were you feeling low?' It was less of a snap. More of a snarl. His temper might not appear often, but it was also lingering more than she would have expected.

Why was she feeling low? She could hardly tell him the truth. She didn't even want to tell herself. 'It doesn't matter. It won't happen again.'

He turned fully to her. With his mouth set like that he looked very different. She could well imagine him cruel and distant. If she'd seen him like this that first day with Annie, she'd have told her sister to run a mile.

Then he took a deep breath and went towards the painting she'd been admiring before.

'Where is Annie?' she asked, reminding herself that his moods were not her concern.

'With your family and my cousin Sir Gerald in the blue drawing room. He's showing them the family bible and waxing dramatic. It is almost time for refreshments. I came to find you.'

'Oh. I should join them.'

'In a moment. You may think you are immune to Dominic, but he has a way of…getting to people. He sees through their defences. It can be very seductive. Be careful.'

She couldn't help laughing at the absurdity of his warning under the circumstances. He flinched and she hurried to explain.

'I'm truly in no danger of making a fool of myself over him, Lord Sherbourne. He is a fascinating person and he clearly cares about your friendship, but he isn't…well, he isn't my type.'

'You have a type?'

His voice was a little calmer, there was even a glimmering of his usual humour underneath, glinting like a live coal beneath a heavy coating of ashes.

She considered. Tim and this man had very little in common.

'I don't think so. But I know what *isn't* my type.'

'You could still be surprised.'

'I could be, but I doubt it will be on account of Lord Wrexham.'

'Yet you let him kiss you.'

There was more curiosity than anger now. She was back to being a conundrum. She didn't know if that was an improvement.

'I don't think that would qualify as a kiss. More a testing of the waters. He was surprisingly polite about it. Too often men think finding a widow alone is an excuse to paw her and lick her like a dog at a soup bone.'

His mouth twitched and more of the annoyance was shoved away by amusement. 'That does sound rather…off-putting.'

'It is. Your friend was more cat than dog. And he didn't sulk when I told him I was not interested. Two excellent qualities.'

'But not enough to convince you to share your soup bone.'

She couldn't help it, she giggled. 'That is one euphemism I haven't heard yet.'

'You started it.'

'I apologise then. That was not a happy analogy. I think it must come from being around too many young men every day.'

He came to stand beside her, looking at the print she had been inspecting. As in the museum and the ball, there seemed to be a point of proximity at which her already alert body began experiencing rather strange reactions. Some she remembered from Tim, but some were new and uncomfortable.

'What *do* you teach the veterans at Hope House?'

'Mostly literacy, but also sums. To the soldiers as well as to their wives and children. We also have a reading circle for anyone who is interested.'

'A noble venture.'

'I think so,' she said rather defensively.

'I meant that sincerely. You needn't raise your hackles at me as you do at your mother.'

'I apologise. I did hear her voice for a moment.'

To her surprise he touched the hair above her temple for the briefest moments.

'I dare say you carry it inside you.'

Her eyes burned as if he'd blown smoke into them. 'Perhaps. Perhaps I'm preparing for the day she discovers what I do. Eventually she will. And then she shall try to manipulate Papa and Annie and Piers to stop me.'

He didn't wave that way. 'What precisely does she think you do in Birmingham?'

'I told her I am companion to a widow.'

His eyes narrowed. 'Something tells me that is not precisely a lie. You said that far too comfortably.'

She laughed, her tension fading further. 'You are right. I told you of my friend in Birmingham. We share rooms and she also teaches at Hope House. In fact, it was she who wrote to me of the opening and gave me the courage to leave home when I was at my lowest point. That is close enough, isn't it?'

'You are on firm ground indeed. And lucky to have such a friend.'

Her eyes burned again. She wished Eleanor was in town, too. She needed someone who could tell her she wasn't an awful person for wanting to lean her head on the shoulder of the one man in

England who was categorically off limits. That this would pass.

She managed a smile. 'I know. I miss our evenings when we return to our rooms and brew tea and talk about everything and nothing...'

He took a step towards her and stopped, turning his head a little, listening. Her heart had tumbled into chaos at his sudden movement, her body frozen in confused anticipation. But he merely shrugged, his expression turning flat again.

'Cousin Gerry must have finished by now. We had best join them.'

She followed him in silence. It should have been she who suggested they join the others. She never should have left them in the first place. Every time she found herself alone with this man the ache right at her centre burned a little brighter.

She pressed a hand to it, but it didn't calm it at all. The sooner she returned to Birmingham, the better.

'You did not try the tapenade,' Juan accused, shoving the tray under Marcus's nose.

Marcus sighed and moved away from the tray and his butler-valet-chef's accusation.

'I'm not hungry, Juan. You should be happy Mrs Walsh and this idiot here did your tapas justice. There's hardly any left.'

'I'll take that,' said the idiot and took the last of

the strips of toasted bread with the olive tapenade. Juan took the now empty tray and left the room, shaking his head at something or other. The door shut behind him with a quiet emphasis.

Marcus turned back to Dom. He didn't want to do this, didn't want to talk about it at all, but he had to be absolutely clear.

'Stay away from Mrs Walsh, Dom.'

Dom licked his fingers and flopped into an armchair. 'You made your point, Marc. Enough. You're not only being redundant and dramatic, but even a tad disrespectful of your prospective sister-in-law. She's a soldier's widow who followed the drum through a bloody, brutal war. She's perfectly capable of slapping me down or kicking me in the ballocks and she knew that.'

'You wouldn't have dared do any of that to Anne.'

'Damn right I wouldn't have, even if I wished to, which I more certainly don't. Besides being your betrothed, she's an innocent. Lily is neither.'

'Then kindly regard her as if she was.'

'Fine, I will, but I think you're being ridiculous. Why not let her have some fun?'

'Fun!'

'Yes, fun. She clearly enjoys crossing swords.'

Marcus clung to the shirt tails of his temper, but he could feel the fabric ripping in his grasp.

'This may be a game to you, but she might take your shallow flirting for something more serious.'

'You're starting to sound like my father, Marc. What the devil is wrong with you? From the way you're carrying on, one would think you—' He broke off, his eyes widening. 'Marc? You…you're not jealous by any chance?'

'Have you lost what little mind you had, Dom? She is to be my sister-in-law. Just stay away from her.'

Dom rose, his expression hard. 'I already told you I will. I would also recommend the same to you. She seems to be having an unhealthy effect on your temper, old friend.'

The door gave a truculent thud behind him.

Marcus stayed where he was, willing down his maligned temper. It had been years and years since he'd lost it so categorically. And with Dom. Whatever Dom's failings he was a loyal friend, once at great cost to himself.

Damn it. Now he would have to apologise. To her as well. She'd borne his attack well, but he had no right whatsoever to dictate to her, let alone condemn her.

Damn idiot. A twelve-year-old would have handled that better.

He left the room as well and went to his study. Ombra peeked out from under the desk. 'They're gone,' Marcus informed him and Ombra huffed, but stayed where he was. 'Any room in there for me, old boy?'

Ombra's nails scrabbled at the wooden floor as he rose, stretched and yawned, vacating his favourite spot. He stood for a moment, cyeing Marcus as if waiting for him to slip in there in his stead.

A faded memory of doing just that when he was a boy came back to him. It had smelled of his father's cheroots and leather slippers. Marcus smiled. It seemed lifetimes ago.

He'd been sulking and had hoped everyone would think he'd run away to join the navy or something equally outlandish. He'd hid there with Ombra's grandsire, imagining with gratification his parents and sisters all coming apart at the seams at the thought of him tossed about in an Atlantic storm and how he would return, having vanquished some pirates and stolen their booty, and then everyone would see he was no baby as his sister Gertie had admonished him.

His mother had found him and sat herself down at the entrance to his little wooden cave and waited until he'd poured out all the frustration and confusion of an eight-year-old who was beginning to realise the world expected a great deal from him that he did not want to deliver.

He remembered her words very well, both calm and warm, echoing in his little chamber.

'Everyone must sometimes do things they do

not wish to. The key is to also do things that are truly, utterly yours so that they fill your world with joy far more than the things you don't wish to do weigh you down. It shall be hard, but try to always keep the balance just a little in your favour, Marco.'

He'd done well in that respect. Until now. Ironic that he was slipping far out of balance because of his mother's own demand that he do something he did not wish to do.

They'd both known it was fear that was driving her demand that he marry before his thirty-fifth birthday. That her demand was unfair, that she was shackling her own unspoken need to survive like a weight about his neck. But neither of them had been strong enough to deny her. She'd consoled him, and herself, that even if he did not truly wish to marry, he did want children.

'Find a good mother for the children you want to have, just as I found a good father for the children I wished to have.'

'You were in love with him.'

'True. I was lucky. To love a man who is also a good father—that is luck. I wish you the same, but if you can only secure one side of that balance, choose a good mother for your children.'

And so he'd agreed and hoped that by some miracle it would just…happen. That doing what he did not wish would somehow become something he did so he could keep that balance.

Choose a good mother for your children.

He had. Anne Devenish was precisely that. No foolish whim on his part could negate her value in that respect.

He glanced at the portrait of his parents in their corner. The frame had the Sherbourne family crest carved into the bottom with their motto: *Praemonitus, praemunitus.*

Very appropriate for his predicament. Forewarned was indeed forearmed.

Now he was forewarned of his stupidity and knew where the horse droppings were, he could stop stepping in them again and again.

Any situation could be addressed by following two simple steps:

Step one—face the facts, most unpleasant first.
Step two—do something about it.

So, most unpleasant fact... *Oh, hell...here goes...* He was attracted to the least appropriate woman on earth. Perhaps his mind was playing a jest on him worthy of the best Greek fables. Not quite Oedipus, but quite bad none the less...

Now, what to do about it.

Since he couldn't very well leave the battlefield

or eliminate his enemy, he would have to ignore it. Her. Mind over matter.

He would be polite and stay the hell out of her way until balance was restored.

She was his betrothed's sister.

That was all.

Chapter Twelve

'We're here.' Dom hopped down from the hackney and Marcus followed. He'd been lost in his thoughts and hadn't noticed where the carriage had turned on their way back from Westminster.

Until he looked up. Those columns…those stairs… St George's, Hanover Square, was unmistakable.

'What the devil are we doing *here*?'

Dom paused with his foot on the lowest step. 'We're here to attend my cousin's wedding. You promised. I agreed to go to your ball and you agreed to come with me today.'

'When the devil did I agree to attend a wedding? I don't even want to attend my own.'

Dom's eyes widened and he flapped his hands in a shushing motion.

Marcus lowered his voice with effort. 'You did not mention it was a wedding, Dom. I would have remembered that, trust me. At least I warned you I was dragging you to a ball. You might have returned the courtesy.'

'I'm not as nice as you. I didn't tell you because I knew you wouldn't come. I must attend or my aunt will inform my father and that means at least four pages of vicious vitriol by the next post. But if I attended alone people might have drawn the very wrong conclusions about my matrimonial ambitions. With you here everyone will assume it was you who dragged me along now that you are set firmly down the path to wedded bliss. Problem solved. Now hush and move.'

He caught Marcus's sleeve and tugged him towards the stairs.

Marcus called himself to order. Irrespective of Dom's perfidy, there was no need for histrionics on his part. It was only a church. He'd been here several times for his friends' weddings and survived intact. He'd just never noticed how noisy it was. And even with the high vaulted ceiling and wide nave with the pews raised on either side it felt…cramped and close.

The wedding party was already there, standing in the nave and filling the pews. There were others in the church, some on their own business and some waiting with evident pleasure for the spectacle. It was cheaper than a penny play and not as stuffy with body odour and tobacco smoke as the theatres.

St George's was a fine place to idle for a stray hour.

Marcus followed Dom to the raised pews on the left, relieved they wouldn't be actually joining the wedding party below. He had his limits. At least he thought he had. As they moved up the side aisle towards the front he glanced around the familiar church, taking in the Corinthian pillars and the barrel vault above the nave, across to…

He froze.

The pews on the other side were populated by a row of young women dressed in various shades of flowers, the silk trimmings of their bonnets catching the light filtering through the high glass windows. They were a delightful sight for the young bucks to ogle. Marcus recovered himself and shoved Wrexham into the first seat that was free.

'Not this far back, Marc,' Dom protested.

'Yes, this far back,' Marcus snarled. 'Anne and her sister are over there. Did you know they would be here?'

Dom shrugged. 'They must be relatives of the bride. Damnably small world, the *ton*.'

A very tall thin man with more hair than head gave them an impressively vicious look over his shoulder and they fell silent. At least outwardly.

Inside Marcus was a cauldron bubbling with several of the ten plagues—there was thunder and lightning and pestilence and a strong urge to do away with the firstborn of the Wrexham family.

If this was Dom's twisted attempt to prove to Marcus he was wrong to be flinging himself into a parson's mousetrap, it was a wasted effort. He'd already come to that conclusion himself. Like most profound revelations, this one, too, had come too late to make a difference.

But it wasn't the scene of his future nuptials that was twisting his gut. It was the sight of the plain straw bonnet with a single yellow ribbon amid the sumptuous millinery confections of Madame Fanchot and her like. Or rather, the sight of the face it framed for a moment as she settled into her seat.

Lily was the very last woman he wanted to see in the venue where he would all too soon be consigning himself to marrying her sister.

Perhaps the Greeks were in the right of it. According to them the Gods delighted in setting humans up to make tragic fools of themselves. They would have delighted in this scene.

'In two months you shall be standing precisely where my cousin is standing,' Miss Morecambe whispered to Anne and gave a gusty sigh.

'Though with someone far handsomer than Geoffrey Pruitt-Smythe. How I envy you.'

Anne gave a perfunctory smile and hushed her friend, her attention on the couple below.

Lily stared at the balustrade that separated them from the nave. She ought to be watching the ceremony and readying herself for the inevitable. In less than two months she must return to London to witness her sister's marriage to Lord Sherbourne.

Tim's commanding officer Captain Denham once told her that the day before a battle he always tried to imagine the worst that could happen. Then he would linger in the image and find his feet in it so that if it came to pass, he'd be prepared. Then he would put that image aside and think only of how he would win.

Lily didn't want to do either. She didn't want to look at the excited couple surrounded by their loving family. She didn't want to sigh over the beautiful bridal dress in the palest pink trimmed with white silk roses at the flounce and sleeves puffed *à la Française* trimmed with white satin points.

She had done her best to join the spirited discussion among Anne's friends as to what fashion would best suit Annie's pale gold beauty. She knew Annie would look far more beautiful than the bride they were watching. She, too, would stand there with roses and pearls woven into her hair, smiling up at the handsome face of her husband-to-be…

Lily took her handkerchief from her reticule. The other girls in their row were clutching theirs to catch the tears of excitement and joy and envy leaking from their eyes. Lily mopped her forehead. Even with the vaulted ceiling high above them and the weather cool outside it was stuffy here and hard to breathe amid the perfumed crowd. She wished she could take off her bonnet. She wished she could walk out. She was at the edge of the pew. She could just leave…

She glanced down the nave towards the entrance and froze. For a moment she remained skewered on Lord Sherbourne's dark gold gaze, the heat turning to sharp crackling ice, covering her like a frost racing across a field at dawn.

She snapped her head forward again.

'Lily?' Anne whispered. 'Are you not well?'

No. Not well at all.

'I am fine. I merely…don't like crowds.'

Anne's hand closed on hers. 'Is it an episode?'

An episode. Mother's euphemism for the attacks that sometimes caught her since the war. Such a nice, neutral word.

'No, I'm fine. Truly.'

She couldn't even mention she'd seen Lord Sherbourne now. Anne wasn't suspicious by nature, but perhaps even she might begin to wonder and that would be unbearable. She would be miserable for Lily if she knew and eventually she would reveal the truth to Lord Sherbourne, by deed if not by word, and then it would be even more unbearably uncomfortable.

Eventually this…infatuation would fade and she would look back on these days with embarrassment. It would. She'd been through far worse than a foolish *tendre* for the absolutely worst possible man in the world and had paid a high price for it. Now she could hardly remember why she'd adored Tim so foolishly. Infatuations came and went. This would as well.

She straightened her back and focused on the ceremony. Both bride and groom were nervous. The groom kept glancing at the bride and his hand shook as he signed the registry, but then the bride laughed joyously and he smiled at her—happiness, relief, love…

A tear dripped out of the corner of Lily's eye and she dried it quickly and glanced at her sister. Annie wasn't watching the couple now, but the pattern on her reticule. It was of a shepherdess and probably one she'd embroidered herself. She looked almost bored, but Lily knew better. Had she seen Lord Sherbourne on the other side of the nave? Was she embarrassed? Upset she hadn't known he was coming?

Worried about her future?

Questions catapulted themselves about Lily's mind. She'd thought she knew Annie inside and out, but she'd changed this past year. Older, quieter, more…aloof. Even from Lily. As if she was already pulling away into her new role.

Or perhaps… Had Annie guessed Lily's feelings towards Lord Sherbourne were not…sisterly? Oh, God, she hoped not. That would sit heavily on poor Annie's soft heart.

The couple filed out, followed by their chattering, laughing family. Annie's friends rose from the pews, excited and laughing as well, and they all made their way towards the entrance.

'Oh, look,' exclaimed Miss Morecambe. 'It is Lord Sherbourne and Lord Wrexham! Anne, you didn't mention they were planning to attend.'

Anne was saved from answering by Miss Faversham jostling her for a better look, her face alight.

'Oh, it is. Isn't Lord Wrexham beautiful? You are so lucky to have danced with him, Anne. Those eyes…' Three of the girls sighed in unison. Lily barely managed not to roll her own eyes. Anne, too, seemed less tolerant of their nonsense. She took Lily's arm and drew her out into the blustery afternoon. The wind tugged at their skirts, slapping their ribbons against their cheeks.

Lily knew Lord Sherbourne would approach

Annie and she prepared herself, brought herself inside as she had every time before the soldiers marched into battle, waiting in the emptied barracks or tents until they returned or an envoy passed through with news, good and bad.

She knew how to gather herself in.

He stood a little to one side, looking out to the street. He looked impatient, just as he had the previous day, and there was none of the usual tolerant humour on his face. He was more handsome as a statue, but less likeable.

She wished that his revealing this side of himself would weaken the hold he had on her, but it was making her worry, not dislike him. Something was wrong and her foolish mind and even more foolish heart wanted to share that burden.

He turned at their exit and approached Anne, looking at no one else. Two of the young women beside them sighed. Lily wanted to shove them down the steps which was unfair because she was far worse. Annie smiled and held out her hand with her usual calm poise. She was truly meant to be a countess.

'I did not know you were planning to attend this wedding, Lord Sherbourne.'

'Neither did I. Dom dragged me here without fair warning.'

Lord Wrexham grinned and bowed. 'I'm an

awful excuse for a friend. It's a wonder he hasn't shaken me off yet.'

'Nothing I do seems to have the desired effect.'

'You have only to ask, old man. Come, Mrs Walsh. I shall escort you home and leave this curmudgeon to the woman who must all too soon bear the burden of his ill tempers.'

'We will walk together. It isn't far,' Lord Sherbourne replied. 'Unless you find it too windy and would rather wait for the carriage, Anne?'

'I would enjoy the walk, Marcus. I enjoy brisk weather.'

Lily and Lord Wrexham followed.

'There go the most envied couple in London,' Lord Wrexham murmured. 'It is to your sister's credit that she hasn't become the most hated woman in town. All that beauty and sweetness nabbing the big prize.'

'Don't he mean '

Lord Wrexham glanced down at her childish remark and smiled. 'I'll try not to be. You two are very close.'

'Very.'

'I envy you, then. My brother is a replica of my father. They are both experts in the art of disapproval.'

'Is that why you and Lord Sherbourne are so close?'

His smile softened further. 'Probably. He's

the least judgmental person I know. We became friends at school though he is two years older than I. He'll thrash me with that damn tongue of his if I make a mistake, but it's never personal. He can't be bothered to be disgusted with anyone.'

'What kind of mistake?' she asked, curiosity pressing aside depression for a moment.

'Oh, in one of my lectures, for instance.'

That was clearly another evasion, but she didn't press. It was evident neither man wished to discuss their work.

'I thought you spoke superbly well,' she said instead and he squeezed her hand between his ribs and arm.

'So did you. Do you know I like you, Lily Walsh? If you were an heiress, I would elope with you this very afternoon.'

'If it is an heiress you need, Annie and I sat next to two this afternoon who appeared all too willing to elope with you.'

'*Not* at any price. I said I like you. That is a pre-requisite to making the worst mistake possible a person could make. If I must give up my freedom one day, I'd rather not want to throw myself into the sea before the registry is even signed.'

'You think it a mistake to marry?'

'I do. It is nothing more than a tool for people with power to control those without.'

She slowed. 'Do you mean women?'

'I mean everyone. It is all about the control of property. Our whole damned…excuse me, dashed society is constructed on a handful of men holding the reins of the majority for their own purposes and that requires a legal structure that will make the tugging of those reins effective. Marriage is merely one part of that structure. There is nothing holy about it.'

'Why, Lord Wrexham, you're a radical. I thought I caught the scent of saltpetre and sulphur at your talk. I would definitely attend a lecture of yours on this topic.'

He laughed and shielded her from a man bearing a tray of something steaming on his head as they turned on to Brook Street.

'I dare say you would, but otherwise it would likely be an empty hall. Besides, I'm not a true radical. Marcus tells me I merely like to grumble because I can't stand my father. Which is damn unfair since his parents were delightful people. I spent most of my time down from school and university at Sherbourne Hall rather than with my own family. People were always trooping through Marc's house. It was noisy and chaotic and the best place to be. And I don't know why I'm telling you this.'

'Because you like me.' She smiled.

'Is this what you do with your students?'

'Do what?'

'Listen. It's very sneaky.'

'I know.'

'Hmmm. I'm learning some good tactics from you, Lily Walsh. Are you certain you're not a secret heiress?'

'Quite certain.'

'Pity. Do let me know if your circumstances change.'

Lily laughed. They'd reached Number Twenty-Three and the footman had already opened the door to Lord Sherbourne's knock.

'Won't you both come in, Lord Sherbourne? Lord Wrexham?' Anne asked prettily. Lord Wrexham moved forward just as Lord Sherbourne stepped back, causing a moment of confusion. Lord Sherbourne gathered himself first.

'I'm afraid we cannot this afternoon, Anne. We have some matters to attend to. I shall be by tomorrow to take you driving in the park. Good day, Mrs Walsh.'

Lord Wrexham's arched brows rose, but he let Lily's arm go and with a quick wink he turned to follow his friend.

Lily and Anne went upstairs and changed out of their promenade gowns in silence.

Now that Wrexham and his nonsense weren't shielding her from herself, Lily's head was back to pounding. She ought to worry about Anne's uncharacteristic silence, but she couldn't. She felt empty. Miserable.

She *ached*.

'I think I shall go rest a little, Annie. My head…'

Annie nodded and smiled, but it wasn't real either.

Chapter Thirteen

'Mrs Walsh. May I have a word with you?'

Lily straightened so fast it was a wonder her spine didn't snap. Lord Sherbourne was standing in the open doorway of the parlour, dressed for driving, his greatcoat filling the door frame, his gaze on the window behind her. Lily tightened her hold on her book. A moment ago her heart had been dragging itself along like a sick tortoise and now it was careening about like a filly with a wasp under its saddle.

'Lord Sherbourne.' Good. You remembered his name. Idiot.

She cleared her throat. 'Annie…'

'Has gone to change for our drive in the park. I wanted a word with you before we went.'

Please don't blush. *Please.*

'A word?'

He finally looked at her, his frown deepening. 'Are you well?'

She touched her hair, wishing she'd asked Ailish to do something with it, rather than merely pulling it back with a ribbon and some pins. Not that it mattered. In fact, she'd thought she'd made it clear to herself that that kind of thinking was strictly forbidden.

She had to stop even regarding herself as a woman around Annie's fiancée. She was nothing but a…an extension. Annie's sister.

'I am perfectly well, Lord Sherbourne.'

'You look…tired.'

I'm exhausted.

'Piers and I stayed up late, talking.' The lie was plausible enough.

He nodded and picked up a sheet of writing paper from the table, turning it over. 'It occurred to me, later, that I never did properly apologise. That day.'

Her mind drew a blank for a moment. 'What day?'

He shot her a quick hard look, as if offended. 'At my home. In the library. I was…discourteous.'

Heat climbed up her cheeks. Strange that he would remember his anger. She remembered how comfortable she had been talking with him afterwards. 'You were angry.'

'That is no excuse.'

'Well, no. I admit I was a little surprised. Annie said you never lose your temper.'

'Rarely. Very little is worth the bother.'

'Lord Wrexham obviously succeeds where others fail.'

He sat down on the other side of the table, folded the paper diagonally and spread it out again, then folded it down the middle. He had large, long-fingered hands, yet he folded the paper with swift, precise moves. He didn't even seem aware of what he was doing. The paper kept becoming smaller and thicker, opening and refolding this way and that.

'I've known Dominic since my third year at school.'

She wasn't quite certain what point he was trying to make and proceeded cautiously, her heart calming a little at his peculiar diffidence.

'I dare say he's more a brother than a friend, then.'

'Yes, you could say that.'

His smile was swift and warm but faded almost immediately. He looked back down and added a fold to his creation, turned something and pulled something else and set it down.

She gave a little gasp of surprise. It was a little bird, wings arched and outstretched, tail reaching for the sky and beak extended. Lord Sherbourne turned a little towards the door and she caught the sound of voices in the hall upstairs.

'I should go.'

He rose and she followed, feeling as awkward as awkward could be. Her pulse was too fast and she didn't even know why. Nothing was happening.

No, more and more of her little island was washing away, the waves licking at her bare feet, pulling her in. Soon she'd have nothing at all to stand on.

'Am I forgiven?' he asked and she forced herself to smile.

'Of course you are. You never said anything truly offensive, at least not to me. Most people would have blamed me, not Lord Wrexham.'

'Your parents, I suppose.'

'Yes, probably. Please don't be angry with your friend on my account.'

'I'm not.'

'No,' she said, watching the tension flicker over his face. She didn't know which side of him was truer—this severe, almost dour man, or the one who let humour and curiosity take centre stage. She wondered if Annie knew.

Annie.

He was Annie's. As simple as that. There was nothing to wonder about. Nothing to puzzle over. Nothing to yearn for.

Marcus, Lord Sherbourne, was to be her brother-in-law.

She would certainly *not* be considering the

offer of employment from London's Hope House. In fact, the sooner she returned to Birmingham the better. This utterly unwanted attraction would fade in time and soon she would be able to meet Annie's husband without her body reacting as if she'd been dropped into the middle of a battlefield.

He nodded. 'Would you care to accompany us to the park?'

Well, that was definitely an uninviting invitation.

'It is kind of you to offer, Lord Sherbourne, but I promised Piers I would read his essay.'

His mouth twisted a little at the corner. 'Enjoy.'

When the door closed behind him she picked up the little bird. A smart woman would toss it into the grate, but she cupped it in her hand and went upstairs to her room and set it down gently by her inkwell.

What kind of man made paper birds in the middle of an apology?

She locked the door and sat for a long while, staring at the fragile little creation with the perky tail.

Chapter Fourteen

'When are you returning to Birmingham?'

Lily looked up from her letter to Eleanor.

Her mother stood in the doorway of Lily's room, her hand on the knob as if prepared to slam the door and run if Lily attacked. In the weeks since her arrival in London her mother often approached her like this—setting a safe distance.

There it was, the familiar, uncomfortable pinch right in the middle of her chest. Lily answered it as she always did: *'She cannot help herself. There is nothing inside her that could provide what I need.'* One day, perhaps, she would accept that and stop hoping that…

'Soon, Mama. If you wish I leave immediately…'

Perhaps it was a good idea she be forced to leave. She was not doing a very good job at self-preservation on her own.

'It is merely that the expenses…'

'Yes, Mama. I understand. I shall leave by the end of the week.'

She touched the little bird balanced on her inkwell. The poor little thing was a tad ink-stained and the tips of his wings as wilted as Lily's soul, but its tail was still as perky as ever.

'Very well,' said Mrs Devenish. 'If that is what you wish.'

Lily didn't bother answering that disingenuous provocation. It *was* what she wished. Or rather, it was time she ought to wish. Remaining in London was only making it worse. She'd learned to put a smile between her and her increasingly bruised heart, but it wasn't easy.

In the fortnight since Lord Sherbourne's forced apology he still came to see Annie, though not quite as often as before. Lily wondered if it was because he'd noticed something in her behaviour. She hoped not. In any case she kept her distance and he no longer made the same efforts to charm her as he still employed with her parents and Annie and Piers.

A smart woman would have long ago retreated to the safety of Birmingham where she knew her worth and had her routine and there were no overly clever men who saw through one and who made her laugh when she least wished to.

Annie entered the room, her gaze moving between Lily and their mother. 'Mama, shall I wear

the primrose pelerine or the hunter green with
the Prussian frogging for the drive to Richmond
Park?'

Mrs Devenish was immediately distracted.
'Goodness, my dear. Neither! Did you not see the
latest article in *Ackermann's Repository*? Sim-
plicity is the order of the day. You shall wear the
striped lutestring spencer over the lovely pale blue
jaconet muslin walking dress Madame Fanchot
just delivered this morning. And I think the leg-
horn bonnet with the blue ribbons. That will bring
out your eyes. Primrose makes you look wan. We
never should have allowed Madame Fanchot to
convince us to take that shade. It is quite too bad
of her.'

In the doorway she paused and glanced over
her shoulder. 'Perhaps you had best stay home,
Lily. You are looking rather peaky lately.'

'Nonsense, Mama.' Annie's tone was sharper
than usual. 'A drive on such a lovely day can only
do good. Besides, Lord Wrexham is coming and
he and Lily rub along well together.'

'Anne! Where do you hear such vulgar phrases?
I dare say it is from Piers and those dreadfully
noisy friends of his. In any case that is hardly to
the point. Lord Wrexham may be as handsome as
the devil, but he hasn't a farthing to scratch with,'
Mrs Devenish snorted in disgust, unconscious of
her own use of one of Pier's vulgar sayings. 'I

don't know why Lord Sherbourne bothers to associate with him. The tales one hears of that reprobate are quite, quite shocking. When you are Lady Sherbourne you must drop a hint in Lord Sherbourne's ear that he is not at all the thing.'

Annie didn't answer, but her mouth was a hard flat line as she and their mother left the room.

Lily sealed her utterly uninformative letter, cursing as she dripped hot wax on her finger. She ought to have jumped at her mother's suggestion she not join the excursion to Richmond Park, but her perfidy ran deep. The perverse part of her was storing up memories and sensations and didn't give a hoot about what was right and loyal.

Chapter Fifteen

'It has been a simply lovely excursion, my dear Mrs Faversham. Richmond Park has never looked lovelier. Don't you agree, Anne, dear?'

Anne paused in her exchanged goodbyes with Miss Faversham and obediently agreed with Mrs Devenish that it had indeed been a lovely excursion. Miss Faversham craned her neck as she climbed into the awaiting carriage, clearly hoping for another glimpse at Lord Wrexham.

Marcus cast a surreptitious look at his pocket watch. Almost three hours now. This was his first visit to Richmond Park in the company of a gaggle of young women and tedious young men and their parents.

He hadn't quite accounted for these types of events when he'd offered for a woman of twenty-one. A drive around Hyde Park was bearable. Balls were a nuisance, but at least one rarely had to talk with any one person for more than a few moments at a stretch. But a three-hour drive and stroll through Richmond Park with perfectly pleasant people who had probably not once been east of Berkeley Square had planted a pain right in the middle of his forehead.

He wanted to be alone for a while. A week at the least. A month.

Anne waved as the Favershams and the Hammonds drove away and then walked towards him, her soft smile in place. She was a picture of English beauty and serenity. He could not have chosen better if he'd been Pygmalion himself and formed her from ivory and had all the gods bless her with every virtue in the book. She was the perfect choice.

The only imperfection was in him. It just ran rather deep.

'Where is Lily?' Anne glanced around.

'I don't know. She went off with Dominic.'

And there it went, a little deeper. At least he'd managed to keep his voice neutral. Unlike his temper. He would have a word with Dom. Again.

'Oh.' Her eyes widened. With hope. 'Do you think…? Is he fond of her?'

'He is *not* husband material.'

She blinked a little at his snap. 'Well, I am aware of his reputation, but they say reformed rakes make the best husbands…'

If he hadn't been so tense he might have laughed.

But something cruel and resentful inside him was yearning to let slip a very poisonous arrow.

'"They" say a great many things. Most of them are either self-serving or ignorant.'

Anne's smile fled. 'I didn't mean... I merely... Oh, look. There they are!' Anne waved at her sister with relief.

Dom and Lily were approaching along the path from King Henry's Mound and Lily waved back. Her bonnet, which was hanging from her arm by its strings, bounced giddily. The sun, annoyingly bright and cheerful, raised auburn and copper lights in her hair. She had her hand on Dom's arm and he leaned towards her to say something and she smiled up at him and laughed.

They looked very comfortable together. Happy.

No. He wouldn't let that happen. Just...no.

Wrexham looked up and met Marcus's gaze. His smile was smug, like a cat warming itself in the sun with a mouse under its paw.

Rage clawed through Marcus, shredding its way along his nerves, tightening a mailed fist about that pain in his head. At that moment, before he caught himself, he could have happily imagined doing violence to his best friend. Bringing down the whole temple about their heads like a roaring Samson.

He turned away. Every time he thought he knew its boundaries, the swampland of his weakness pressed forward, swallowing more solid ground and squeezing him into a shrinking island of sanity.

This time he didn't even look at Anne to centre himself. That only made it worse.

'Oh, no, Lily. Your pelisse is torn at the hem!' Anne exclaimed and Lily glanced down with a frown.

'Oh, dear. She must have ripped it when she landed.'

'She?' enquired Mr Devenish as he and Mrs Devenish joined them.

'A dog had chased this poor tabby up a tree and Lord Wrexham coaxed her down. It took him ages which was why we were so long. What a pity she did not shred your coat instead of my skirt.'

Dom laughed. 'It was your fault for cooing at her as if she was a turtle dove.'

'I was trying to calm her,' Lily objected.

'Well, next time remember cats haven't a romantic bone in their body. They're opinionated malice with fur and whiskers pasted on, bless their fastidious hearts. But since it was my fault she jumped out of my arms I'll make good and buy you a new pelisse. I think… Yes, something bold. Claret-coloured to bring out your hair.'

'That is very considerate of you, Lord Wrexham,' Mrs Devenish said with a clear snap in her voice, 'but quite improper.'

For once Marcus completely agreed with his future mother-in-law. Still, he held his peace as they walked towards the remaining conveyances awaiting them by the gates. The afternoon might have ended on that slightly sour but perfectly normal note if Mrs Devenish could have contained herself. But she barely waited for Dom to swing himself on to Pegasus and trot away through the gates before turning to Lily.

'Must you embarrass us so, Lily? It is a good thing the Hammonds and Favershams had already departed before you made a spectacle of yourself.'

'Mama…' Anne said, but Mrs Devenish talked right over her.

'It is bad enough you dawdled behind with *that man*, but that utterly foolish tale about rescuing a cat, when it was quite obvious you two…'

'Mabel!' Mr Devenish intervened with a rather alarmed glance at Lord Sherbourne.

'There *was* a cat, Mama.' Lily's voice was as flat as a millpond in midsummer.

'Well, that's bad enough.' Mrs Devenish gave a gusty sigh. 'You were ever thus, Lily. Even as a child. There was that cat of yours that ran under the carriage wheels. What was her name? Ella? Emma? That's right—Emma. She was quite an ugly little runt, but still, a pity.'

Lily Walsh gasped as if she'd been stung. Her

eyes fixed on her mother, wide and empty. Mr Devenish turned faintly grey as well, his voice raw.

'*Mabel.*'

'What?' Mrs Devenish asked with a casual insouciance that was wholly unconvincing. 'Oh... oh, dear, how foolish of me. Forget I even mentioned it.'

'Forget?' Anne looked very like her father—pale and stricken, though not as pale as Lily.

Only a moment ago Lily's expression had been utterly, blankly indifferent. Now her freckles stood out on the bridge of her nose and her lips looked bruised as if she lacked air. Marcus had no idea what Mrs Devenish's words meant, only that they were unusually cruel. He wanted to push that woman away, far away, until she went over a cliff into the abyss where she belonged.

But she wasn't done. 'Oh, come now.' Her voice was soft, conciliating. 'My dearest Lily, one cannot go through life walking on eggshells and worrying about ever mentioning a name. It is not as if you are the first woman who lost a child.'

God in heaven.

His anger and resentment and confusion fell away. Even the wielder of that cruel sword fell away and all his attention and pain fixed on Lily. She held one fist to her sternum, like an oath, but her hand was twisting in the fabric of her pelisse and her voice shook.

'The kitten's name was Helen, Mother, not Emma. After Helen of Troy because Papa and I were reading the *Iliad* at the time. You knew that, Mama, because you thought it was ridiculous to call such an ugly beast after a beauty. *Your* words, Mama. I dare say you would have said the same of Emma had she lived long enough to return to England with me because she was small and had straight brown hair and not your beautiful golden curls any more than I had.'

For the first time Mrs Devenish seemed aware of her audience. 'I suggest we change the subject. I'm certain Lord Sherbourne is bored by our little family disagreement.'

'Boredom isn't my usual response to viewing someone being tortured, Mrs Devenish.'

They all turned to him, as if his words were the anomaly in this family drama. Perhaps they were. He ought to climb into his curricle and go, but the thought of leaving Lily with this witch... He turned to her father.

'It is still a fine afternoon so, if you don't mind, sir, I shall take up Miss Devenish and Mrs Walsh in the curricle and see them back to Brook Street.'

'I...yes, of course. Thank you. Capital idea.'

Marcus didn't wait for the others to recover. He took Anne's arm in one hand and Lily's in the other and led them towards his curricle. They said nothing and Lily didn't even demur when he handed Anne up first so he could sit beside Lily. It was wrong, stupid, but at that moment he didn't care. He was damned if he was leaving Lily exposed after that.

He would take what he could. Even the torture of her leg pressed to his. Denial wasn't working. Perhaps an immersion in agony would.

Her thigh was firm and warm against his and he wanted so badly to put his arm around her and thaw away that careful covering of frost she donned around her mother. He could understand it so much better now.

Why hadn't he known this? In the report he'd commissioned about the Devenishes there had been no mention of a child. A daughter named Emma.

He wanted to know everything now. How old the babe had been. What had happened. Everything.

Hell. He wanted to kill Mrs Devenish. With his bare hands.

'My lord?' His tiger's surprised admonition brought him back to reality and the approaching sharp turn on to the London road. He checked his team and himself.

'Are you quite certain you two aren't foundlings?' His question won a choke of laughter from Lily and a sniff from Anne as she hunted in her reticule for a handkerchief and blew her nose, shoving it back with more force that she usually allowed herself.

'I don't understand why she must say such horrid things. It is as though there is a…a beast inside her sometimes.' Anne's voice was watery and Lily placed her hand over hers, turning a little towards her sister. The motion brought her thigh even more securely against Marcus's.

'I don't think she can help it, Annie. When she is upset she must lash out.'

'Then she should take up boxing and leave her daughters alone,' Marcus intervened.

Annie gave a snort of laughter and Lily's thigh softened against him as she turned to him this time. Her colour was back and her smile was warm with laughter, bringing her dimples to life. Pure yearning impaled him like a lance.

'Is there such a place, Lord Sherbourne? A boxing salon for women?'

'I'm afraid not, Lily. Pity. Though if there were I dare say it would be overrun by men coming to watch.'

'We wouldn't let them in. You men have your own boxing salons, don't you?'

'We do, but I rather think the appeal of your boxing salon would outstrip the appeal of watching a couple of pasty, paunchy and puffing men try to pop one over the other's guard. What would you wear, by the way?'

'Marcus!' Anne admonished, but she leaned forward with a smile, looking to Lily for guidance. Lily's face was upturned, as if the image was engraved on the fluffy white clouds floating above them.

'Breeches and short chemises tucked into the waistband. Something simple and comfortable that won't get in the way.'

Simple, maybe. Definitely not comfortable. At least not for him.

He wished his imagination wasn't so active. It was doing its damnedest to slip Lily out of her borrowed clothes and into her boxer's costume. Did she have freckles anywhere else? There would be a dusting of them on her bare shoulders, hidden by the fall of her hair. No, she would have to gather her hair if she was to box... Lily-in-his-mind obliged by gathering the reddish-brown waves in her hands, winding it up, her arms rising and pulling at the soft, sheer fabric of her chemise, her generous breasts pressing against it...

'And gloves,' she continued, clearly determined to continue in this lighter vein. 'It looks rather painful to hit someone with one's bare hands.'

He could use a good blow at the moment. He resolutely lowered the curtain on Lily-in-his-mind.

'Is boxing painful, Lord Sherbourne?' Anne asked, her voice hushed as if her mama was sitting behind them rather than his tiger, Blunt.

'It can be, Anne, if you don't do it correctly. For example, never fold your thumb into your fist if you want to plant someone a facer.'

'Is that boxing cant?'

'I'm afraid it is.'

'There seems to be a great deal of it. Cant, I mean. Sometimes I don't understand what Piers and his friends are saying. I am forever asking Lily to translate.'

'You understand canting lingo, Lily?'

'Being surrounded by soldiers one must, or remain in ignorance of half of all that is being discussed. I learned Spanish, Portuguese *and* flash lingo, so if you swell and gentry mort think you can have a pull at me, you'll soon be sherked.'

Anne laughed. 'Is this what you teach them in Birmingham, Lily?'

'This is what they teach me. We have a fair trade and teach each other. Most of the children are really darlings and they do try so hard.'

'I dare say if I had you as a teacher I would make every effort to study, Mrs Walsh,' Marcus said.

'Were you a good student, Marcus?' Anne asked, her eyes wide with interest.

'A veritable angel. All my teachers remarked on it. As good as gold.'

There was a suspicious grunt from behind and Marcus cast a quick glance back at Blunt, his tiger.

'You didn't even know me then, Blunt.'

'No, my lord. But that's not to say I don't know those that did.'

'Your syntax leaves a lot to be desired, Blunt. And Sparks's version of events is as suspect as his master.'

'Who is his master, Lord Sherbourne?' Anne asked.

'That sad rattle, Wrexham.' He really shouldn't have brought up Wrexham. He could still see his friend leaning down to kiss Lily while she stood there, eyes closed.

It should have been him.

No. It should *not* have been him.

'And this Sparks is his groom?'

'No, Sparks is his valet. His groom's name is worse.'

Blunt, completely lost to all sense of propriety, sniggered.

'What is his groom's name, then?' Lily demanded and Anne seconded the motion.

'Yes, Marcus. What could be worse than Sparks?'

'Brisket,' admitted Marcus.

Both sisters burst into laughter. As usual Lily's laugh tumbled through him and he made the mistake of looking down at her.

For the briefest moment London disappeared. There were no genteel buildings and fashionable gentlemen striding along the pavements. No clopping of horses and cries of sweeps. No beautiful betrothed sitting just a few inches to the right. Nothing but a woman who had somehow thrust her hand through his chest and twisted his dried prune of a heart into rampant idiocy.

He had no idea when he'd crossed the line from lusting after the most unsuitable woman in London to…to whatever this damned uncomfortable feeling was. Probably watching her battle her demons as her mother thrust home the knife.

He hated seeing her hurt. It was unbearable.

A faint nudge from Blunt behind him brought him back to earth and Brook Street and he guided his team to a halt. Blunt went to the horses' heads and Marcus helped the sisters down.

Form helped. Lily thanked him and went inside and he stood for a moment with Anne while that rebellious entity inside him tugged him in Lily's wake. He ignored it. As soon as he was back in Curzon Street he would have words with the rebel. Right now he had to fix his attention on the woman tied to his life.

'I apologise for my mother, Marcus. That was awful.'

He smiled at her. None of this was her fault, poor thing. She was a good, sweet woman.

'You aren't responsible for her, Anne. And it seems you and your siblings have developed reasonably good defences against her. You certainly needn't worry about me.'

'No, you dealt with her very well. She is rather frightened of you.'

'Good.'

She laughed a little. 'Yes, it is. She wants to come to Sherbourne Hall when you must travel to Prussia in the autumn. To keep me company.'

He didn't want to think of what the future must bring, but he forced himself to smile.

'That won't happen. I promise you.'

She sighed in unveiled relief. 'Thank you. And thank you for being so kind to Lily and distracting her. That is the greatest gift you could bestow on me.'

His guilt expanded like a hot-air balloon. Damn, he was a complete cad. She didn't deserve this.

What if he told her this was wrong? *They* were wrong? That he didn't want to marry her?

What if he told her…?

No. There are certain rules you don't break. An honourable man doesn't shoot someone in the back unless they are about to kill someone else. And an honourable man does not jilt the woman he asked to marry him. Only women had the prerogative of breaking an engagement. They had so few rights in society, but this was one that was wholly theirs. For a man to jilt a woman… Casting her off would spell ruin on far too many levels. It would have brutal consequences for Anne and her family. For Lily, too. He could not jilt Anne any more than he could walk up to a child and strike him.

'You'd best go rest, Anne.'

He waited until the door closed behind her before mounting the curricle again. They drove for a while in silence, navigating the crowded streets. He barely noted the flow of carriages and carts and horses, his mind churning itself into a soggy lump of misery.

How had this even happened? Lily satisfied barely three out of the ten requirements on the bride-choosing list he'd made out two years ago when he started down this disastrous path. His image of married life—pleasant, distant, connecting with his wife around their children and involving as little of himself as possible—seemed almost childish.

But that still didn't explain Lily. She was nowhere near as beautiful as Anne. Brown hair and grey eyes and a smattering of freckles and those two squiggled scars along her jaw couldn't compete with Anne's gold and silver loveliness. But Lily's attractions not only competed with her sister's, they completely outstripped them. Apparently the truism of beauty being in the eye of the beholder was absolutely true because Anne's beauty now seemed tepid and stale compared to the vivid play of expression on Lily's face. He had to struggle not to search her out when he entered a room. Not to listen for her voice.

Behind him Blunt cleared his throat and Marcus surfaced from his tangled thoughts.

'I've known you a dozen years, haven't I, sir?'

Oh, hell. Here it comes. Blunt did choose his moments.

'Fourteen years, Blunt. If you're planning to live up to your name, get it over with quickly. We'll reach the mews any moment now.'

'Fourteen years, is it? Boulogne seems like a lifetime ago.'

'This morning seems like a lifetime ago.'

'We did well at that blockade, didn't we?' Blunt sighed, still caught in nostalgia.

'We did. And after. What of Saragossa?'

'Ah, that was a fine moment. But my point is, sir, that I've been with you through some narrow passes.'

Marcus gave up attempts at diversion. Blunt was hound-like when it came to following the scent.

'Your point?'

'My point, sir, is that they are nice young women. It's not like you to muddle the reins.'

'I wish I could say it's not like you to muddle your metaphors, Blunt.'

'Getting huffy won't change facts, my lord. Here we are now.'

'Thank goodness. I need some whisky.'

'Whisky won't change the facts either, sir.'

'I know, Blunt.'

Blunt sighed and fell silent and when they pulled up by the mews and the undergroom hurried to the horses' heads, Blunt took the reins from Marcus and cleared his throat again.

'You always had a way of getting through a narrow pass, sir. You'll come right here, too.'

Marcus didn't answer that empty assurance. Coming through a tight spot during battle was one thing; extracting himself from the biggest mistake of his life was a challenge of a different order of magnitude. It could not be done and he had best resign himself to reality right now. This instant.

Eventually time and abstention would do their jobs and smother pain and memories and empty wishes under its numbing layers. Time excelled at turning hopes and needs grey. It would work its magic on this mess as well.

It was a hell of a thing to wish for.

Chapter Sixteen

There's something about a mask.

The Queen of Hearts in the great gilt-edged mirror of Atherley Hall smiled at Lily, bathed in the light of a hundred-candle chandelier. Sparks of reddish fire glistened in her hair and the claret silk of her Tudor-style gown shimmered. She looked utterly foreign and wondrously dashing.

Lily resisted the urge to tug up the square neckline; it was certainly cut much lower than the portraits of the Tudor Queens it was modelled upon. The only hint to her costume's identity was in the row of tiny golden hearts embroidered along the neckline and flounce. Otherwise the dress was simple and yet daring, with a tightly fitted bodice and waist and a flaring skirt whose folds shaded from blood red in the candlelight to dark purple in the depths that shifted and swirled as she moved.

The mask was a shade between—darker than red, but not yet purple. Beneath it her mouth looked as if she'd been well kissed. Under the shield of her gilded fan she touched her lips. The only kiss she'd even been close to recently had been one unwanted almost-kiss from a beautiful rake. And far too many imagined kisses from the least suitable man in the world.

It was a ludicrous costume for someone like her, but when Madame Fanchot had showed it to them Lily knew she wasn't strong enough to reject it. She *loved* it. Even the irony of dressing as the Queen of Hearts while her own heart was breaking didn't ruin her pleasure at the freedom promised by the masquerade.

In a few short days she would leave London, her beloved sister and brother, and her heart. Just for tonight she would set everything aside and revel in being anonymous and dressed at her best. She would close this chapter in her life by not allowing even the slightest tinge of regret that Lord Sherbourne would not be attending. Any such thoughts would be banished to the arctic realms the moment they formed until she overcame her foolishness.

Beside her red and gold dress, Annie looked the image of innocence in her shepherdess costume with its wide flounced skirt, a cotton cap with sky-blue ribbons tucked over her golden curls, and a curlicue staff with a knot of forget-me-not ribbons.

Mr Devenish had merely donned a black domino, but Mrs Devenish had also indulged and was dressed as a Roman empress. Probably the kind who poisoned their political rivals, Lily thought uncharitably.

They had barely stepped through the doors into the ballroom when a slight figure dressed like a corsair, complete with sword and doublet, placed himself before them.

'May I beg your hand for this dance, my Queen of Hearts?'

Lily glanced at Annie, but her sister merely elbowed her indelicately in the ribs and all but pushed her into the corsair's arms. Lily curtsied.

'You may, Sir Francis.'

It was a wide shot, but it struck home and the mouth under the heavy mask curved. 'Ah! I am acknowledged at last. By the Queen I live to serve. Now I can die happy.'

Lily followed him into the dance, laughing at his nonsense. She had no idea who he was, nor did she wish to, and when the dance was over and her hand was sought by his friend and then another she forgot about him and enjoyed a series of flirtations with a Roman centurion, a harlequin, an admiral of the line, her corsair once again, and a few who were either not bold or imaginative enough to wear more than masks or dominoes, but who were very appreciative of her costume.

She'd never quite realised the power of a plunging neckline, but clearly it was formidable.

Masquerades were nothing like balls.

There was a sense of excitement and chaos, people bumping into each other, drinking glass after glass of the ever-flowing pink champagne, laughing immoderately... A sense of freedom and of the remnants of the debauchery that London had been so famous for before the Revolution and the wars had caused a break from Parisian hedonism. All this was apparently still alive and well and waiting for an excuse to surface. Inside her as well.

She no longer knew where her family was and didn't care one whit.

She didn't care one whit about anything at all.

At some point the corsair returned and danced her out into the gardens which were lit with Chinese lanterns and already buzzing with pucks and fairies and pharaohs and footmen with trays of more champagne. Everyone seemed to be laughing a great deal, hovering on the thin line between gaiety and abandon.

That was probably why she didn't immediately notice when her faithful Sir Francis danced her out of the circles of light cast by the lamps and behind the sharply cut yew hedges that separated the lawn from a darkened rose garden.

She definitely noticed when his hand slipped from her waist to her behind.

He definitely noticed when she knocked his arm away.

'Absolutely not.'

'Just a little kiss from my queen.'

'Not unless you want a black eye to go with it,' she muttered, her enjoyment fizzling out in an instant. She ought to have known it would end thus. She turned back, but in two steps he grabbed her from behind, nuzzling her nape.

Oh, for heaven's sake. She yanked his hands apart.

'You've had too much champagne, sir. I suggest you find a bench and sleep it off.'

'It's not the champagne, it's your delectable bosom that is intoxicating me.'

She really ought not to giggle. Now he not only looked like a failed actor, he sounded like one, too. Her head might be fuzzy with pink bubbles, but she knew it was best not to turn her back on him again. She stepped back in the direction of the lawn and rammed into something far more solid than the yew hedge. Another pair of arms came around her, steadying her, and a voice rumbled above her.

'Is this some new form of dance you two are practising? *La Chasse au Corsaire*, perhaps?'

The words were light, but Lord Sherbourne's

tone wasn't. There was a bite and a warning to it. She should have been mortified to be discovered in such an ignominious position, but she wasn't at all. Her sigh was wholly involuntary—relief and something far worse.

'Is she yours?' the corsair asked, sounding genuinely puzzled and more than a little worried as he assessed his challenger's size.

'No, but she made it clear she most certainly isn't yours.'

The corsair inspected her, wavering a little. He must have had more champagne than she.

'Pity that. I like you. You make me laugh.'

Lily melted a little, but Lord Sherbourne's heavy arm tightened around her shoulders at these unthreatening words.

'You can go to a penny theatre if it's laughs you want, now go inside.'

To Lily's surprise the corsair obeyed and slipped past them without a word. He must be younger even than she'd thought.

She realised she was still standing tucked under Lord Sherbourne's arm. She closed her eyes briefly, gathering that sensation and placing it with care in her forbidden memories' chest. The nerves that had been stretched thin by the corsair's transgression were now humming hungrily at a completely different threat.

She ought to step away. He was Annie's.

She tried to honour that resolution by pushing against his chest, but that made the world sway and for a moment she felt weightless and unformed, like a hot-air balloon unmoored. Then his arm was around her once more, tucking her against his length and she braced her hand on the nearest surface which was his chest and found her feet again. They were still under her, though a little woolly.

She searched for something urbane to say that would befit her status as Queen of Hearts, but her words were as childish as the corsair's.

'I'm so sorry. You must be dreadfully displeased with me.'

Displeased.

In the long, long line of emotions currently plaguing him that would have stretched all the way to Hadrian's Wall if he'd laid them end to end, displeasure was loitering somewhere near Newcastle. If that was what she saw when she looked up at him with those damned luminous grey eyes framed by the crimson mask, she was not as perceptive as he had thought.

Which was a good thing.

Marcus wished his evening wear had pockets. He needed somewhere safe to put his hands. He would very much have liked to put both of them around the throat of that golden-haired corsair. In fact, he'd been wanting to do so any time since his arrival half an hour ago as he'd watched the red queen dancing happily from one popinjay's arms to the next. He hadn't approached, but he hadn't been able to look away, either.

He ought to have gone looking for Anne, but he told himself it was his duty to keep an eye on Lily while all those men were buzzing about her and plying her with champagne. He knew what they were thinking. Of her lush curves encased in a tight red dress and her glorious hair gleaming in the candlelight and that gut-clenching laugh that promised so much...

At least he knew what *he* was thinking and if those Bartholomew babies were contemplating even one-hundredth of the images that were plaguing him, he didn't want them getting any ideas, such as dancing her down a darkened path.

He wished that amorous sprig had resented his interference; it was damnable he'd folded so swiftly. He needed *some* outlet for this...

'I didn't realise we'd danced away from the rest,' she said into the silence, her words carefully measured as if she had to pick them out one by one from a box. 'I think... I think perhaps I had a trifle too much champagne.'

It was her night for understatements. He tried to think of something to say that wouldn't be damning, for him or for her, but his mind was busy hoarding the sensation of having his arm around her, her palm splayed on his chest echoing his chaotic heartbeat and her hair warm and silky under his chin as she leaned against him.

She didn't smell of lilies or of lavender or anything soft and pliant and chaste. Her scent was orange blossoms mixed with the climbing jasmine vines with those vivid pink and white flowers that burst into life at night and would tempt him down into the garden when he spent that summer in Cadiz. He wanted to draw her back so he could imagine her there—long before he'd set his life down the wrong path.

He ought to say *something*. She was clearly waiting for some sign of absolution from him. He wasn't her keeper, damn it. He wasn't her anything and he was soon to be her...

God help him. He would have to bed Lily's sister. He couldn't do it.

When the devil had Anne become 'Lily's Sister'? It should be the other way around.

But it wasn't.

And he couldn't.

'Lord Sherbourne? Marcus?' She spoke his name on a rising note. 'Marcus, are you unwell?'

He almost laughed. She had a point. It *was* a form of malady. And like a malady it would pass. It might feel as though it would kill him, but that was nonsense, wasn't it? This agonising ache wasn't a bullet or the plunging sharpness of a bayonet breaking through skin and muscle and blood vessels, shattering bone.

It was just an ache. A regret. The only thing that would wither and die would be a fleeting fantasy based on an unusually fierce physical reaction to this unlikely woman.

And on how…how *right* he felt with her.

What if…? What if they were found here together…?

She arched her head back, her lips parted. He wished there was more light, so he could fix this image in his mind.

'Marcus,' she whispered. 'Did you come outside because you are feeling ill? Do you need to sit down? Say something!'

He finally found his missing wits and his temper. 'I came outside because in the half-hour since I arrived you had three glasses of champagne and that damned nursling was clearly doing his best to ply you with more. When he coaxed you outside I felt it was time to intervene.'

'You were watching me?' Her voice rose in a squeak.

'Well, someone had to. When you let slip the reins you do so with abandon.'

Even in the darkness and with her mask he could see the flush spread over her neck and face. She brushed the edge of her silk mask with her finger.

'It's the mask. For a little while I forgot who I

was. It was nice. The champagne and the dancing. There are no masquerades in Birmingham. Or at least none I am invited to.'

She sounded so forlorn. The stupid part of him wanted to rush up north and establish a whole festival of masquerades for her with rivers of champagne running through them. Without any corsairs, preferably.

'In a few days I must return there,' she continued, spreading her free arm wide, her voice wobbling a little. 'I wished... I don't know what I wished.'

A few days.

Don't leave.

He grabbed the stupid part of him by the scruff of the neck and shoved it, ache and all, into a deep dark well. He hoped it drowned.

Tell her to go inside. Better yet—find her father and have him take his tipsy daughter home before she did something foolish.

Before *he* did something foolish. Like stand here with her in the dark while people were milling about only yards away, dancing and laughing and probably doing a great deal more in the many dark walks that graced Atherley's gardens. It was his role to keep her safe, not damage her further. Keep her safe from herself and from him.

Keep her, Stupid's voice whispered from the depths of the well. Marcus dropped a full bucket of water on him.

'Don't be angry,' she said.

'I am not angry.' Though to be honest, angry was not quite as far as displeasure. Perhaps hovering near Islington, eyeing its chance to make a dash for the front of the line. 'I am concerned.'

Concerned perked up from where it had been languishing by the side of the Great North Road east of Leeds.

'Oh. Well, you needn't be. I'm not quite so... floaty any longer. I should go inside, shouldn't I?'

No. Inside there were more glasses of champagne and corsairs.

'I think it best you return home. You'll have one hell of a head tomorrow.'

She rubbed her temple and a lock of shimmering hair fell over her brow. Before he could even think, he slipped it behind her ear. And stayed there, his fingers resting on that peach-soft skin, on her pulse. She shivered, her head tilting a little so that his fingers slipped into the warmth of her hair.

His cock strained further against his breeches. *That's right, Marcus my boy, just another step and everything will be perfect*, Stupid cackled from the well.

He withdrew his hand as if he'd accidently stuck it into a sleeping bear's mouth. It felt twice the size of his other hand and his whole arm was tingling. And he didn't have the excuse of half a bottle of champagne.

'Come. We'll find your family. It's time for you to return home before…'

'Before?' she asked curiously as he peeked around the yew hedge. He slammed the lid shut over Stupid's well and took her arm, guiding her around the shadowed edge of the garden towards the patio. He needn't have bothered with circumspection. It was approaching midnight and everyone was hurrying about in search of the best position for the night's unmasking.

Nobody would be calling for their carriage at this hour.

Lily must have been more tired and tipsy than she appeared. She came with him like a docile lamb, leaning a little more on his arm when they turned corners or descended steps.

In the race to defeat his defences, tenderness was now running neck and neck with lust and he couldn't decide which was worse.

He settled her in one of Atherley's empty front parlours far from the raucous ballroom and went to make the necessary arrangements.

When he returned to the darkened room it took him a moment to notice the lump on the sofa. She was curled up into a near ball, her cheek on her hand, the tips of her stockinged feet peeping from the long silk skirts spilling on to the carpet. He rubbed the spot on his chest where she'd grabbed his coat and shirt when she'd almost fallen. Her fingers had scraped hard against his skin and the atavistic creature inside him that was struggling against its chains hoped she had left a mark.

'Lily. Wake up.' His voice was a little too sharp and she shifted with a sigh, her eyes opening.

'Oh, hello.' In the darkness her smile was a sultry benediction and without thinking he sank down on one knee beside her. Luckily he landed on one of her discarded shoes, the short heel sending a well-deserved arrow of pain up his leg. He gritted his teeth.

'The carriage is outside. I brought your cloak. I told your father I shall see you home.'

She blinked a little at his clipped words and then surged into a sitting position. It was evidently a mistake since she winced and pressed a hand to her masked forehead.

'Do you need to be ill?' he asked unsympathetically as he rose.

She shook her head. 'No. It's my head, not my stomach.' She glanced up at him, looking more sober and quite wary. 'I learned to hold my spirits in the army. At least I thought I had. I am apparently out of practice.'

'I'm glad to hear that. Come. Your carriage awaits. Or rather my carriage, but we won't quibble.'

'I should wait...'

'I've already told your father I am seeing you home. Let's not complicate matters. Everyone has already taken off their masks so unless you wish for an embarrassing reunion with your golden corsair, I suggest you take my offer and leave at a high point.'

She didn't argue, but she also waved away his offered arm. They passed in silence through the empty hallway, accompanied by the sounds of music and mirth from the other side of the house. Inside the carriage she slipped all the way into the corner and untied her mask without once looking at him.

He removed his domino as well, tossing it on to the seat opposite.

Despite the waxing moon it was dark outside, only the faint glimmer of the lamps swinging from the box casting shifting shadows through the cracks in the thick curtains. They touched her profile with a faint glow, picking out the tips of her lashes like pinpricks of frost.

They were already past Kensington when she spoke. 'I haven't made such a fool of myself in a very long while. I'm sorry I ruined your evening.'

He was a whole clumping mass of aches and this just set them all off again. He didn't move towards her, but his voice was softer when he answered.

'You made up for it by giving me a good excuse to leave early. You might enjoy masquerades, I don't.'

She gave a little shudder, like Ombra did just before he settled on the rug by the fire. 'I have never been to one. But it is true that I enjoyed… not being Mrs Walsh.'

'Who were you instead?'

She brushed her hand over her skirts and a slight shadow filled her dimple. 'Can't you tell? I am the Queen of Hearts. Like the card.'

'You chose the costume?'

'Oh, no. It was the only one Madame Fanchot had immediately available that could fit me. The poor woman who had commissioned it had to flee London to escape debtors' prison. Madame Fanchot very kindly sold it at a fraction of its price. I didn't want to take it, but Annie insisted. She wanted me to be happy.'

In went the knife and stayed there.

He tried to stop the words but they came out anyway. 'I'm glad she insisted. You look beautiful.'

She looked at him, her eyes wide. Without the barrier of the mask he could see again how large they were, the grey as luminous as mercury.

She shook her head and went back to the contemplation of her skirts. 'Annie was right. In her letter asking me to come to London she wrote that you were nice and kind. I thought that was Annie being Annie, but it is the truth. Thank you for helping me. I don't think anything would have happened, but I might very well have made a fool of myself and given Mama even more fodder for her dislike of me.'

'She doesn't—' He cut himself off. 'I think it is more complicated than dislike.'

'Yes, I know.' She sighed and yawned. 'It doesn't matter.'

It did matter, but she was tired and he was shattered so he didn't answer. London already had them in its grasp. He could feel its pull at the carriage wheels, in the smells of smoke and humans that chased away the cool scent of woods and night. Brook Street was moments away.

He wanted to tell his coachman to keep driving. Through the city, past sleeping villages and foxes hunting in the hedges and on to some mythical place where he could reverently unveil the Queen of Hearts and do something about this thudding ugly-beautiful ache.

But the carriage was more dutiful than he. It stopped before the modest house on Brook Street and he waited at the bottom of the steps as the door opened, bathing the tired queen in the light of a single candle held up by the maid. In the doorway Lily turned.

'Thank you. Goodnight.' Her smile was rather

sad and a welling of utter misery held him there
after the maid closed the door.

'My lord?' the coachman ventured after a moment. 'Where to, sir? Sherbourne House?'

Marcus shook his head. He didn't want to be
alone with his thoughts. He would go to his club
and get good and drunk. He hadn't done it in
years, but it felt like an excellent idea right now.

Pink champagne was the devil's brew.

It must be close on dawn because the light
clawing through the curtains was a dirty grey and
it hurt her eyes. It hurt her everything.

Pink champagne and the light of day were not
good friends.

There was justice to it, though. She'd drunk
too much of the bubbly sweet concoction because
her heart had ached. Now her head and stomach
and quite a few of her muscles had joined in the
misery parade climbing up and down her insides.

It was Annie's fault.

If she hadn't sent that foolish letter forcing Lily
to come to London weeks before she'd meant to.

If she hadn't decided to be the perfect daughter
and add the perfect match to her already perfect
repertoire of filial achievements.

If she hadn't been the best person in the world,
which made it utterly impossible to even indulge

in foolish daydreams of her slipping off a bridge and Lily consoling her distraught once-fiancé.

That last one was particularly horrid of Lily and now her eyes and throat were burning, too. Served her right.

And to top it all off she'd made an utterly abysmal fool of herself last night. What had she been thinking? Or rather why *hadn't* she been thinking? It was all confused, some moments brightly bold and others murky and indistinct.

She remembered feeling warm and safe when he saved her from her amorous corsair. It was a peculiar feeling—it wasn't like anything she had experienced. Tim certainly hadn't given her that sensation. Their union had been based on excitement and rebellion and then on the strange life of a soldier's wife with all its challenges and privations and intensity.

No one had ever made her feel safe. That had been up to her and she'd never questioned it. Now she would. Damn him for that as well. It was even worse than turning to syrupy mush every time he smiled at her. Or touched her.

She slid her hand out from under the pillow and placed her fingers below her ear. Had he touched her there or had that been part of her champagne-soaked dreams?

He had. Slipped her unruly hair behind her ear.

She'd probably looked a complete hoyden. But in the carriage he'd told her she looked beautiful.

She covered her head with the pillow.

Stop it. He is Annie's. And Annie and Piers are the only two people you truly love in this whole wide world. You would do anything for them, including put an end to this maudlin infatuation.

From this point onwards you will not think about him, or moon over him, or flirt with him.

I do not flirt with him! exclaimed a horrified voice.

She gave it a firm shove back into place. *You most certainly do. Every time you tell him things you don't tell anyone else or try to make him laugh. And when you leaned against him as though he was your sole source of support that was* precisely *what you were doing. And you will stop all of this right now, not out of shame or because it is improper, but because you love Annie more than anything. As if she were your daughter. As if she were Emma. You would never,* ever *want to hurt her.*

Hot tears leaked out of squeezed shut eyes and she let them come even though she knew they would make her headache worse.

In the end she fell asleep again, but there were no pleasant dreams.

Chapter Seventeen

Resolutions were damnable.

'Are you quite certain you won't come, Lily? It is Edmund Kean after all and you did so enjoy his performance in *The Fatal Accusation* when we went a fortnight ago.'

Lily smiled at her sister and shook her head, holding firmly to her resolve to stay away from Lord Sherbourne.

He appeared to be doing the same. That horrid night two days ago was still a little on the murky side and she hoped she had not revealed something embarrassing. Anything more embarrassing than being drunk and disorderly.

She probably had because he was clearly uncomfortable with her. Now he stood talking with Mr Devenish and he'd barely even nodded at her when he arrived that evening to escort Annie and her parents to the theatre.

'No, dear. I must see to my packing. The coach leaves early tomorrow.'

Annie moved closer, her head and voice lowering. 'I wish you wouldn't go. You said you could stay until the end of the month and that the school is closed during the summer months. Why not stay until—'

Lily cut her off. 'I shall return for it. But I need… I need my own place, Annie. I need some quiet. If it were only you and Piers…'

She was cracking and she tried to smile. Annie touched her hand and nodded, but her eyes were red, too.

'When I am married you shall come and stay with me often.'

Lily nodded and bade everyone a pleasant evening and went upstairs and once her ragged little portmanteau was packed and her dark blue wool dress laid out for the morning, she crawled into bed and cried herself to sleep.

'Lily! Wake up… *Please* wake up! Oh, this is *terrible*…'

The whisper pushed its way into Lily's dream, slipping past the image of the blazing streets of San Sebastian crowded with drunken soldiers and flowing with blood.

That was precisely what Lily had thought as she searched for Tim among the bodies being stripped of rings and buttons and coin by the scavengers: *Oh, this is terrible.* Again and again and again.

She surfaced into the darkness and realised she wasn't in Spain. Hadn't been there in five years. And that hadn't been her voice...

'Annie?' She scrambled into a sitting position, squinting into the darkness. Her sister was half kneeling on the side of the bed, her eyes wide. 'Annie! What happened? What is wrong?'

Annie held up something pale. 'Piers was waiting in my room when we returned from the theatre. He brought a letter. From John!'

'John? John *Smithson*?'

'Of course, John Smithson. What other John is there? A friend of Piers is in the Foreign Office and he brought it all the way from Constantinople. John writes he knew it best to have Piers deliver it to me than risk it being intercepted by Mama and Papa. Oh, what shall I do?'

Lily sat up against the headboard, trying to force her fuzzy thoughts into order. 'But... You haven't spoken of him in years. Why would he be writing to you?'

Annie made a strange sound, between a choke and a groan. 'It is my fault, entirely my fault. I wrote... I thought... I felt it right to...to inform him. It was foolish and I regretted it the moment the letter was sent...'

'Annie, slow down, what are you speaking of?'

'I wrote to John months ago. When Marcus first spoke with Papa about me. I know it has been years since we… But still, it felt proper. Oh, I cannot explain. In any case he never answered and I thought: there, see? I was right to forget all about him and so I accepted Lord Sherbourne's proposal. But he says here that the letter was first sent to his previous post in Rome and lingered there for a while before it was sent on to Constantinople… I truly thought he had forgotten me. I was *determined* to forget him, but… Oh, Lily, I cannot bear it. Read it!'

She shoved the letter at Lily and Lily took it, but her gaze was on her sister. Annie rarely cried, but her face glistened with tears and they kept coursing down her cheeks even as Lily watched.

'It's too dark to read here, love. Tell me.'

Annie took the letter back, pressing it to her chest. 'He writes he had meant to put me out of his mind for ever, knowing he could never be good enough for me, but when he received my letter he was devastated far beyond what he had thought possible and he knew he had to Risk All and tell me the Truth of His Feelings. He says that if I love Lord Sherbourne he shall wish me happiness with all his heart. But he knows of Lord Sherbourne's reputation and he fears this is a marriage promoted by Mama and Papa and if so he begs me not to… He says that he has Never Loved Another.

That all his thoughts are still of me. Oh, what shall I do? I cannot jilt Marcus. It is *unthinkable*.'

Lily clasped Annie's hand in hers and she realised both of them were shaking. She drew a deep breath.

'Annie. I want you to do something for me. I want you to imagine yourself as Lord Sherbourne's wife in two years' time.'

'What?' Annie's voice squeaked upwards.

'Indulge me. Close your eyes. You have been married two years to Lord Sherbourne. You are at the breakfast table with him.' Lily considered mentioning events preceding breakfast, but she felt neither of them were best positioned to contemplate that scenario. 'Can you do that?'

Annie's right shoulder rose a little, her mouth pinched in a hard line, but she kept her eyes shut. Lily waited for a moment.

'Now do the same with John.'

Annie drew in a deep breath and burst into sobs.

'Well, there you have it,' Lily said.

'But I cannot *jilt* Marcus! It would be *ruinous* of me. I shall have no reputation left. And Mama and Papa *depend* upon me. You know they do. He is so very wealthy and we… Besides, I *like* him and don't wish to do him harm. He has been nothing but kind and considerate towards me and…

and how would I even go about it? Oh, it is impossible. I'm *doomed*.'

Lily almost laughed at Annie's uncharacteristic dramatics, but her own nerves were strained to snapping point and she was feeling a tad dramatic herself. Still, her course of action was clear. 'I shall speak with Lord Sherbourne.'

Annie's sobs hiccoughed to a stop. 'Lily… Oh, would you? You always know what to say to him. And I know he respects your opinion, and you shall find some way to explain… Oh, my darling Lily, would you do this for me?'

Guilt roared in Lily's chest like a chained bear at a taunting crowd. 'Of course I shall, Annie. First thing in the morning. And I suggest you write to John and tell him he must ride *ventre à terre* or sail close to the wind or whatever he must to reach England before Mama and Papa foist you on to some other wealthy suitor.'

'But you cannot possibly visit Lord Sherbourne at his home alone,' Annie said, aghast. 'That would be shockingly improper.'

'I shall wear my gloomiest widow's weeds and crepe veil, love. You would be surprised how often widows are overlooked. Those degrees of freedom are almost worth four years' marriage.'

Chapter Eighteen

Sherbourne House looked perfectly unthreatening. Even inviting. Like its neighbours it had a classical façade though it was larger than most and set a little back from the road. Otherwise it was unremarkable. There was certainly nothing about this pleasant building to cause alarm.

Except that she had to walk up to that door and demand to see Lord Sherbourne.

She pressed her clasped hands together against the thumping in her chest. It was making far too much noise. She closed her eyes and opened them and for a moment the carriages and carts that had been rushing past were gone, the road empty like the parting of the Red Sea. Before she could think she hurried across and up the three steps and raised the knocker. For the briefest of moments she hesitated and then struck it, twice.

The deep metallic reverberation was still thrumming through her when the door opened and the butler, Juan, stood there, a look of very English boredom on his round face. He stared at her, a frown gathering, and she remembered she was still draped in her veil. She raised it and rushed into speech.

'Good morning, it is very important I speak to Lord Sherbourne. Could you please tell him Mrs Walsh begs for a moment of his time?'

Juan's eyes widened and he cast a glance past her on to the street, but to his credit he stood back immediately, his face emptying of expression.

'Of course, Mrs Walsh. I think perhaps you should wait in the study.'

The study had not been on their tour of Sherbourne House and she could understand why. It was far less orderly than the drawing rooms they'd been shown, with books and papers stacked on a sideboard that ran along the shelves on one wall and a haphazard collection of rugs marking different corners, as if this space was separated into little fiefdoms, each with its own purpose.

For a moment curiosity pushed panic out of the way and she stood there, absorbing this room where every element spoke of its owner. She wanted to go object by object and discover its meaning because she knew it was there, just as it had been in the little paper bird.

The first thing that caught and held her gaze was a framed drawing near the mantelpiece. It wasn't merely the skill of the artist, but that she recognised its subject—it was a sketch of the narrow mountain pass above Astorga in Spain. A deer stood on a rocky outcropping above the pass, looking directly at her, its eyes glistening.

She remembered the pass because of that sharp finger of rock scratching the sky, but when she and Tim had passed through there as part of General Moore's retreat in 1809, the area had been cloaked in muddy snow and sullen clouds and Napoleon's cavalry had been nipping at their heels. Someone clearly sketched this in spring—the details of the flora and fauna were exquisite, down to berry-heavy bushes and the...

Lily braced on the mantelpiece and rose on tiptoe to gain a better look.

'Admiring the view?'

Lily whirled around, almost knocking a small jade figurine of a wolf from its perch on the mantelpiece. She caught it just as the front legs tipped over the edge and set it back with care.

Her heart had been at a canter since Annie woke her, but now it was in full gallop.

She cleared her throat and turned. 'Lord Sherbourne, thank you for...'

Her words and thoughts ran aground.

Men in shirtsleeves, or less, were not a novelty for Lily. She'd been married and spent four years following the army drum during a protracted and brutal war. The sight of a man, albeit an unfortunately handsome and well-constructed one, wearing no coat or waistcoat and with his sleeves pushed up to his elbows should have had no effect on her whatsoever.

This sudden loss of breath was merely surprise. Or nerves.

Definitely nerves.

He raised his dark brows. 'For?'

'For?'

'You began to thank me for…?' he prompted.

'For seeing me.'

'Seeing you is always my pleasure. Though I admit to being puzzled why you have graced me with your presence. Is all well in Brook Street?'

When he made his voice so…flat, he almost looked like a stranger. It had been a while since she had seen Lord Sherbourne amused or relaxed, his deep, languid voice tinged with honey and a hint of laughter.

That was the man she had hoped would be present this morning. The one who appeared not to take life seriously at all and who was willing to forgive human foibles because to do otherwise would require too much energy. The man who laughed at life, but without malice.

It was hard to imagine the man who faced her now laughing at anything, let alone taking kindly to her news. She very much hoped the other Lord

Sherbourne was present somewhere under this forbidding exterior.

'Actually, Lord Sherbourne, it isn't…all well, that is.'

'That sounds alarming. Why don't we sit down, then? I have the feeling I might need the support.'

He didn't look particularly alarmed, but he was still watching her very carefully and far more directly than he had since she'd disgraced herself.

Just as he was about to close the door a dark form slipped inside. For one wild moment Lily had the fanciful thought that the jade figurine had become a real-life wolf. But as the dark grey canine padded along the wall and scooted silently under an enormous mahogany desk, she realised it was merely a dog and a rather timid one at that.

Lord Sherbourne didn't seem to notice. He waved her towards a chair placed before the desk and she sank into it gratefully, resisting the temptation to peek under the desk to see what the wolf dog was doing.

'Lord Sherbourne, I…'

'Marcus.'

'I… What?'

'My name. Marcus. I have a feeling our conversation is about to become awkward. Perhaps some informality might help?'

The appearance of a hint of green-gold laughter in his deep eyes set her heart beating even faster.

Marcus.

He wasn't helping at all.

'Is it money?' The drawl lengthened as his cynicism rose to the surface.

'Money?'

'It hasn't escaped my notice that your parents are living rather beyond their means in town. Nor that you have been attempting, with indifferent results, to rein them in. Are they being dunned? If they need dragging out of the River Tick, I would rather you come to me with such problems than go to the cent-per-cents.'

'It isn't money…' At least, not yet. That pit was yet awaiting them if she succeeded in her mission today. She continued with new resolution, 'Lord Sherbourne… *Marcus.*'

Oh, dear, that sounded good.

He leaned forward, his elbows on the desk. He wore no cravat either, and the opening of his shirt fell forward, revealing the strong lines of his throat and collarbone and the shadowed skin of his chest.

Good lord, how was she going to do this?

She rushed forward before something else diverted her. 'Annie… Anne doesn't wish to marry. She's in love with someone else.'

His eyes narrowed into hot golden slits, like a jungle cat emerging from the undergrowth. Lily realised her hands were clasped to her chest as if in prayer and she dropped them to her lap. His glance flickered to her chest and back up. She was as flushed as a beet, she knew it, but there was nothing she could do.

'Just so I understand. Anne is in love with someone else and doesn't wish to marry me,' he repeated in a measured, emotionless voice.

'Yes. That is it. Precisely.'

The silence stretched and stretched, but it wasn't still. He seemed to vibrate with some tensely held emotion. So much so she was almost afraid to breathe too deeply for fear of setting something off. But when he spoke again his voice was as bland as boiled rice.

'Is this a new development?'

'No, no. She was in love with John ages ago, but—'

'John Smithson.'

'You know John?' Surprised chased away a portion of her discomfort.

'I know *of* him. I understood there was a youthful attachment some years ago, but it came to nothing.'

'Did my parents tell you?'

He cocked his head a little at her suspicious tone and a dose of that disconcerting humour was back in his gaze. In fact, the iciness in his face and eyes was completely gone. There was no sign she had just dealt him a mortal blow. Her lungs loosened a little.

'No. I made it my business to enquire about Anne's past before I offered. I thought it sensible. Don't you agree?'

'Cold-blooded is more accurate.'

He leaned back. He was openly smiling now. Had she missed something? Perhaps he hadn't understood her. She thought she had been very clear.

'If you wish... Lily.'

She squirmed a little at the way his voice dipped into her name, wrapping it about in silken warmth.

'So, to continue,' he said with sudden briskness as she remained as mute as the dog under his desk, 'you are here to tell me I am discarded. Dismissed. Cast off. Traded in for her young love. I would have thought it was for her to deliver my *congé*, but knowing your sister, I can well see she sent you into the line of fire in her stead. I was quite correct—this is most awkward.'

'You don't seem very put out.'

'I was never one for *"the trappings and the suits of woe"*, Lily.'

'Yes, you are an expert at hiding your thoughts.'

'Am I? How nice to have one's skills appreciated. Would you care to have a guess at what my thoughts are right now?'

He was being purposely flippant, but after a

month of acquaintance she knew he was anything but.

'You are thinking...' she said slowly.

'Does it show?' he asked, his brow knotted in comic worry, and she couldn't help smiling.

'Since you can be most flippant when either annoyed or serious, then, yes, it shows.'

He laughed, a low rumbling sound that seemed to reach her through the floor, shimmering up her legs. She pressed them together more firmly.

'How transparent of me. But you cannot be surprised I might be annoyed at such a blow... To have the diamond of the past three Seasons prefer a man more than ten years my junior and... well, I don't know that he has any property at all, so financial comparisons won't help here. Have you any suggestions as to how to repair my sadly crushed vanity?'

Though he was taking this far, far better than Lily could have hoped, she couldn't help a surge of annoyance.

'Your vanity has been bolstered by years of adoration, toadying and downright sycophancy, Lord Sherbourne. I am quite certain the vacuum created by my sister's desertion will be so abhorred by the *ton* that you will be showered with written applications for the position of your Countess within the week.'

He appeared to consider her statement in all

seriousness, rubbing his jaw in a thoroughly annoying way. 'Well, perhaps not written.'

Her temper tried to slither out of her grasp, but she grabbed it and hauled it back. She would not give him the satisfaction. 'If your heart were engaged, I would be more inclined to feel sorry for you.'

He sighed and pressed a hand to the region of said heart and her eyes were drawn despite themselves to the impressive breadth of his chest.

'Ah. And what if my heart *were* engaged?'

Her heart hitched at the hint of something different in his tone. Not the light, languid tone he so often employed. Something...real?

'Is...is it?' she stammered, suddenly unsure. Had he come to care for Annie over the past month? It was possible. Annie's mothering warmth drew men to her like kittens to a bowl of milk. She tried to see past his expression, but his armour was legion. There was nothing there but that faintly sardonic smile that widened a little as she sat there, stewing in fear and discomfort.

'What do you think, Lily? You seem to be on top of everything.'

'I'm not.' She shook her head. 'I merely know it would be a mistake for Annie...for *both* of you to enter into this alliance while she believes herself in love with John.'

His fingers tapped faintly on the table and then

stopped. 'I heard you disapproved of her marrying this fellow at the time.'

She took a deep breath. 'I did. I like John, but they were mere children. Seventeen and nineteen.'

'You were seventeen when you wed Tim Walsh.'

'Precisely. I know the pitfalls. My marriage was happy for one fourth of its duration because I was too young to distinguish between stubborn charm and strength of character. Tim was an excellent soldier for the same reasons he was a deficient husband.'

In the silence that fell she could hear the rhythmic huffing of the dog under the desk. Another anomaly in her long list of this man's anomalies. She wished she could read him. She hated feeling so lost.

'I hesitate to point out the obvious,' he said at last, 'but you and your sister are chalk and cheese. You should have guessed she might be more judicious than you.'

'She is. She was. But seventeen is seventeen. And I didn't disapprove of John, I merely thought they should wait until she was older and he more advanced in his career. It was my parents and his that convinced the two of them they were ill-suited. But I think even they must accept that if they have remained constant in their love for four years despite their separation...'

'Constancy towards a dream is called religion, Lily. Not love.'

Lily couldn't help laughing at this blasphemous observation and again his eyes crinkled at the corners. It was a damnable habit of his to topple her defences so easily. She *needed* them.

'Founded on fact or not, do you really wish to be wed to a woman who will pine for a dream for ever?'

The amusement disappeared as he observed her and again silence fell. 'It has its advantages. The logic of marrying someone like your sister was to have a wife who would not importune me with her emotions.'

'Charming,' she snorted.

'Well, perhaps not that. But convenient.'

'So you could go about enjoying your many mistresses. Conveniently.'

His brows rose at her crude comment. 'I don't have a harem, Lily. I'm afraid I would find it very tiring and I'm past the age of such…exuberance. To be quite honest, your sister's appeal was that she appeared quite unexcitable. I would have, of course, made every effort to please her and eventually I think I might be better, ah, qualified to achieve that than her youthful love. Mostly I hoped all her natural kindness would be bestowed on our children.'

A slash of pain turned her voice sour. 'Children

being the true purpose behind the marriage. Oh, I beg pardon—not children, an heir.'

He leaned back and locked his hands behind his head, looking up at the sky-painted ceiling. His shirt parted from his waistband, revealing the hint of a taut abdomen carved as neatly as a statue's.

Lily's mouth went dry, her cheeks cold, then hot. Damn him. Was he doing this on purpose? Had he noticed her watching him? Probably. The man was as canny as a fox.

'Unfortunately, yes,' he said. 'It is rather expected of me. And I, unlike her darling John, am no longer young.'

'Thirty-five isn't in the least old,' she objected and he laughed.

'Thank you for that prompt defence, Lily-fox.'

'Fox?' she asked, startled at his reflecting of her thoughts.

'Your hair,' he explained and she reached up self-consciously to touch the unruly waves she'd pinned up in a poor imitation of Ailish's efforts.

'It's brown.'

'Not when the sun is on it. Then your true colour shines through, I'm afraid. A grey-eyed fox. The trickiest kind.'

'That's absurd. There is no such thing. I'm no more a fox than you are a wolf.'

There was a faint *woof* from under the desk

and she started. She'd completely forgotten about the dog.

'But she doesn't know that, Ombra,' Lord Sherbourne addressed the dog in complete seriousness and she couldn't hold back a helpless giggle.

'Doesn't know what?'

'That one of my many and very regrettable names is Wolfram. After some poet or other. My mother had a romantic streak, though she would never admit to it.'

'Wolfram.'

'I'm afraid so. It's a burden I must bear. Do you know that when you try not to smile you are betrayed by your left dimple? Your right one is much more obedient. No, I take that back. There it is. Hello, dimple.'

'Lord Sherbourne…'

'Marcus. Marcus St John Wolfram Septimus Endicott, to be precise.'

'Septimus?'

'Worse than Wolfram, I know. I think my parents believed in adversity as a path to virtue.'

'Well, either they were very wrong, or you haven't suffered much adversity.'

'I rather think they were wrong. Well meaning, but wrong.' He gave her a smile that was both wolfish and sweet at the same time.

Her dimples were betraying her thoroughly, but she was saved from answering by a little puff at her ankles. The dog's—Ombra's?—dark snout and darker eyes peeked up from below the desk.

'Hello, fellow,' she addressed the dog. 'I don't remember seeing you when we came to visit here.'

'That's because he was hiding under my desk that time as well. He isn't fond of crowds.'

'And rightly so. What a clever dog you are. Have you come to commiserate with me? At least someone here is acting the gentleman.'

'Unfair. I'm the wounded party here,' protested Lord Sherbourne.

'It certainly doesn't feel like it at the moment. And we are straying from the point.'

'Dear me. Which is?'

'Which is that you could replace Annie with another one like her in a week if you wished. Written applications or not.'

'What if I don't want "another one like her"?'

Her insides rolled again. She wasn't on dry land at all. She was on a ship…no, a raft and this man kept trying to tip it over. Was she wrong about his lack of attachment to Annie? Or was he merely toying with her?

The latter, most likely.

'Is that really what you want, Lord Sherbourne? Last night when my sister came to me in tears with John's letter, I asked her to imagine two futures. One was sitting with you at the breakfast table in two years' time. The other was sitting at the same place with John. That did it.'

'I doubt we'd be having breakfast together. I wake abominably early.'

She thumped her thigh with her fist. 'You are being purposely obtuse. You know what I mean.'

He shrugged and looked away, but not before she caught a glimpse of something harsh. Tension and…yes, there was undoubtedly anger there. Her annoyance faded. He might be toying with her, but he wasn't as impervious as he seemed and he had every right to be angry.

'Lord Sherbourne,' she continued in a softer tone, and then amended, 'Marcus—'

'Why even come to me?' he interrupted, lowering his mask further. 'It is your sister's prerogative to jilt *me*. You seem to be holding this stick at the wrong end.'

'It is her prerogative in theory only, Marcus. She hasn't the resolution to hold her ground if you side with my parents and insist she honour her betrothal. She needs to know you will stand down.'

'Abandon the siege, stop the cannonade and let the town burn…'

It was so sudden it caught her utterly unprepared. Her breathing choked off and a thousand tiny darts of pain shot through her. The room receded, the tall dark figure seated before her, so vivid a moment ago, became murky and indistinct.

Not again. Not *now*.

She did what she'd learned. Hold tight. Breathe. Hold tight…

'Hell…' He surged from the chair and was gone, as if she'd vanished him out of existence, or vanished herself. Then he was before her, his eyes luminous like the moon reflected in a pond. His hands closed on her shoulders, touched her face, his palm warm against her cold cheek.

The room finally began to take shape out of the mud. His face—she could see the gold flecks in his eyes, the skin stretched over his cheekbones, the roughness of stubble along his jaw.

'I am sorry.' She sounded calm, which felt wrong. She didn't feel calm.

He shook his head, withdrawing his hand from her cheek, and she wished he hadn't. She shivered.

'Don't. That was damnable of me. I'm the one who should apologise.' He sounded truly contrite and there was a strain in his voice she hadn't heard before: genuine regret and something else. She blinked and drew a long calming breath.

She always told herself the next time it struck she would remember to breathe it away directly, but somehow when it attacked she couldn't think of breathing. Or of anything sensible at all. Perhaps next time.

'You knew,' she said dully, 'that I was at San

Sebastian when the soldiers rampaged after the siege.'

He held silent, one hand still braced on the arm of her chair. There was a battle in the golden-brown eyes and she wondered if he would admit or deny the truth. He drew a rough-edged breath and straightened.

'Yes. Your brother mentioned you were hurt while looking for...for your husband. He didn't tell me any details and I didn't know what it had done to you. But I know it was hell on earth that week. That was unforgivable.' He moved away, his usually long fluid movements choppy. He opened a cabinet and poured amber liquid from a decanter into two glasses and handed her one.

'Drink.'

'It is ten o'clock in the morning.'

'Whisky isn't a factor of time; it is a factor of need. You need this. Drink.'

She did as she was told. It burned her raw throat and filled her stomach with fumes and fire and it made her want to cry, but she didn't.

'I hate when it happens.' The words burst out of her and he touched her shoulder briefly.

'Not that it should be any consolation, but you carry that scar remarkably well. Too well, I think. Poison needs to be aired, not stored in jars until one accidentally breaks.'

She pressed her fingers to her forehead. 'I am not here to discuss my flaws.'

He gave a slight, unamused laugh and took his glass to sit opposite her again. 'Of course not. You are here to discuss mine.'

'No, I am here to ask you to support my sister in her decision.'

'And so we circle back to my question. What do I get as reparation?'

'Freedom from what promises to be an unhappy alliance.'

'That is *your* interpretation.'

'What more do you want?' she snapped, still raw and exposed and sinking under her own confusion.

He considered her again for another long moment, swirling his whisky in his glass and stretching her nerves to breaking. 'My quandary goes rather a little deeper than my wishes, Lily. You see, I gave my word.'

'But Annie is willing to release you...'

'Not to Anne. To my mother.'

He nodded towards something past her left shoulder and she turned, half expecting to see a tall female version of Lord Sherbourne glaring at her from the corner, but it was only a portrait. It was an excellent likeness, clearly by an artist of talent, and yet there was no drama or embellishment to it at all—just a couple standing beneath a wide tree, doing nothing in particular.

The man was smiling at something either inside him or far beyond the viewer. Though his hair was pale brown to Marcus's black, in looks he was very like Marcus, but not in expression. The woman was the opposite—she was not a particularly handsome woman—shorter and rounder and darker than her distinguished husband, but her expression was very direct and with that same humorous tolerance Lily had often seen on Lord Sherbourne's face.

Lord Sherbourne continued. 'I have four older sisters. The eldest was twenty-three and youngest twelve when I was born and my parents had abandoned hope of having a son. My mother was forty-four and my father fifty years old at the time. They were already grandparents to two bouncing baby grandsons. I was rather a shock.'

'I dare say your sisters doted on you. That might explain a few things.'

He grinned. 'That doesn't sound complimentary.'

She sighed. 'It is actually. You may be annoyingly self-confident, but the other side of that coin appears to be generosity and kindness. I cannot fault your regard to Annie in any way.'

He cleared his throat and she realised she'd embarrassed him again. 'Well, the point I was making was that when my mother learned she was ill less than a year after my father's death...' he glanced at the painting, but his expression was back under control '...she became very worried that I was letting my comfortable life sweep me along with it and would never marry and more importantly never have children.

'And before you mention heirs again, she was not in the least concerned with heirs to the Sherbourne title. She came from a large Italian family and always believed that was far more important than wealth or station. That was what mattered most to her. So she very ruthlessly used my love for her and fear about her illness to extract a promise from me that I would marry before my thirty-fifth birthday. At the time four years seemed a damnably long time.'

He spoke the words lightly, but they were as thin as a breeze and beneath them she sensed a whole landscape of love and pain and loss and accountability. Her heart ached, as if she was witnessing that moment right now.

His word to his dying mother. She could not fight that. Her heart plummeted.

'So, as I said...' he picked up a pencil lying on the side of the blotting pad and traced some invisible inscription on the gold-embossed leather edge 'you've placed me in something of a quandary. It took me two years to identify a woman I could consider marrying.'

She nodded, but her neck felt stiff. 'If I may…if I may ask, when will you turn thirty-five?'

The corners of his mouth kicked up very briefly. 'End of October.'

She ought to have felt a modicum of relief that it was four months away and not four weeks. But the thought of him being married in four months to anyone at all… 'That would still give you several months to find someone else.'

'Well, in theory, yes. But I shall be travelling ahead of the English delegation to the Congress in Aix-la-Chapelle which shall take place in October. Through Paris first and possibly Vienna. I shall be leaving by mid-August.'

'I see. And…and there was no other woman…' Oh, God, she could not say it. She had to. She cleared her throat, but he was already speaking again.

'In light of these considerations, I think I have a solution for both our quandaries.'

'You have?'

'Yes. If Anne is indeed in love with her old flame and wishes to marry him, I'm willing to set her free. But as I would be doing you a favour, you really ought to do me one, as well.'

'You want my help finding a bride?' Her voice squeaked upwards alarmingly.

'In a manner of speaking.'

'But… I couldn't,' she answered, choking over the words. 'I am the least qualified person to advise you on…on—'

'I didn't mean I wanted your advice,' he interrupted a little brusquely. 'I meant you could always offer to take Anne's place. That would solve quite a few problems, don't you think? I would be able to honour my promise and you could solve all your family's difficulties in one fell swoop.'

She could hear the dog breathing. The clock ticking. Her heart beating. Everything was suddenly very, very loud.

'Anne's place.'

'As my wife,' he elucidated, the pencil flitting between his fingers like an acrobatic snake.

His wife.

His *wife*…

His wife.

It made no sense. One did not trade a Miss Anne Devenish for a Mrs Lily Walsh. Dozens of Anne-like ladies could be found in any London ballroom and most would leap at an offer from Lord Sherbourne. He was *not* serious.

Was he teasing her? Punishing her a little?

Think. Calmly and rationally.

'Lord Sherbourne. I realise you must find my request upsetting and…and perhaps insulting, but…'

'Are you trying to tell me that my counter-offer is upsetting and insulting, Lily?'

'No! No, not at all, but I know you cannot truly be serious. Surely your mother intended you to make a good match and I am most certainly not that.'

'Oh? And why not?'

'Why *not*? I'm a widow.'

'Like many others and through no fault of your own.'

'Well, yes, but I'm not…'

Oh, hell.

She took a deep breath and jumped into the pit. 'I am not…pure.'

It was an awful word, but she could think of no other acceptably virginal euphemism.

He rubbed a hand over his mouth, but his eyes were sparkling with sudden laughter. That was *not* the response she'd expected.

'You know what I mean!'

'Yes, I rather think I gathered the gist of it.' His voice shook. 'But being, ah, *pure* was never on my list of requirements. In fact, there were two widows on my list.'

'Well, you could marry them, then,' she snapped.

'Both? I'm willing to stretch the boundaries a bit, but that is excessive. Besides, they were stricken from my list for reasons unrelated to their lack of so-called purity.'

'Well, I am certain I never would have made your list in the first place.'

'How can you be certain if you don't know what my criteria were? The fact is, I think you and I would manage together very well. You have never once bored me.'

As far as compliments go, it was mild, but her stupid heart flopped on its back like a panting puppy waiting to have its belly scratched.

'In fact,' he continued, considering her with an air of a man eying a mare at Tattersall's, 'in fact, I think you might suit me better than Anne.'

That was several miles too far. Her suspicious instincts flared into being. 'I sincerely doubt that is true.'

'Oh, it is. Witness this conversation. I can't imagine speaking so openly with her. I thought she possessed more depth than the other women on my list, but I find you far easier to talk with and I think you find it rather easy to talk with me as well.'

'Not when you're being slippery and clever.'

He smiled. 'You do very well even then. I like that.'

I like it, too. Damn you... Marcus.

It was awful that he'd even suggested this. He would all too soon regret even thinking it. She could well believe he didn't relish going back to his list and settling for second best. But whatever he said, she would never have even made that list.

Though to be fair, it might well be true that he valued the unusual honesty that had developed between them… No. Once he thought it over he was certain to see there were a thousand reasons not to marry someone like her. It was her duty to at least point out several of them.

'I am naturally flattered, Lord Sherbourne…'

'But?'

'But though you might consider me a possible replacement, society won't.'

'Ah, society. I'm not marrying for society's sake, but my own. I played their game for two years during this interminable search, but once I wed I shall go back to ignoring them as much as possible. So if it's balls and Almack's you are pining for, I'm afraid you've come to the wrong man.'

She laughed at the admonishing note in his voice. 'I'm not speaking of Almack's and you know it. I'm speaking of being tainted by the scandal of my elopement. Of how society will regard… Once you have…'

Oh, God, she couldn't talk about children. While they'd been theoretically Annie's that had been hard enough. But now he'd opened Pandora's box, the image of Emma…

She pressed a hand to her chest. She would not crumble again. Breathe.

'You're speaking of children.' His voice was soft, pulling a shawl of warmth around that cold fist inside her.

'Yes.' She forced the words out, concentrating on her keeping her breaths even. 'Yes, I am.'

'I see.'

'I don't think you do, Lord Sherbourne. I'm not…as eligible as Annie. You could do far, far better.' There, she sounded perfectly rational and the nail-studded fist in her midriff was shrinking. There was no possible way she could tell him she could not bear the thought of suffering through that again. She couldn't.

She waited for him to probe and press and object, but he didn't. The watchful expression was back and she wondered what he saw. Or thought he saw. Nothing good, probably. He was probably already regretting his outrageous offer. Well, she would not hold him to it, though it would serve him right if she did. She wanted this over with.

It was too *hard*.

'I realise you are upset by Anne's rejection, but once you consider a little you will realise it is for the best and be grateful I didn't accept your flattering offer.'

'I see you have arranged it all in your mind. Very well, we won't belabour the point right now, but we still must settle the issue.'

'What issue?'

'I think it only fair you offer some form of reparation and, since you seem convinced the only damage being done is to my vanity, you should offer something appropriate.'

'You want…compliments?'

He smiled, some of the lighter amusement returning and she felt her own tension fade. She was far too attuned to this man's moods.

'I would prefer something rather more concrete.'

'You can't mean money. You must know we haven't any.'

'No price could heal my wounded heart, anyway.' He pressed his hand over that organ once again and she barely stopped her hand from rising to touch the tingling rush of warmth that spread out from the same spot on her own chest.

'You are very annoying,' she snapped.

'And you are a serious thorn in my…side,' he replied with a bow. 'So we are quits. At least in that respect. Not in this. What will you offer?'

'I don't see why I must offer you anything but good common sense.'

She sounded ridiculously stuffy even to her own ears and she wasn't surprised when he laughed.

'"O, when she's angry, she is keen and shrewd! She was a vixen when she went to school; And though she be but little, she is fierce."'

It took her a moment to place the quote. '*A Midsummer Night's Dream*. I was never fond of that play. Too fantastical.'

'Of course it is,' he soothed. 'You are far too practical to be swayed by the intervention of Pucks and potions. But we are digressing. What will you offer?'

'What do you *want*?'

'A balm for my bruised pride. You could try kissing it better.'

Her jaw slackened.

'Three kisses,' he continued, unperturbed by her shocked expression. 'I think…spread over, say, a week?' He glanced at the calendar set out on the side of his desk. 'How fortuitously symbolic. It is Midsummer's Day in a week. Three hot, midsummer madness kisses culminating on the longest, sunniest day of the year when the Oak King cedes to the Holly King and spirits abound, wreaking havoc on mortals. Anything might happen. You might even decide to accept my offer.'

His voice kept sinking lower and the roiling heat inside of her kept rising, but she clung to the slipping shreds of her dignity.

'Are you mad?'

'That has been debated. Perhaps. Sometimes quite certainly.'

'And if I refuse?'

'That is your prerogative. If you consider the

prospect of kissing me distasteful all you have to do is say so and I shall withdraw my suggestion and leave you to think of some other offering.'

'This is extortion.'

'Not at all. I think it very fair. Think of the advantages. You've been a widow now for how many years?'

'Five, but…'

'Other than Wrexham, have you kissed anyone since then?'

'No, and as I told you at the time I did not kiss your friend, nor did he kiss me, but…'

'Well, that is a sad shame. Did your husband put you off it?'

'He… No, he most certainly did not. But…'

'Do you plan to never kiss anyone ever again?'

She opened her mouth to state precisely that, but stayed there, like a landed fish. What on earth was she arguing about? He was offering Annie's freedom in exchange for kisses. *His* kisses.

She went scalding hot. Did he know? Oh, God, he had to know. She must be as transparent as rice paper. She swallowed.

Three kisses for Annie's freedom.

'And…and you would not dispute Annie's wishes?'

'Not for a moment. She is, as of this moment, fancy-free. I hope her sainted John rides to the rescue sooner rather than later, for she shall find her position both in your home and in society a trifle uncomfortable once the news spreads.' He stood. 'In fact, you'd best go and inform her she is footloose and I shall make my own way over at a slightly more civilised hour to formalise the situation with your parents. I suggest you be on hand to comfort them as they mourn the loss of a fortune… Sorry, a son-in-law.'

She stood as well, a trifle unsteadily. It was either the shock or the whisky—she wasn't certain. She hesitated.

'Do you…don't you wish to, uh, collect?'

'Does that mean you are willing to accept the trade?'

'I… Yes. Yes, I am.'

She sounded far calmer than she felt, which was good.

'Good. That means you shall have to postpone your plans to leave London.'

She straightened. That seemed so far away from her now.

'Of course. I couldn't leave Annie now in any case.'

'Of course not. Are you certain there are no pressing…ah…commitments awaiting you in Birmingham?'

'What? No, nothing until September.'

'Then why were you so pressed to return?'

'I wasn't… I mean, I was, but that was merely…'

She groped for a reasonable reason and tossed her mother into the ring. 'My mother wants me gone.'

'I see. Charming. Well, the burden of your presence shall soon be eclipsed by Anne's scandal so we needn't worry about that. Now I'd best arrange for Juan to see you home. I shall send word where and when I expect my first instalment.'

Oh.

'Not now?'

'Definitely not while you are still so unsettled. I prefer you take your time deciding whether you are willing and I certainly prefer you to be fully concentrated on the act rather than on your sister.'

'But how do you know I shall honour my side of the bargain if you have already released her from the engagement?'

His mouth curved. 'I trust you, Lily-fox.'

Damn him.

She fumbled to arrange her veil over her face and he tugged on the bell-pull without removing his gaze from her.

'Just so we are clear. This is only if you are willing. I have no interest in reluctant sacrifices. So if…'

'I would not have agreed if I weren't willing, Lord Sherbourne.' Her words sounded dreadfully stuffy and she was glad for the cover of her veil and even more so when he smiled.

'No, you are far too honest. For better and for worse. Very well. Three real, willing kisses.'

Heat flared over her, pinching at her cheeks and spreading through every inch of her.

Real, willing kisses. Yes, she could manage that.

All too well.

Unbelievable.

Marcus sank back down on to his chair as the door closed and let his breath out slowly, reaching down to stroke Ombra's scraggly head.

He must have once done something very, very good to deserve such a stroke of luck.

Not just luck—a blasted *miracle*.

He surged to his feet again and glanced at the clock. Almost eleven. This was no time to be sitting down. He needed to be at Brook Street as soon as decently possible to confirm his release from impending disaster. The last thing he needed was for Anne Devenish to get cold feet and send this golden opportunity up in a puff of smoke.

He looked over at his parents' portrait that hung between the bookshelves. 'This is a turn for the books, isn't it? I know I promised to marry before my thirty-fifth birthday, but I think you will agree this change of plans is for an excellent cause.'

His father, ever the optimist, smiled on, while

his mother, also quite typically, managed an impressive mixture of resignation and contentment.

Ombra gave a jaw-cracking yawn and padded after him as he strode out of the study and up to his room. As they passed the great mirror that hung midway up the stairs he caught his expression and allowed himself a complicit smile.

Five years without a real kiss. Well, he could work with that. He would have to go gently, though.

He paused halfway up the next flight of stairs, his hand tightening on the banister as he remembered her shock when he'd mentioned the siege and the fire.

That had been cruel of him. Not that he could have known she would react like that, that the memory and the wound ran so deep. But still, knowing what he did about her life, he never should have stooped so low. His only defence was that she'd breached his own defences so thoroughly.

And that foolishness of mentioning children. He'd been hoist by his own petard. He'd wanted to convince her of the importance of honouring his mother's wishes, but he'd misinterpreted her reaction in Richmond Park. She might have loved her daughter, but clearly the thought of having another child terrified her.

He would tread more carefully from now on.

The very last thing he wanted to do was hurt her or scare her away. He wanted something entirely different and now he'd been granted the opportunity to reach for it.

To think—only yesterday he'd been the most miserable among men.

What a difference a day made.

Chapter Nineteen

Not a word.

Two days had passed since she made her deal with the devil.

Two days of nothing.

Well, that was not true; quite a bit had happened, Lily thought guiltily. The house was in an uproar and her parents in a panic. She'd known her parents' finances were unsound, but she'd not realised they were disastrous.

She'd not been invited to take part in the discussion that followed Lord Sherbourne's tête-à-tête with Annie yesterday, but that hadn't stopped her from shamelessly eavesdropping, her ear glued to the drawing room door from the safety of the adjoining parlour. Her parents had done their best to protest, bully and beg, but luckily Annie had stood firm.

Or rather sat and cried, but still—firmly.

Lord Sherbourne had remained mostly silent,

occasionally repeating in his languid drawl that he respected Miss Devenish's right to make up *her own* mind and spend *her own* life with a person of *her own* choice.

These subtly emphasised reminders were well timed to bolster Annie when her resolve flagged. After half an hour of this tail-chasing, His Lordship appeared to lose his patience and he bade them farewell and good luck, assuring them he would settle the matter with society in the most advantageous way for the Devenishes—whatever that meant—and then he left.

Lily had to hold firm to the doorknob to prevent herself from rushing into the hallway to thank him—and remind him that she took her promises seriously and would of course honour their verbal contract.

Luckily, she'd held back.

He *must* have been funning with her. Punishing her a little, perhaps. She'd thought him serious, but why on earth would he be? He was known to have had several beautiful mistresses and, despite his protests and hasty offer, he had probably already compiled another List of London's Most Eligible Ladies. Why on earth would he be interested even in kisses from a plain widow past her first youth and who reminded him of a fox?

Damn him.

Stupid her.

'Mrs Walsh.'

Lily lurched out of her chair. She hadn't even heard Annie's maid enter the parlour. 'Yes, Ailish?'

Ailish, her eyes bright with conjecture, held out a sealed letter. 'A message for you, Mrs Walsh. The lad didn't stay for an answer.'

Lily broke the seal, her heart thumping.

As far as clandestine missives went, it wasn't impressive. It read:

> *First*
> *Today*
> *Noon*
> *Hilliard's*
> *Natural Philosophy*
> *M.*

Lily sat down. *Today. Noon.* That was in an hour. Midsummer madness indeed.

First. Of three...

She surged to her feet. Thank God Annie had insisted on adjusting her old gowns for Lily's use. She was damned if she was wearing her widow's grey or even lavender to her first real kiss in five years.

When she was ready she stood before the mirror. The pale-primrose promenade dress and the bronze pelisse with the darker frogging across the chest wasn't the first stare of fashion, but it suited her foxy colouring.

For the first time in many, many years she wished she was as beautiful as Annie. Or at least taller.

She sighed and turned away, making herself a promise. Whatever came, she would make the most of it.

She's not coming.

Damn, he must have been mad to think she would. She'd secured her goal, after all.

She might at least have had the decency to send someone with a note so he didn't have to skulk between the bookshelves like some lovelorn fool who…

'Excuse me, could you help me reach Erasmus Darwin's *Botanic Garden*?'

Marcus turned, his heartbeat scurrying ahead faster than a cat up a tree with Ombra at its tail. How the devil had she sneaked up on him? His instincts were shot to hell.

He did his best to keep his expression bland as she looked up at him. She wore a thin lace veil, but, though it covered her face, it was no real barrier. She wasn't quite smiling, or rather her eyes were, but her mouth was a carefully controlled line. Her left dimple, however, was hovering at the edge of existence, which was a good sign.

Simply for something to do he reached for the book she'd mentioned and opened it. '*A Poem, in Two Parts... The Economy of Vegetation*? Good Lord. I've never heard a less poetic name for a poem.'

She plucked the volume from him. 'It is an ode to scientific advances like the steam engine and men like Benjamin Franklin.'

'What has that to do with vegetation?'

'I admit the name is rather...unfortunate, but he has many fascinating ideas about what the future might bring, like submersible sea balloons that can carry people underwater, for example.'

'Fulton built one in France twenty years ago. The *Nautilus*.'

'Well, this was written thirty years ago so perhaps your Fulton stole the idea from him.'

'And then there was Bushnell's submersible almost fifty years ago. It went by a slightly less edifying name—the turtle. And one hundred years ago there was a Russian design with flame throwers. And then two hundred years ago there was the Dutchman, Drebbel, who—'

'Now you are merely showing off,' she admonished.

'Guilty. Are you impressed with my esoteric and utterly useless knowledge?'

'Terribly. A little puzzled how flame throwers worked underwater, though.'

'They didn't. The poor fellow never did succeed, though to his credit he almost died trying.'

Her left dimple was in full bloom now and he plucked the book from her hands and returned it to its spot safely out of her reach.

'There's a newer edition in the back room,' he suggested, taking her arm.

'I happen to prefer older editions,' she said primly, but both dimples were in evidence now and he gave in to his relief and smiled.

'I'm glad to hear that. Nevertheless...' He took her arm and with a glance down the empty aisle he guided her swiftly through the door at the end and shut it behind them, turning the key in the lock.

Her eyes widened and he held up his hands and hurried to reassure her.

'Please don't worry. I locked it so we won't be disturbed. I'll leave the key in the lock if you wish to leave at any moment. That is always your prerogative.'

She gave a faint laugh and looked around. 'I'm not worried.'

She truly didn't sound worried and that both calmed him and made him tense all over again. This seemed to be the pattern of his responses to this strange woman—whatever she did, he seemed to be plagued by two opposing forces that did nothing to cancel each other out.

'This is Anszel's private room,' he explained.

'He meets here with printers and publishers to review upcoming book lists. He agreed to…uh, lend it to me.'

'Anszel?'

'Mr Grozny. The proprietor.'

'Mr Anszel Grozny? Then why is it called Hilliard's Bookstore?'

'Anszel felt the name Hilliard would draw a larger crowd than Grozny. He is probably correct in our narrow little world.'

'Probably. Unfortunately.'

She went to look at one of the many stacks of books reposing on a table long enough for a knight's dining hall. 'You appear to know him well.'

'I dare say I do. I knew his son. We were up at Oxford together.'

'Knew. What happened to him?'

Damn, he didn't want to touch any nerves. But lying wasn't possible when she was looking at him like that. 'He was a soldier.'

She gave a slow, grave nod.

'He was excellent with languages. Spoke ten of them,' he added by way of distraction.

'That must have been useful in Spain. Was he in Spain?'

'Yes.'

'What regiment?'

Ah, hell.

'He served with Wellington. Ah, good, Anszel even left some brandy in the decanter. Come, we need to toast our pact.'

She cast him a look that said clearly she knew a diversion when she saw one. She was a damned suspicious woman.

'Do you often hold your…meetings here, Lord Sherbourne?'

'Never. But I needed some place…neutral where we won't be disturbed. And I'm too old to collect the kisses I'm owed in carriages.'

She laughed, that tumbling joyous sound that had caught his attention from the beginning. He should have known he was in trouble when every time she laughed he had to struggle to stop himself from searching for her face in the crowd. And now he was not only free to look his fill, he was about to taste as well…

'Come. A toast. To midsummer madness.' He kept his voice quiet and clean of triumph.

He handed her the glass carefully, trying to fight the surge of heat that coursed through him as her grey eyes met his, her mouth still curved in a tentative smile.

He looked away from her lips to the slight scars that zigzagged up her jaw and ended near the lobe of her ear. He wanted to know how they had happened, whether it had hurt, what…

Not yet.

'I thought you were jesting,' she said. 'About the kisses. Punishing me a little.'

'Did you? I rarely jest.'

'You always jest. It is a perfect façade.'

His smile widened against his will. 'I'll amend my statement. I rarely jest on matters of importance.'

'And kisses are important?'

'Of course. What is more so?'

She considered. 'Loyalty? Duty?'

'Important, but very dull. I have enough of those without seeking them out.'

'Rumour indicates you have enough of the other. Without seeking them out.'

'Rumour is wrong. I am far more discerning than you give me credit for, Lily. Are you here only out of loyalty and duty? If so, tell me and I shall return you to Brook Street, your debt repaid in full.'

It was a risk and even as he said it he cursed himself, but she merely shook her head.

'It is not merely that.'

He waited for her to add something, but she sipped her brandy and looked about the room.

'Will we meet here for all three kisses?'

His heart hitched and he set down his glass. He'd never felt so gauche in his life. Or if he had, he couldn't remember it. 'To be honest, I haven't thought that far ahead. I didn't know if you would come. For all I knew you might have accepted your victory and hared back to Birmingham.'

The frown line appeared between her brows. 'I would never have done that. At least not without informing you. And I could hardly leave Annie now. Not while the household is still...seething.'

Annie. Of course.

'Why not? She has what she wanted. Freedom from the odious attentions of the reprobate.'

She smiled and shook her head. 'Nonsense. In any case, I didn't wish to leave. And I find it rather insulting you think I would go back on my word.'

'I didn't mean it in that way. Merely that you might have changed your mind about the terms of our agreement. I meant what I said, Lily. If at any point you do change your mind you tell me, yes?'

'Very well. But I shan't.'

Her voice was light and she looked younger, too, like a girl on an excursion. She certainly didn't look like a sacrifice chained to a rock, awaiting a dragon.

His nerves slackened a little more and he gave in to temptation and took her hand. Her fingers curved over his palm, settling so naturally that for a moment he merely stood there, watching the tan-coloured glove against his skin. He'd wanted to kiss her but right now what he wanted most in the world was to feel the soft slide of her palm shaping itself against his, her fingers pressing between his, tightening as he moved towards her...

When she pulled her hand away his breath caught and he had to stop himself from taking it back.

Rules. Boundaries. He rarely had to remind himself, but he rather thought today he would have to do quite a bit of that.

When she unfastened the button, he wasn't quite certain what she was doing. It took him three buttons and two fingers to realise she was pulling it off. Then she held out her hand once more and he took it.

Tingling heat spread through him like fire in dry hay—snatching cell after cell, licking and burning its way along nerve ends, deep into his muscles, making them stretch and ready as if he was about to enter the boxing ring—or head into battle.

Absurd.

Undeniable.

He was on fire from holding this woman's hand. A kiss from her would likely incinerate him.

'I don't like gloves,' she said, her voice low, almost dreamy. 'I like to feel the world.'

'Yes.' He held on to her hand and brushed his knuckles along the line of her cheek with the other. The twin scars were a little puckered and he wanted to touch his mouth to the contrast between the velvety skin and those ridges. He touched his thumb to the line of her lower lip, settling on the soft, deep rose-coloured pout.

Her lips parted a little, her breathing shallow.

So was his. He hadn't even done anything yet and his insides were already caving, his skin in flames.

One kiss today. Only one. Don't be greedy.

He bent, touched his mouth to hers and had to stop, holding tight against the need to groan.

He proceeded carefully, brushing his lips against hers, buffing them like a cat. Her hand fluttered against his waistcoat before settling, her fingers curling into the fabric, dragging it against his skin. Cascades of sparks spread over his chest and downwards, adding to the growing heat in his groin.

God, he'd known it would feel right. He'd known it.

'The day I came,' she whispered, 'you weren't wearing a waistcoat.'

'How improper of me,' he whispered back and touched his tongue to the succulent middle of her upper lip. Her body shivered against him, her hands twisting deeper into the fabric of his coat.

It was going to kill him to go slowly.

'I want you to be improper again,' she whispered against his mouth. 'Take it off.'

He drew back. 'Take it off?'

'Off.'

'Here? *Now?*'

She flicked a button. 'Here and now.'

He didn't wait for further invitation. He tossed his coat and waistcoat on to the table and she laid her hands gently on his shirt, the corners of her mouth picking up.

'Better.'

He locked his legs. *Steady on, now.* 'Your pelisse. Tit for tat.'

Her dimples deepened. There were only six buttons worked into the dark frogging and she slipped them off without coyness and laid her pelisse in a rather more orderly fashion on the back of a chair.

'This doesn't mean I agree to anything else,' she said with a quick look and he shook his head.

'Nor I. Just a kiss today.'

'Just one?' she asked.

'I prefer to space out my treats. Come here.'

She laid her hands on his chest as she had before and raised her chin. There was so much in her eyes when she wasn't being cautious. Excitement, worry, laughter. He gave up trying to understand either of them, cradled her face in his hands and kissed her.

And lost himself entirely.

Her lips opened under his, soft and pillowy and

fitting to his as if they'd practised this a dozen times.

To be fair, he'd fantasised about kissing her often enough recently. Practically every time he'd come within two yards of her or had to hand her up into a carriage or take a cup of tea from her or in that treacherous time in his bed between waking and sleep… That had been the worst. But those dreams had been nothing more than a soldier's drill and now finally he was going into battle. But war was hell and this…this was pure heaven.

She tasted of peaches and blackberries plucked from hedges by the stream. And he was ravenous.

He broke free for a moment, his mouth against her cheek as he struggled to find his balance, his control. Slow, don't hurry, don't scare her. Slow…

She made a sound, between a mewl and a moan, and an answering groan rose up in him like the cries of souls trapped in purgatory. To hell with slow.

He raised her on to the table, his fingers pressing into the soft skin at her waist. Her eyes were half-closed, slumberous and distant, the grey misty and blurred. He couldn't seem to look away.

His hands weren't frozen though—they slipped from her waist to her hips, his fingers pressing into the lush curves as he moved closer, his thighs pressing against her knees and suddenly… oh, miracle…they parted, slipping him between them until her skirts held him at bay. Her hands moved up his chest, leaving shimmering trails of jealous need in their paths until her fingers left linen behind and found flesh.

She stopped, catching her lower lip between her teeth.

He stopped as well. The sensation of her fingers resting so lightly on the taut muscles of his neck, just brushing the hair at his nape... She was branding him, his skin absorbing her mark for ever. She licked her lip and continued, her fingers slowly threading into his hair, retreating, then deeper. His scalp tingled and vicious streaks of heat coursed down his back. With each stroke she pulled him deeper into a warm ocean and it was frightening and wonderful.

Her lashes rose and she smiled up at him, pulling him under completely. He groaned and leaned down to press his mouth against her neck, the peach-soft lobe of her ear, his teeth scraping the skin below it.

'Yes.' She breathed the word, a shudder rising through her, her hands pulling him closer. When her mouth returned to his, he gave up whatever resolution he'd formed that morning of a slow, clever seduction, spaced out and rationed. He sank into her, gathered her hard against him, her skirts running up to bunch between them, and kissed her again.

Her mouth was silky warmth, those little moans demolishing him. Her tongue played with his, her lips brushing up against his when he pulled away, parting when he sank back in. She opened with a totality that was exhilarating and horrible because he knew it might be up to him to stop and he wanted everything.

When he finally brought himself to a halt he was one big, pulsing mass. He was hard against her skirts, his heart thudding like a great gong.

Being right had never scared him so much in his life.

'Lily.' He breathed her name against the warm perfume of her neck. 'Lily…' He closed his teeth hard on the need to say her name again and again and again.

It could not have been more than five minutes, perhaps ten, but he was a damned wreck.

He moved away, looking back from a safe distance. He'd tumbled her hair. It lay in a soft mass of waves over her shoulder. Her mouth was parted and reddened and her eyes…

Another step back put more distance between them and the need to do something very, very foolish. Thirty-five was far too old to be impulsive.

He held up a finger, reminding them both.

'One.'

Chapter Twenty

Second
Noon
Today
Black carriage
Corner of St George and Maddox
M.

Carriage?

Lily folded the note with a faint huff. She had hoped for something more...well, something more. She'd waited almost two days for this second note, turning over her resolution so often she'd churned it into butter, and this was the best he had to offer? A carriage?

Well, he might be setting the terms, but as he'd pointed out it was her prerogative to accept or reject. They would see about this carriage business.

As promised, a black-panelled carriage was waiting at the corner. A footman stood by and when he saw her, he gave a slight bow and opened the door. Casting caution to the wind, she hurried inside before she could reconsider.

Lord Sherbourne was seated at the far end, a dark form in the gloom that settled on them the moment the curtained door shut behind her. He made no move towards her and she slipped into the opposite corner and crossed her arms, inspecting her nemesis.

In repose his face looked precisely as his reputation would have advertised. Harshly handsome, with sharp-cut lines, a sensuous mouth that served his sardonic smile well and eyes that always seemed to say *I know you and I know you are hiding something.*

Well, after well over a month watching him with Annie, Lily felt she knew him rather well, too. And she knew he was most definitely hiding something under all those urbane layers. Something definite, powerful and very private. Something she quite desperately wanted to reach.

But that was her foolishness.

'I thought you said you were too old to collect kisses in carriages,' she said, breaking the silence.

He smiled, his eyes lighting with an amber-gold light that shone in the gloom like a great cat. 'I wouldn't waste one of your kisses on a carriage ride, Lily.'

Oh, hell. She was melting again. How was she ever going to find any equilibrium if he kept doing that? She wanted to tell him she didn't mind at all if he kissed her in the carriage. In a bookshop. In the street. In the middle of Almack's. Everywhere and anywhere.

No, she didn't want him to kiss her yet, because then their peculiar pact would be more than half over.

He moved a little towards her and held out his hand and she laid hers on it. He threaded his fingers through hers and warmth wove itself up her arm and cocooned her whole, tingling along as it went, like a series of feathery kisses.

'You came prepared,' he murmured.

'I did?'

'No gloves.'

His hand tightened on hers as he moved even closer, resting their joined hands on his thigh. Just like that day she'd first danced with him her hand looked dainty in his. She smiled at the sight and he raised their linked hands and brushed his mouth along her knuckles.

'This doesn't count,' he murmured, turning her hand over and touching his lips to the inside of her wrist. 'I like that you hate gloves, Lily. You smell like orange blossoms.'

She gave in and moved a little closer, too. Her other hand clenched against the need to touch the dark head bent over her hand.

'You smell like the forest I used to run away

to when I was little,' she whispered, leaning towards him. His breath huffed against her wrist and his mouth moved up her arm, pressing the pelisse before it.

'That may not be a good thing,' he murmured against her skin, his voice warm with laughter.

She gave in and lowered her head to brush her cheek against the dark silk of his hair and breathed her fill.

'It is an excellent thing. I can't describe it—pine and earth and freedom and sunshine and...'

He drew back and for a moment she wondered if she'd said something wrong. Then she was pulled on to his lap, his arms hard around her, his body as tense as if he was bracing for a crash. The carriage rolled on sedately, but he still sat there, his cheek against her hair, breathing carefully, his arms caging her, but warm and comforting. Finally, the tension eased, his hand smoothing the fabric of her dress against her waist.

'You really ought to take up boxing, Lily. You have a way of popping a facer over one's guard.'

'Is that what I did? Just by telling you how wonderful you smell?'

His laughter rumbled against her. 'Apparently. Damn, we're here already.'

'Here?' The carriage made a sharp turn and through the crack in the curtains she saw a stone wall and iron gate. Marcus slipped her off his lap and when they stopped he jumped out and helped her down. She had a swift glimpse at a grey stone façade and tall trees before they stepped inside.

'Where are we?'

'Chiswick. A place I come to when I need quiet. You are perfectly safe here.'

'I know,' she said without thinking.

No one came to greet them, but when they entered a large room that looked to be a cross between a study and a library a tray of tea and cakes was waiting on a table.

She walked along the shelves, alight with book envy, and stopped before the window. A wide lawn rolled down to a sheltered stream lined with willows that spread their roots and dipped their leaves into the water. In the middle of the lawn was a wide-boughed plane tree under which a table and two chairs faced the water.

'This is lovely! Do you often come here?'

'Not as often as I would like.'

'Pity. But those chairs don't look comfortable enough for that view. You need a deep armchair with an ottoman and plenty of cushions.'

He laughed. 'I'm not in my dotage. Yet.'

'It has nothing to do with age. It has to do with indulgence.'

'There is your answer, then.'

She shook her head, watching him as he poured the tea, his hair falling forward to cover his brow.

Her hand tingled with the memory of it slipping through her fingers, but she tried to concentrate on the man, not his undeniably attractive physique.

He was a puzzle. She'd known that from the day they'd been introduced upon her arrival in London. She still wasn't certain what to make of him and now it mattered more than ever.

'Do you know,' she said, turning to look out at the calm and calming view of the willows, 'I thought you disliked me from the outset. You never tried to charm me as you did my family.'

She felt rather than heard him come up behind her.

'Do *you* know,' he replied, turning her towards him, 'that you are not always as clever as you think you are?'

'I don't think I'm clever.'

'You are *convinced* you are. You are accustomed to out-thinking those around you and you've developed a bad habit of assuming you know people better than they know themselves.'

She wanted to be offended, but there was a smile in his eyes that took the sting out of his damning assessment. 'Guilty as charged. What has that to do with you disliking me?'

'You *are* clever. Figure it out.' He touched a finger to her temple. His hazel-gold eyes narrowed against the sun, but she felt the same sensation of being *seen*. She'd felt it from the first day she'd met him. Even when he was across the room when he looked at her she felt…*this*. It was as unsettling as those dreams where one realised one was walking through the centre of town stark naked.

'When did you first think of kissing me?' she asked abruptly and his eyes narrowed further, flickering down to her mouth. She swallowed.

'At Lady Sefton's ball.' His tone was abrupt. 'I had no choice but to dance with you. A damned waltz. I could tell you didn't want to either, but we did our duty and halfway through you looked up at me and laughed. That was not a good moment.'

She stared. There was no laughter in his eyes now. His face was stripped of the veil of humour, his voice divested of its careful drawl, revealing the hard-cut base beneath.

'I was nervous,' she admitted. She remembered that moment all too clearly. 'I didn't even understand why. You made everyone else around you comfortable, but you made me nervous.'

'Now you know why. I didn't want to make you comfortable and you certainly made me as uncomfortable as hell. It is generally not good form to want to bed the sister of the woman you have committed to marry.'

'You wanted to bed me?' Her voice wobbled between croak and squeak.

'Want.'

She held still through the chaos that single word unleashed.

Want.

She wanted it, too. *Desperately.*

She swallowed, preparing the words.

'Don't ask questions you don't want answers to,' he said abruptly, returning to the tea tray. 'Come and have your tea.'

That command was so out of place she couldn't help laughing. His shoulder twitched, but he didn't turn from his task of filling the two cups. She went to him and touched his arm.

'Not yet.'

He looked at her and she hurried on, throwing caution to the winds.

'I thought of kissing you before that. Which is far worse. Annie is my sister, after all.'

She braced herself on his arm and rose on tip-toe to brush a quick kiss over his cheek. His arm came around her, holding her there. She let her eyelids sink closed, cloaking herself in darkness as she absorbed him with her other senses. She'd been right about the forest, mysterious but familiar, and his warmth that wrapped around her even when she was several feet away. This close it was like sinking into a warm bath. She sighed and slid her palm up his chest, finding the line between his waistcoat and the linen shirt.

'I meant to wait, take you down to the willows...'

he murmured and she shifted, touching her mouth to his.

He froze, a deep, almost audible reverberation coursing through him as his arm tightened around her, his hand sinking into her hair, clamping about her head as if he would pull her away. She rested there for a moment, absorbing the texture of his lips, the sensation of waves and eddies of electric need pulsing through her. The anticipation was sweetly painful.

'Marcus,' she murmured against his mouth, touching her tongue to the tense line of his lips.

That broke him.

The kiss at Hilliard's had been a revelation. Like growing up thinking the full range of blues was limited to the pale shades of dawn, only to find oneself by the seaside on a clear summer day facing a whole universe of blues, bright and muted, dark and jewelled, all just waiting to be experienced.

That had been marvellous enough, but the second kiss was a completely different kind of revelation.

She *owned* this kiss. She owned the feel of his skin on hers. His taste, that distant and familiar scent that reached up through her roots. She was right at the centre of the fire with him, like a phoenix resurrecting herself against his body.

Want. She wanted, wanted, *wanted* this…him. Marcus.

Three kisses were *nowhere* near enough.

She moaned, pressing herself harder against his length as his hands moved over her, caressing her back, her hips, his hand closing on her backside, pulling her up against him, his legs parting to accommodate her. She wished she were taller or he shorter or…

Her thoughts stuttered as she was lifted off her feet again and she found herself on the table, the tea tray shoved aside. Her eyes opened to the brown-gold fire in his, like a sunset striking amber.

'This kiss isn't done,' he muttered, his hand still tense on her nape.

'We're merely getting comfortable,' she agreed in her primmest voice and he gave a little choke of laughter as he ran his hands from her waist down her thighs, easing them apart.

'Very comfortable.'

She smiled back and he groaned and gathered her against him, moving between her legs which opened all on their own. The table was thankfully quite tall and her legs clamped shut against his. She could feel them shake, feel his breath uneven against her neck as he held her for a tense moment. Then he breathed in and softened his hold, his hands resuming their exploration, his lips touching her temple, her cheek, pausing for a moment on her jaw.

Her scars…

She froze.

'No.'

He drew away slightly, but his breath was still there, warm, comforting.

'Does it hurt?'

She shook her head slightly, her hair buffing his cheek. Somehow, she knew he'd know where she'd gathered those scars. He would tie them to her reaction back in his study, linking her story together like daisies in a chain and there was nothing she could do to stop him.

'Don't hide yourself from me.' He touched his mouth to them again, resting there, warm and soft and devastating.

Something awful was happening inside her, not an episode, a beast climbing out of a pea-sized pebble, growing and stretching and pressing everything out of its way, laying claim. Taking her over. Relentless. She could barely breathe.

'Oh, sweetheart,' he whispered, melting her.

There was pity there, and heat, and she didn't know what to do with it. She wanted to pull away, but she didn't want to waste this kiss on sadness and pain so she wrapped her hand around his nape and brought his mouth back to hers.

He wasn't gentle this time. He all but crushed

her against him, his mouth devouring her as his hands roamed at will. She'd worn a simple muslin gown in a pale peach colour, wanting as little as possible in the way if he touched her as he had at Hilliard's, and he made full use of the thin fabric.

This time he didn't wait for her to unbutton her pelisse. She barely noticed when he slipped it off, but she noticed when he eased one sleeve off her shoulder and released her mouth long enough to trace that curve, his breath slipping down her arm, over her chest, into the darkness between her breasts. His mouth just brushed the embroidered ribbon along the line of her bodice, heat shimmering through the thin fabric.

She wanted it off. She wanted… Suddenly it was absolutely clear she'd come for far more than kisses. Here where they were completely alone, an island apart from her life.

'More…' she whispered. 'Please…'

He stopped and leaned his cheek for a moment against the hard curve of her shoulder, then turned his head and pressed a light, butterfly-wing kiss against the side of her neck and withdrew.

Her hand slipped off his shoulders, over his chest, and fell into her lap.

He was breathing hard and for a moment they remained side by side in silence, she seated on the table, he leaning back against it. His hand was a mere inch from her hip, but it felt very far all of a sudden.

'I went beyond our agreement. I'm sorry, Lily.'

'I'm not. I didn't stop you.' She slipped off the table and adjusted her dress before moving towards the window. Behind her, she heard the burble of liquid in the cups.

'The tea isn't even cold.' He sounded surprised and she smiled. He was such a strange mixture of light and dark and she was never quite certain which side would surface. 'Come, we'll take our tea down to the willows.'

Reason and love keep little company together nowadays.

He almost spoke the words from *A Midsummer Night's Dream* aloud as the carriage swept out of Chiswick. Instead he watched her profile—the slope of her eyelashes and the kiss-reddened pout of her lower lip.

This was going by *far* too quickly. Why the devil had he asked for three kisses? He should have demanded a dozen, at least. He was the world's worst negotiator.

'Anne received another letter from John,' she said abruptly.

'Two letters in one week. Is he trying to make up for lost time?'

Her dimple shivered, but was sternly chased

away. 'Apparently he will be following his letter as soon as he secures leave and on no account is she to marry a rake and reprobate.'

'That's a pretty picture she's painted of me.' He tried to sound disgruntled and was rewarded by a flash of laughter in her eyes.

'Anne thinks very highly of you and has never said a mean word about you. It is your reputation that precedes you, my lord, and I rather think the tales of your escapades suit you very well. But it hardly matters; she is feeling very cherished at the moment and walks about with her two letters clutched to her bosom, oblivious to the gnashing teeth and tear-reddened eyes around her.'

'I presume you aren't being afforded the same luxury of being oblivious. Have they discovered your part in this?'

'Not yet. Annie might eventually let word slip. She was never good at keeping secrets from Mama and Papa.'

'What will you do if she does?'

'Oh, nothing. I am accustomed to disappointing them and I only plan to stay with Annie until John arrives.'

'I see.'

'What do you see?' she asked, her head canted to the side, like a watchful sparrow.

What did he see? Quite a few things, but the only one that concerned him at the moment was that he didn't want Lily to disappear from his life. He shook his head. He wasn't ready for this conversation. He knew full well he wanted her in his bed, but other than that he didn't know what he wanted, not unequivocally. And if he did, he wasn't quite certain how to reach for it without ruining everything.

He reached for her instead, pulling her on to his lap. She gave a little sigh, her arms slipping around his neck as if it was utterly natural. Then she tensed.

'I thought you said you were too old for kisses in carriages.'

'I was wrong. A rare occurrence, but there it is.'

'This isn't kiss number three,' she insisted.

'Hardly. Two and a half. Damn, we're already at Mayfair.'

'We shall have to be quick, then,' she said and kissed him.

Chapter Twenty-One

'Where have you been?'

Lily paused with her foot on the bottom stair. Her mother stood in the open door of the back parlour. She looked pale and there were purple smudges below her blue eyes. Lily's stomach twisted, caught between guilt and pity.

'I went to a bookstore.'

'Again? Books are expensive and we are in no state to pay unnecessary bills now your sister…' Mrs Devenish's voice thickened and trailed off as she retreated into the parlour. Lily hesitated and followed, closing the door behind her.

'I didn't purchase anything, Mama.'

Her mother sank on to the sofa. 'What difference does it make? Everything is simply awful. We cannot hide it much longer. We are quite, quite ruined. We had expected… There was no reason not to…'

Not to live beyond their means, fully depending upon another to save them. Lily didn't say the words and her mother suddenly raised her hands and her voice in a wail.

'Lord Sherbourne was everything that was generous and amiable and distinguished. Why John Smithson of all men? Could she not at least have had a fancy for someone with a comfortable independence? Not only must we leave London, but Mr Devenish said we might have to lease out the house and lands in Kent as well and find some tiny hole in a dreadful provincial town like Cheltenham or Harrogate or worse. And now we cannot pay Piers's fees at Oxford he shall have to come as well and we shall be dreadfully cramped.'

'Piers! But he *must* continue his studies.'

'Of course he cannot continue. We cannot afford the fees and in any case he shall have to find a position, though goodness knows what he can do. And all this after we gave your sister three seasons in town and all those lovely gowns and presented her at Court and everything of the very best. Oh, I cannot bear it!'

For well over half an hour Lily did her best to soothe her mother. But the gap between the life Lord Sherbourne had promised and looming ruin and disgrace was too wide to be bridged by platitudes. Eventually Lily rang for her mother's maid and when her mother hobbled upstairs on her trusty maid's arm, she went down to the kitchen to ask the cook send up a tisane for her mother.

On the way to her room she passed by her father's study and for a moment her hand rested on the knob, but she let it slip and continued upstairs. It was foolish to turn to him for a more sensible approach to their quandary. In his own way he was suffering as much as her mother—walking about in silence, avoiding everyone's eyes.

Guilt and worry stewed inside her as she climbed the narrow stairs to her room. Her stomach ached from it. It was only made worse every time Annie came to her room to hug and thank her before rushing back to reread her cherished letters. The promise of John's love seemed to wrap her in a fog of positivity. If Lily hadn't been so happy for her and so relieved for herself, she might have found it annoying.

She wished she were strong enough to tell at least Annie the truth. That she was no saviour. That the chief reason she'd agreed to help was because she couldn't bear the thought of Annie marrying Marcus... Of *anyone* marrying him.

Except herself.

She sat on the side of her bed and let loose the thought that had been chasing her since her fateful visit to Sherbourne House: what if she accepted his offer?

It was a solution. For all of them, her family

included. It was true that she was not a suitable match. She wasn't beautiful or a social asset like Annie and her reputation was tarnished by the scandal of her elopement and would be even more so if...*when* it became known, as it must, that she worked at Hope House.

Then there were his criteria. What had he said? That he'd chosen Anne because she was unexcitable and kind and warm. Well, she could hardly claim to be unexcitable and she wasn't certain she was kind unless it was to people she cared about, and as for warm...that depended on what one meant by warm.

She shoved that unsatisfactory list aside and reached for the positive side of the ledger. She'd never seen Marcus show a smidgen of physical attraction towards Anne, so Lily most definitely, and rather mysteriously, had an advantage there. And she made him laugh and didn't bore him, which she rather suspected Annie sometimes did.

And she liked him and he liked her. Perhaps that was most important of all? *It's a bit more than liking on your part, Lily Walsh.*

She pushed that thought aside as well. He might not wish for a wife who wanted him more than he wanted her, but Lily could keep her thoughts and needs to herself. It was a little dishonest, but not very. After all, perhaps this *was* merely an infatuation and in a few months this...this gut-churning, skin-tingling, heart-pounding all-over ache would settle into something more manageable and they could move along quite merrily together without him even knowing she had thought herself head over heels in love with him.

She let the word finally settle at her centre: love.

This was a strange and foreign beast. It didn't feel at all like what she had felt for Tim. She and Tim had tumbled into it full of enthusiasm and conviction and physical excitement, but she didn't think it had gone this deep. She could not remember this…wrenching feeling. This warmth. This need to open her arms to a man and invite him to lay himself safely in them. This trust. It was just…different.

But when all was said and done, for Marcus marriage meant one thing above all: children.

She froze, but didn't stop the idea. Just let it come, bit by bit. Children. He wanted children. Not an heir. Children. A family.

He would want a son, wouldn't he? A boy like him—with sparkling tiger's eyes and a smile that melted you. A boy who would be kind to animals and curl up with Ombra under his father's desk…

He would want a girl, too. He'd grown up in a house full of sisters and nieces and nephews and he had so much warmth to give to a daughter.

He might not love Lily as she loved him, but

he would love his children with all his generous heart. She knew that. That capacity was in every line of his being. In the way he spoke of his parents and sisters and their children, in the way he was with his friends. In his kindness and care towards Anne and now towards her. He would love his children without the reserve he often set between himself and the wider world.

She pressed her lips together, hard, waiting for the pain that always came when she thought of Emma. There was the burn at her innermost point. But also the image of Emma lying on a blanket near their tent outside Salamanca, trying to shove her pudgy pink foot into her mouth, her brow gathered in concentration at this Herculean feat.

Lily smiled. A daughter. Not Emma. Emma was dearly loved, but gone. Someone new and cherished. She picked up her shawl and pressed it to her burning eyes.

She'd never allowed herself to think of children again since Emma. The possibility of being a mother once more had ceased to exist, become as irrelevant as a dream of sprouting wings and flying.

But now it was possible. Children. A family. A husband.

Marcus.

She lowered her shawl, folding it slowly. She

wasn't at all certain she could do it. Not when the moment of truth came. But she knew she could no longer evade considering it.

In fairness to him, she ought to give him time to reassess his options as well. He'd given her the power to force him into another engagement he might not want any more than his first. If she cared for him, she ought to protect him, even from his own chivalry and impetuosity. She ought to give him time to think. She ought to give herself time to do the same.

That was what she would do. She would tell him that if he hadn't found a better prospect by October...

She took a deep breath and let it out slowly, meeting her eyes in the dressing table mirror. If he had no better prospect by October, she would marry him.

The knock on the door was timid, but Lily jumped anyway. Her nerves were as thin as gossamer. She had best pull herself together.

'Come in.'

Annie slipped inside. 'I heard Mama crying downstairs earlier when you were with her. I feel horrid. Is it very bad?'

'It is manageable. It will require economies, but we are still far better off than most people. It is merely that Mama and Papa don't know how to live within their means. Or rather Mama doesn't. Once they leave London they shall find it easier.'

It was neither quite the truth nor quite a lie, but it was enough for Annie. She sank on to the bed beside Lily with a sigh and leaned her cheek for a moment against Lily's shoulder.

'I feel so guilty. If I were a truly dutiful daughter, I never would have let you tell Lord Sherbourne I didn't wish to marry him...'

'What?' The door crashed open and Mrs Devenish roared in. Her shriek was so loud they were both on their feet before they realised it was their mother.

'Robert Devenish! Up here. Now!'

Annie scooted back, as white as the linen sheets, hands clapped to her mouth. A little too late.

'What? What is it?' Mr Devenish asked in confusion as he ran into the room headlong. 'What has happened?'

'I shall tell you what has happened... No, *you* tell him, Anne Devenish. Repeat what you just said.'

'I didn't say a thing!'

'Liar!'

'Were you eavesdropping, Mama?' Lily intervened. 'That is hardly good *ton*.'

'Don't you talk to me about good *ton*, you hussy! Is it or is it not true that it was your idea to tell Lord Sherbourne about Anne's infatuation with John Smithson? I knew Anne didn't have the gumption to break her engagement. I *knew* it.'

'No! Oh, no, Mama. It was I who—' Annie's attempt was swiftly interrupted as Mrs Devenish turned to her, finger outstretched and damning.

'Just *when* did you tell Lord Sherbourne you did not wish to marry him, Anne Devenish? I am quite certain that when he left us at Brook Street after the theatre there was no thought in your head about breaking the betrothal, yet the following morning here he was, talking about *your* wishes. *When* did you tell him?'

Tell her you wrote to him. Lily tried to force the thought into her sister's mind, but Anne was already in retreat.

'I… I went to see him.'

'You went to see Lord Sherbourne at Sherbourne House. Alone. *When?*'

'I… That morning. Early.'

Mrs Devenish's head moved slowly from side to side, like a cork bobbing along a brook. 'You never could tell a convincing lie, Anne Devenish.'

Lily waited for the inevitable. Her mother turned. 'So it is true. I should have seen that right from the start. *You* did this. You vicious little slut—'

'Mabel!' Mr Devenish finally spoke and his

exclamation shook Anne free. She ran to his side, tears streaming down her pale cheeks.

'Father! It's not Lily's fault. I told her about John and begged her to help me. It's not her fault.'

'Not her fault?' Mrs Devenish's voice gathered like a fist. 'Not her fault she encouraged you to throw away a fortune and a position in society you couldn't attain in three dozen lifetimes as if it was no more than a soiled handkerchief? Not her fault we must all slink away from town disgraced and penniless? Are you so simple you don't realise what you have allowed her to do to you? She has ruined your life. She has ruined *all* our lives!'

Anne was as pale as her muslin morning dress and the tears kept coming and Lily's insides ached at the truth of it.

'Enough, Mother. You are quite right; it is my fault.' She would have done better to remain silent. Nothing could placate her mother in this mood.

'Don't you dare play martyr with me, you wretched girl. It is ever the same with you. You are never content. You must have *everything*. Coming between me and your father. Between me and the children. You've always been jealous of me, ever since you were a child. Now you're ruining Anne's life as well…'

'Mabel! *Enough.*' Robert Devenish held out his hand, half remonstrating, half supplicating.

'Enough? Enough? It is *never* enough for her.

Don't you understand? She was the one who turned Anne against Lord Sherbourne. She ruined our lives, Robert. She ruined everything.'

Mr Devenish turned to Lily. 'I think it's best you both go to Anne's room for now. Your mother is distraught.'

'Distraught! When will you wake up, Robert? We are *ruined*! We shall end up in debtors' prison.'

'Nonsense, Mabel. Lord Sherbourne recognised that breaking the betrothal might have unwanted consequences for us and was so generous as to accept his part in its failure. Therefore, he has settled all our outstanding debts so we may return to Kent unencumbered.'

Silence. They all stared at Mr Devenish.

'You spoke with Lord Sherbourne? When?' It was a demand, not a question, and Mr Devenish wavered, as if he wished to take a step back. He tightened his arm around Anne's shoulder.

'He, uh, sent for me the following day. Felt it would be best done in Curzon Street.'

'And you didn't think to tell me?'

'He felt it was best kept between us and I agreed.'

Mrs Devenish waved that answer away like a buzzing fly. Her eyes were bright again, a smile softening her mouth. She looked like Anne suddenly. 'But…that means we could yet stay in London, Robert. There is still a chance—'

'No.' Robert Devenish's voice had a completely uncharacteristic snap to it. 'Lord Sherbourne and I agreed it would be best for everyone if we were to remove to Kent for the remainder of the Season. When John arrives—'

'John!' Mrs Devenish interrupted in her turn. 'There is no possibility I shall allow Anne to marry a third-rate clerk. She was almost a countess! There are far more eligible men who would yet jump at a chance to wed her if we cannot yet convince Lord Sherbourne her objections are merely girlish nerves. Why, she might yet become a marchioness.'

Anne was staring at her mother, all her pain and disappointment laid bare. Robert Devenish was breathing rather noisily, like a bellows beginning to work after many years lying in the corner of a cellar.

'Mabel. I gave my word and I mean to keep it. We will *not* remain in London, frittering away funds we do not have and betraying the trust of a man who owed us not a single farthing and who might instead have sued *us* for breach of contract. We are *not* putting Anne through the agony of refusing her heart's choice for the second time. She will *not* be a marchioness or a countess or anything so empty. She will marry whom she chooses and she will live with her choices, good or bad. Not ours.'

Lily held herself very still. She knew her mother would never stand down now. This silence was only the beginning. It was the worst kind of silence, worse than a cannonade, because she knew what was coming and wanted it over with already. Just like in the war.

But before Mrs Devenish could roll out her big guns, Robert Devenish shook his head.

'It is settled, Mabel.' He spoke softly, his voice shaking a little, but there was finality in it as well. 'This time you have lost. You can either return with us to Kent or remain here on your own. You shall have to find somewhere else to lodge and there won't be much pin money for the foreseeable future, nor will tradespeople extend you much credit, but I dare say you will manage. You always do.'

The guest room door did not slam in a very satisfying manner, but Mrs Devenish made up for that with the door of her own bedroom. It shook the house quite nicely.

They waited another long moment before releasing a collective sigh. Anne sank back on to Lily's bed.

'Thank you, Papa.'

His smile was neither happy nor proud. More resigned. 'You are welcome, angel. Why don't you lie down in your room for a spell? You look quite worn.'

Anne nodded and rose, as stiff as an old woman. At the door she turned. 'Lily?'

'I want a word with Lily, Anne.'

Anne nodded without curiosity and left.

Lily waited, still as tense as the reins of a horse at full gallop.

Robert Devenish rubbed his greying hair and sighed. 'What do you say we take a turn outside before it is too dark, Lily?'

They walked and walked.

Not to the park where they would have to be polite to acquaintances, but all the way south past Charing Cross to the river. They didn't speak much, just walked arm in arm until they reached the water.

The tide was flowing in and the scent of mud and fish and salt reminded Lily of the cramped rooms she and Tim had shared by the port in Lisbon when they'd just married. She'd still been hopeful then, drunk on freedom and sexual awakening. It hadn't mattered that Tim was rarely there. She'd been free in a magical new world.

'I almost hope she does remain in London, Papa. It might be better for you both.'

He pressed her arm against his side. 'She is not

quite as bad as she paints herself, Lily. She merely wants the best for you children.'

Lily felt a familiar churn in her stomach. She wished for once her father would see what she saw. Or at least feel what she felt. But it was foolish, childish, to expect anything else from him. He could not afford to draw back the veil too far.

And in fairness, her mother knew how to keep her worst demons at bay most of the time. To the world Mrs Devenish was a lovely, charming woman. If Lily ever said otherwise to anyone other than Anne or Piers, she was thought to be envious of her pretty and sociable mama. For years she'd needed someone to believe her that the charming Mrs Devenish was not all that charming. Tim had seen through her façade. Perhaps that had been part of his attraction.

But her father had too much to lose. Still, he had stood up for Anne. And his invitation to walk was as much of an admission as he was probably capable of. That mattered.

She let silence fall again and soaked in the last sights of the city. The sun was hanging low in the west, staining the choppy waves with brass. The barges cut darker swathes in the water, their captains calling insults and jests to each other. On the far embankment mudlarks were gathering their day's finds as the water crept up.

She would miss London. Birmingham was so far from Marcus.

She closed her eyes. All the misery that she kept so carefully shackled was beating against her battlements. She tried to shove it back into its dungeon. *You promised you wouldn't start moaning and pining. You* promised. *Be happy with what you have.*

I am happy with what I have. I have Marcus.

'For now. Only for now.'

'What did you say, Lily?' her father asked.

She shook her head and they fell silent once more.

'I wish…' he said, his voice rising like a goose trying to take flight. 'I wish we could have given you a more comfortable life, Lily. It has been more of a struggle for you than it ought to have been.'

She patted his arm. This wave of pain wasn't as sharp.

'I have a good life, Father. I am luckier than most.'

'You make your own luck.'

She wasn't sure this was a statement about her or about life. But he was right. Waiting for fate to deliver the goods was a fool's strategy. She might not like all the cards life had dealt her, but it was up to her to make the most of them.

Chapter Twenty-Two

Third
Noon
Today
Hilliard's
Natural Philosophy
M.

Lily sat down on her bed with a thump, her back to the bright sun outside as she stared at the message.

Somehow she'd expected something…else.

She had *hoped* for something else. After the house in Chiswick, her expectations had run high. She'd based her plans on those expectations and now…

Lily smoothed the creases in the paper, imagining him at his desk in his shirtsleeves, his dark hair falling forward, his mouth a controlled line as he wrote this all-too-dismissive summons.

What was she to do? By the end of the week her family was to leave Brook Street which meant she must be on her way to Birmingham. Even if the offer for employment at Hope House stood, it would only be as of September by which time Marcus would be on his way to Prussia.

And married.

Her own mouth hardened, her back as tense as a fully drawn bow as she inspected his note once more. Was this a message? That he was regretting his rash proposal? Even if it was, she had no intention of collecting her last kiss in between Mr Grozny's meetings with publishers and bookbinders.

I don't think so.

She stared at the message for a long, long while, searching for some certainty either way. The only thing she was quite certain was that though she might not be anywhere near as experienced as he, he hadn't feigned passion at the house or in the carriage on the way back.

He might not wish to wed her, but he definitely wished to bed her. And that would *not* happen in a back room of a bookstore.

She smoothed the sheet and picked up her quill.

The chapel was very well placed. From the sheltered doorway she could see up Curzon Street to Sherbourne House. The boy she'd given a coin to deliver her note was still standing on the top step, waiting to see if there was an answer.

It was taking far too long. Marcus might not be there, or he might not wish…

She straightened as the door opened once more and a footman handed something to the boy. Lily sank back into the shadows and waited, her heart thumping as the boy dashed towards her, dodging between carriages and horse droppings.

'Here, miss. They gave your letter back.' He panted, grinning.

Oh.

The boy took the extra coin she handed him with a little whoop and was off before she could thank him. Alone, her shoulder against the cool stone wall, she unfolded the sheet without enthusiasm. And straightened.

Marcus had written nothing else, merely circled her amended location. But beneath it there was now a drawing.

A very fine drawing of two armchairs set before a river and framed in long-boughed willows whose leaves trailed ripples on the water. The armchairs were populated, too. There was a rather shaggy wolf and a sleek, bushy-tailed fox. It was an exquisite drawing—skilled and whimsical and full of life.

She stared at it, her already uneven heartbeat bouncing around her like billiard balls being swung in a sack. She had an absurd urge to burst into tears.

From within the chapel the deep chords of the organ reverberated through the stone and she clutched her treasure to her and hurried home, alight and impatient and even more utterly smitten than she had been ten minutes before.

Marcus was waiting for her on the stairs of the house in Chiswick, his hands in his pockets. He wasn't wearing a coat or a waistcoat and the midsummer sun transformed his linen shirt into a bright gleam of light which caught her eye the moment the carriage pulled through the iron gates. At his side Ombra was living up to his name by standing very still and dark.

She'd worried a little when she'd entered the waiting carriage on Maddox Street only to find it empty. Well, not empty. A sheet of paper had lain on the seat—another quick but incredibly evocative sketch of a wolf dressed in a vest, standing by a stream and frowning at his pocket watch which showed two minutes past noon. She'd laughed, her tension ebbing away.

Whatever happened, she could not believe this was the last time she would see Marcus. But even if it was, even if she could not change that, she would never regret this.

She would miss him, though. Damnably. Impossibly, deeply, painfully. Awfully.

But she would regret not one moment of this.

'Hello, Lily-fox.'

He opened the carriage door and held out his hand. It felt so good, her hand in his.

'Hello, Wolfram. I didn't know you could draw so beautifully. I love my drawings.'

They were ascending the stairs, so she couldn't see his face clearly, but she was certain a flush of colour spread over his cheekbone.

'It was a scribble.' His voice was gruff and she tightened her hold on his hand. She wanted to do much more, but he probably wouldn't appreciate if she hugged him on the steps.

'They are lovely. And if you consider them scribbles, you must truly be a master. Do you often draw?'

He let out a huff and showed her into the same lovely room. The tea set was waiting, a slow swirl of steam rising from the spout.

'Sometimes. I used to more often than now. It was useful.'

Useful.

Something clicked in her mind. The drawing she'd seen in his study. It had been so familiar she'd felt a shiver of memory. Not fear, but wonder. Other little things clicked into place. Tail ends of rumours and the way he'd spoken of Spain. The presence of Juan and his delicious tapas.

'The drawing in your study of the deer in the mountain pass above Astorga. That is yours.'

He'd just picked up the teapot, but he set it down again and glanced over his shoulder at her accusing tones. 'So? I've travelled extensively. I often draw when I travel. It relaxes me.'

'I cannot think travelling through enemy territory during the war would have been very relaxing.'

'You cannot know when it was drawn.'

'But I can. It showed part of a battlement built by the French at the narrow point of that pass after Moore's retreat. I know when it was drawn because that same structure was torn down by cannon fire when Wellington led the army back into Spain the following year. Which means you were there during the months that area was held by the French.'

'Are you saying I'm a French spy?' He cocked one dark brow.

'No, an English one. I dare say that was what Mr Grozny's son was, as well. You mentioned his facility with languages.'

The corner of his mouth quirked up. 'You are annoyingly observant.'

'So it's true.'

'It is true that my own skill with languages

and drawing were useful during the war. As was my mother's Italian heritage. I made myself useful by travelling as an Italian naturalist from the University of Bologna, studying the indigenous animals of the Iberian Peninsula. It was an excellent excuse to draw landscapes for reconnaissance purposes and hire local Spanish or Portuguese guides. I even used to volunteer sketches of the French soldiers when we came across them. My drawings are likely in a few French homes.'

His casual admission struck ice through her heart. It was foolish to feel fear now for someone who had survived the war and was obviously thriving, but still...

'They would have killed you, had they known the truth. If you travelled as a civilian, you didn't even have the protection of parole that officers in uniform were accorded if they were caught.'

'Parole would have been rather useless in my case. I might have been an officer, but my value as a spy would have been higher than as an object to exchange for French officers. Colquhoun Grant carried out his reconnaissance in full uniform and yet Marmont didn't respect parole when he caught him. If Grant hadn't escaped, he would have found himself a guest in a Paris dungeon. Besides, this is old history. I was lucky.'

'Lucky!'

'Very.'

She knew that sound. He didn't wish to speak of it. Fair enough. She could hardly expect him to respect her boundaries if she didn't respect his. Besides, she didn't want pain and memories to mar what might be her last hours with him. She wanted something very different. And she had other bones to pick before she put her cards on the table.

'Papa told us that you settled our debts.'

His brow furrowed. 'First, they aren't *your* debts. Second, that was to remain between your father and myself.'

'That was rather hopeful of you. My father is no better at subterfuge than Annie. Especially not when my mother is screaming blue murder.' She debated telling under what circumstances that slip occurred, but decided that, too, was a topic that would mar the moment. 'In any case, thank you, Marcus.'

'If you came here to thank me—'

'I most certainly did not,' she interrupted hurriedly before they went down completely the wrong path. 'I came here for my own purposes entirely, but I cannot ignore what you did.'

'If you wish to thank me, you will do precisely that. I have my own guilt about Anne and it was a very small price to pay to appease my conscience. And I don't wish to discuss it any further.'

She raised her hands in surrender and tried very

hard not to smile. She rather liked him when he was grumbling. He caught her look and sighed.

'Your blasted dimples are a menace, Lily-fox. Let's take our tea outside, shall we?'

He opened the glass door out on to the patio. As they walked across the lawn she noticed an addition to the landscape. Beyond the low-hanging boughs of the willows with their arrowed leaves were an armchair, a sofa and a table. There was even an ottoman and an array of cushions.

'Does this meet with your approval?' he asked as he held aside the curtain of leaves for her to pass.

'It is perfect.' She resisted another urge to hug him. 'How lucky it isn't raining.'

'Ah, that isn't luck. I made a devil's bargain for sunshine on Midsummer's Day.'

'Oh, dear. Midsummer's Day is a dangerous time for bargains if the myths are anything to go by.'

'It is well worth the risk. Drink up before your tea turns cold.'

She sank on to the plush sofa and he settled on the other side. Just a few feet away the stream gleamed green and gold and the sun filtered through the leaves and danced on her tea. She was about to say she could stay there for ever, but caught herself in time. Instead, she raised her second grievance.

'It is so lovely here. I admit I was rather disappointed when you suggested we meet at Hilliard's again.'

'Were you?' He leaned back and locked his hands behind his head, raising his face to the sun.

'I don't trust that look, Marcus. You look like a big cat sunning himself after raiding the larder.'

He turned to her, but his attempt to look hurt failed utterly and he laughed. 'I always meant to bring you back here. But my cunning plan was to meet at Anszel's and then...ah...discover we could not use the back room after all. Anszel was quite looking forward to his role in sending me packing. Luckily my carriage would be standing by...'

'Marcus! How devious!'

'I'm afraid I am. Though you would have seen through it in a moment, no doubt. But I rather prefer your direct approach. You are a very brave woman, Lily-fox.'

'Brave! I'm a sad coward, I'm afraid. You saw me come apart at the seams that day in your study.'

'True bravery is the other side of a damaged coin, sweetheart. Only fools have no fear and only people with no depth remain unaffected when they suffer tragedies. I hate that you have to suffer for your depths, but I wouldn't erase them merely to spare you pain. They are part of what makes you wonderful. Damn, I've made you cry. Come here...'

He pulled her on to his lap and she turned her face into the curve of his neck, tears leaking out of her closed eyes. She didn't want to cry, not today. She didn't even know why his words had struck her so hard. She only knew that leaving this man would hurt more than anything that came before.

It terrified her.

She took the handkerchief he gave her and wiped her eyes and blew her nose and went to stand by the edge of the water, watching a family of ducks weave between the reeds.

He came to stand beside her and she took a deep breath. Now or never.

'My parents are returning to Kent at the end of the week. I know this is our last assignation, but I wish… I wish to talk with you.'

'To talk?'

'Yes. I have been thinking a great deal about… about your offer.'

'Have you?'

'Yes.' She cleared her throat. 'You have probably changed your mind and I shan't blame you, but that day I came to your study you suggested that perhaps… Are you still intending to honour your promise to your mother?'

He was watching her very closely. 'I have not changed my mind, Lily. My offer is still open. Does this mean you are interested?'

She held up her hands swiftly, panic and need

swamping her from all sides. 'Only if you cannot find anyone else before you leave.'

'Hmmm…'

She had no idea what that *hmmm* signified. She'd gone as far out on that limb as she dared. She stood there as stiff as a wet sheet hung out in midwinter.

'So if I cannot find anyone willing to marry me in a month, you shall marry me?'

She swallowed and nodded, then shook her head. 'I am certain you could find someone willing to marry *you*. I meant if you have not found anyone *you* are willing to marry.'

'Are you offering because of your family's finances?'

Guilt kicked her in the behind. 'Not entirely.'

'Did I say I appreciated your honesty? I take that back. What other considerations do you have?'

'I didn't mean to upset you. And though it is true I would be relieved to help my family, I would never marry for money. The truth is…' No, not the whole truth at least. She corrected course. 'It is as you said of me: you don't bore me and I want to bed you.'

He choked and coughed. 'You wield your honesty like Blücher deployed his cavalry—with occasional brutal abandon. The question is—can I trust you?'

She clasped her hands together. 'Trust me to do what?'

'To honour your offer if the need arises.'

Now came the hour of truth. And honesty. She drew a deep breath. 'That is the point I wished to discuss. I don't know.'

'You don't know if you can honour your word?'

'It... I... I would like to suggest a compromise.'

'How, precisely?'

'I think we both need time to consider. Properly. You wish to honour your mother and have a family and that is very commendable. I think you also feel a degree of guilt about the broken betrothal and this is a way to assuage your conscience. I know you will say that isn't true, but I think it is. But that is not my chief concern.'

'Let me guess. Your concern is the "family" part.'

'Yes,' she said, relieved he understood. 'The truth is I do not know if I can go down that path again. You told me you want a large family and all I can think of is...losing them. I know I am denying myself something that is wonderful, because I know how wonderful it is far better than you. I loved Emma with all my heart. But after that... I don't think I can go through that again. I simply don't. You deserve someone like Anne who wants a family more than anything. Perhaps you think all women must naturally want children...'

'No. I don't,' he intervened and his expression had that horrid flatness again which gave her no clue as to his thoughts. He guided her back towards the chairs with only the lightest touch on her arm and they sat, remaining silent for a while. She could feel him thinking, probably grateful for the door she was opening for him to withdraw. She gathered herself to make her proposal before he completely withdrew, but he spoke first.

'I have a compromise of my own to offer, Lily-fox.'

'You do?'

'I do. I suggest we both take a month to consider our decision.'

'Oh.' That hadn't been quite what she'd aimed for.

'During this month you will remain here and we shall become better acquainted.'

That was more like it.

'Very well, I shall find a boarding house in town and—'

'No,' he interrupted. 'Here in Chiswick. Only Juan and Blunt and Blunt's wife Mary come here. You will be quite protected here, both in body and reputation. If you wish to go to town you will have a carriage at your disposal and Juan or Mary may accompany you. During this time we can meet when you wish and on whatever terms you wish.'

Whatever terms. Was that a euphemism, too?

She hoped so. That was far, *far* better than her wildest dream. To stay here, summon him when she wished, which would be daily—hourly, most like.

No, surely this wasn't feasible.

'It is perfectly feasible,' he said as if she'd spoken. 'No one comes through those gates unless they are invited. You like it here. There are books and there is room to walk and I shall even leave Ombra to keep you company. A month for you to consider.'

'And during this month you will explore other marital options?' It was necessary to be fair.

'Oh, certainly.'

Her stomach clenched. That was what she wanted, wasn't it? She didn't want him regretting his offer.

'And what will *you* be considering during this month, Lily?'

She lowered her eyes. 'Whether I feel I can be a mother again.' Her voice wavered. Even saying so much terrified her.

'What if I told you I am perfectly willing to contemplate a marriage without children?'

She smiled and shook her head. 'I would say you are carrying gallantry too far. I know you don't wish to make me feel like the damaged goods I am, but I could not contemplate marrying you without knowing I am truly willing to risk being a mother again. Don't argue with me on this head, Marcus. I am serious. That is a line I shall have to decide to cross or not. If I cannot, then I cannot wed you. That is why I need time to think.'

He stretched back, looking at the sky, his jaw hard and a muscle flickering beneath it. She wanted to draw closer to him, feel his warmth, but that was cowardly. This must be settled first.

'Very well. You shall have time. But here. I don't trust your turn of mind when you're on your own. You can think all you want, but you must commit to sharing at least part of your thoughts with me.'

'That is fair.' She allowed herself to relax a little. Still, there was an issue they had not fully resolved yet.

'I have one more condition, Marcus.'

'I don't know if I can take any more conditions. Is it bad?'

'That depends. If I am to stay here, I want us to share a bed.' He straightened and she hurried on. 'You cannot be unaware that I enjoy your company and your kisses. I think it only natural to, ah, progress to the next level. It will allow us to better ascertain if we are compatible in the physical sense. We are neither of us children.'

'That is undoubtedly true. Though I am rather hurt that you still need to question our compatibility in that arena. I thought we had established that beyond doubt. Clearly I need to brush up on my skills.'

She giggled, some her tension fading. 'Now you are truly fishing for compliments, Wolfram. You know I find your embraces more than convincing.'

'Yes. I know that. And that I don't bore you. I'm overcome.'

He spoke lightly but she rather thought she had hurt him a little and he deserved better. Far better. She leaned forward and laid her hand on his bare arm—she loved touching him. If she stayed here, she'd be doing this all the time. Poor Marcus.

'You are the finest man I've ever known, Marcus St John Wolfram Septimus Something-Something. If I wasn't so twisted inside I wouldn't hesitate for a moment to throw my lot in with yours and consider myself blessed to have found such a good man to spend my days with. But this is how I must do it. For you as well as for myself.'

He went as still as a cat at that last moment of stalking a bird in the grass. Then he breathed out and touched the back of her hand as it rested on his arm.

'Very well. We shall proceed according to your plan, Lily-fox pain-in-the-arse. Bed-sharing and all.'

Marcus watched the carriage disappear through the gates. Ombra lumbered after it up to the gates and back, his tongue very pink against his dark pelt.

'You're happy, too, boy? Wanting her back already? I agree. The sooner we have her here, the sooner we can work on those blasted fortifications she surrounds herself with. Come, let's see if Juan has something for both of us.' He paused halfway up the stairs and smiled. 'She wants to share a bed, Ombra.'

Ombra woofed and danced ahead and Marcus shoved his hands in his pockets and continued, thinking hard.

A month. He'd taken risks in his life. Sometimes very foolish ones. This risk was in a whole different category.

A month.

A month for her to convince herself this was a mistake.

A month for him to convince her it wasn't.

He'd never entered a negotiation with higher stakes.

Chapter Twenty-Three

'Annie?'

Lily slipped into Annie's room and her sister looked up, her face shining. She waved a letter. By its unwilted state Lily guessed it was new.

'From John?'

'Yes, he writes he has been granted leave and will be sailing on the HMS *Swallow* a week after the ship carrying this letter, which means he is already well on his way! I cannot believe I shall see him in a matter of days. It is beyond anything I ever hoped! And it is all thanks to you, my darling Lily.'

She laughed and pulled Lily into a hug. Lily returned it, happy for Annie. And for herself. Perhaps this would make it easier to reveal what a horrible person she was.

'Annie, I have something I must tell you.'

Annie untangled herself. 'What is it, love? Is something wrong? Is it Mama? Or money?'

'No, no, nothing like that. But I have done something I am very ashamed of and I must tell you everything. I'm afraid you shall hate me.' Oh, no, she hadn't meant to start crying.

Annie took her hands and drew her to the bed. 'I could never hate you, no matter what you did. No matter how awful. You *know* that.'

'Well, you might. And it *is* rather awful. It is about Marcus.' Lily took a deep breath. Best lay it all out at once.

'I didn't want you to marry him. Perhaps that's why… No, that *is* why I volunteered to help. Not merely for you and John. I mean of course for that as well, but also it hurt terribly to think of you and Marcus together.'

She waited for the bolts of lightning. Annie was still staring, her jaw a little slack.

'And I've seen him since,'

More than seen. Tell the truth, all of it. She shut her eyes and forced out the words.

'And kissed him. And he asked if I wished to marry him instead of you to fulfil his promise to his mother. I don't know if I can because that means children and I'm terrified of going through what I did with Emma. So we agreed to a trial. For a month. To see if I can do it. But I told him he must explore other opportunities as well, though I couldn't bear it if he does.'

'Lily.' Annie's voice was reedy and she cleared her throat. 'What...? Are you in love with Marcus?'

In love.

She wanted to push that final cut of the blade away, but instead, finally, she let it fall. 'Yes. Oh, Annie, I'm so sorry. I'm the most disloyal person on earth.'

Annie took her hands in hers. 'But this is wonderful!'

Lily blinked. 'What?'

'Why did it never occur to me? I must have been so blind, thinking only of myself... You are perfect for one another.'

'What?'

'He was always far more himself with you than with me. And he certainly never kissed me. I don't know if he even wished to very much, which was probably why I was so comfortable with him. Oh, Lily. This is simply wonderful. I was so dreadfully guilty, but if he were to marry you that would solve everything! I needn't feel guilty about him or Mama and Papa and Piers.'

Lily struggled to keep apace of Annie's enthusiasm. 'I didn't say I would marry him, merely that he offered.'

'But if you love him of course you must marry him.'

'He wants children. He said he doesn't if I don't, but he does. And I don't know if I can.'

Annie's enthusiasm dimmed. 'Are you still so afraid?'

'Terrified,' Lily whispered. She felt cold all of a sudden. 'Sometimes I think…perhaps Emma died not because of the typhoid but because of something I did, or didn't do, or something inside me. Something…wrong.'

'Oh, Lily. My darling sister. She died because the world is a horrid place, not because of you. Never that. I know how much you loved Emma because I know how much you loved Piers and me even when you didn't know how to make things right. I never doubted that. It hurts me dreadfully that you doubt yourself. You are the best mother I know.'

The sat a long while in silence until Lily stopped sobbing, Annie stroking her back.

'I dare say this means you won't be coming with us to Kent.'

Lily shook her head and blew her nose. She had cried more in a month that she remembered in a lifetime. It was very tiring.

Chapter Twenty-Four

Her new home. For a while.

Marcus stood in the doorway as she inspected the room. He was a little blurry through the mist that insisted on covering her eyes.

It was his fault. She could see his effort, his touch in every aspect of the rooms. In the new curtains, a thin pale yellow that glowed like woven sunlight. In the sage-green carpet that connected the bedroom with her own private parlour. He'd brought the beautiful garden into these rooms. For her.

There was a thought of her in every corner. In the cushion-covered window seat overlooking the lawn and stream, in the shelves already filled with books, in the beautiful scroll-topped writing desk complete with the lovely enamelled music box that played a slow, tinkling waltz. And in the middle of the desk was a jade wolf, sunlight winking off its back.

How could she ever leave?

She turned her back on these joys and stalked towards their author. His brows rose and he looked even more wary than when he'd led her up here.

She grabbed the lapel of his coat in one hand, raised herself on tiptoe, and kissed him deep and hard, for a brief moment showing everything, everything, even if she didn't dare speak.

He groaned and gathered her against him, his arms so tight she felt her ribs creak. She had the lead of the kiss only for a moment. Her breaking dam swept his with it and his hand moved to cradle her head, his fingers deep in her hair as he angled his mouth over hers, his tongue brushing and teasing hers as he raised her higher until she was balanced on the tips of her toes.

I love you, love you, love you... The words burst through her, wave after wave of heat spilling out of her.

He pulled back from the kiss, but still held her hard against him. 'I wasn't planning this now. Juan prepared tea...'

She wriggled out of his grasp, giving him a firm shove in the direction of the bed. 'What is it with you and tea? I don't want tea. I want you. I don't want to wait any longer. Not even a moment. What if the world were to come to a fiery end in an hour? What would you rather do meanwhile? Have tea or me?'

He fell back on the bed, laughing, bringing her on top of him. 'Even if the world doesn't end in an hour, and I sincerely hope it doesn't, I would far rather have you. I was trying to be considerate. Give you time to...' He sucked in his breath as she lay herself on top of him, her knee sinking between his legs. 'Give *me* some time to adjust.'

She stayed there, braced on her arms, looking down at the most beautiful man on earth. 'Adjust what, Marcus?'

'Your leg, to start with.' His voice was a rumble of thunder.

'Oh...' She shifted guiltily. 'Am I hurting you?'

He caught her as she moved to slide off him, bringing her more firmly on top of him and easing her leg back between his until it rested firmly against the thudding pressure of his erection.

'I thought it was patently obvious I am in agony. That I've been in agony for an eternity.'

She shifted again, more gently now, watching his eyelids flicker and lower, his lips part. She smiled. 'Hello, Marcus.'

'Hello, sweet Lily. You look very vixenish at the moment.'

'I feel it. I feel...happy.'

His lips pressed together hard, but it wasn't a rejection. She could feel the echo of that sensation in him, the pleasure, the warmth, the certainty that this was right. At the moment she didn't think of anything else, of the future, of fears or worries or failing. Only them, only now. She touched his cheekbone, the soft skin over hard uncompromising bone. Kissed it, breathing him in.

I love you.

The words curled deep inside her, clenching her stomach hard. She brushed her lips over his cheek to the warmth just below his ear where she could taste his pulse, swift and hard. His life's force, swifter now and harder because of her.

I love you, Marcus. With every part of me.

She nuzzled him there, soaking up the warmth of his body under hers, the insistent pulsing of his erection against her thigh, the rhythm of his breathing, his hands moving over her, gentle and firm, as if he were forming her from clay, bringing her to life.

You bring me joy.

She touched her mouth to his, a promise. A hope.

I want to bring you joy, Marcus. More than anything I've ever wanted. Even more than…

Her mind separated suddenly, rearing its head in panic.

'Lily…' his voice was rough, lost '… I don't know how you do it, but you're killing me.'

She shook her head, panic receding. 'That's the last thing I want. I want to make you happy.'

'You make me happy.' He gave a faint laugh, his arms holding her. Safe.

She had him for a month. A whole month. A month of *this*.

'So do you, Marcus… Oof…' She let out a puff of breath as he rolled her over.

'What are you thinking, Lily-fox?'

She gathered her courage and told the truth. 'Of a month of this.'

Perhaps the truth wasn't always the best idea. The thoughtful, distant look came back. Then he smiled, his hand slipping under her skirt, settling on her thigh and brushing gently upwards.

'A month of this. And this. And this…'

Marcus let his eyes drift shut for a moment, absorbing the warmth of her thigh under his palm as he stroked the smooth skin.

How long had he wanted *this*? Wanted *her*?

It felt like for ever. The need to feel her body against his, her heat, her scent… To touch the warmth of her skin, close his hand on the pliant flesh of her thigh without layers of fabric between them. To have her come willingly…

To have her come…

He tensed, holding back another surge of need before continuing more slowly. He wanted her to come apart in his hands, against his body. To let go of her fears and controls and worries and lay herself bare for him. He wanted her naked in so many ways.

Naked meant trust.

God, he wanted that more than anything—that trust.

He didn't have it yet. She might have initiated the first step this afternoon, but there was still a chasm of wariness between them. He could feel it in the tension shivering along her muscles as she held back.

There was no rush. A prize worth winning was a prize worth waiting for. And working for. In this case, work was also pleasure.

He trailed his fingers in feathery strokes up and down the softness of her inner thighs, just brushing the silky curls at their apex. She shivered, her legs tensing, a moan catching in her chest. That little stifled sound was as erotic as a full display of nudity. It filled him with pleasure and hope. He'd known she was responsive. Passionate. He was dying to discover how much.

'I want to move and I don't want to,' she whispered. 'I want you to keep doing that. It's like being pulled apart thread by thread.'

'I'm afraid you'll have to move at least once,' he whispered back. 'If I'm to unravel you properly, we'll need to be rid of your dress.'

She opened her eyes, but they were heavy as

if he'd just woken her. He smiled. He'd see that, too, soon enough. Waking her. Often, hopefully.

'And your clothes, too, Marcus. I want to see you. All of you.'

'Your command is my wish, Lily-fox.'

He removed her dress and chemise slowly and laid her back on the bed as he removed his own clothes rather less patiently. For a moment he just stood above her, inspecting his riches.

Slowly, slowly, he cautioned his greedy side that was panting to touch and kiss and taste every inch of the glorious curves that were finally revealed to him. There was nothing he could do about his erection, though, it was reaching for her as if it was drowning and she was safe harbour. All those nights of unwanted fantasies were there with him, half disbelieving they were actually here, at the moment of truth. That he'd earned the right to finally make love to her. It felt almost suspect, as if this time, too, he'd wake from the dream and find himself alone.

He'd never dreaded being alone in his life, but somehow her curse had brought that, too.

She closed her eyes again, but he suspected it had more to do with embarrassment than passion this time. He could see the change come over her as he'd slipped off her chemise, her eyes sinking from his, the flush of heat overtaken by a blush of uncertainty.

He leaned over her, bracing one arm beside her as the other gently smoothed along the line of her shoulder, down her arm and back up again. He didn't mind that she wasn't looking at him. That allowed him the freedom to look at her openly, explore the beautiful landscape before him. The heavy breasts that had taunted him when they'd all but burst from her Queen of Hearts costume, the soft curve of her stomach, the flare of her hips, full and waiting for him to sink against her, as beautiful as a painting and all his.

'I know I'm not slim like Anne.'

He smiled reflexively at her worrying about precisely the wrong thing.

'Thank goodness. My taste lies in very different, and curvaceous, directions. Precisely these.' He traced a light hand over the curve of her breast and down over her stomach to her hip. His hand would remember that shape for ever. If he never touched her again, it would remember that contour against his skin.

'Then why choose Anne?' Lily opened her eyes, but her gaze was fixed on the wall, for all the world like a resigned virgin.

He restrained his laugh and kissed the warm curve of her shoulder, his hand still following its own path of discovery.

'I chose her for attributes other than the physical. And you do know it is very bad *ton* to be discussing your sister right now?'

She turned back to him, her mouth softening. 'That was rather juvenile of me, wasn't it?'

'Awfully. What must I do here to have you touch me?'

Her smile finally won. 'Ask.'

'That's far too easy. You do know I'd beg if you told me to?'

'I don't want you to beg. I want you far too much for that. And please don't stop. That feels so good. But I need you to be closer.'

'Like this?'

'Yes…'

'And what of this?' His fingers parted the curls that covered her sex, finding the slick folds of her womanhood. Lust gave a great roar of triumph, almost sinking him under its weight. He was so hot he felt singed from the inside.

He struggled through the urge to take, keeping the slow motion of his hand as he stroked, back to her thigh, up over her abdomen, her breasts. It was hard. Now he'd touched her there, his mind was fixated on that target, hot and hungry. It didn't help that her hands were demolishing him from the outside as well, exploring, touching, her little whimpers of contentment and encouragement curling over him.

'Marcus…' she kept whispering his name, as

if discovering it anew. Each time was another layer stripped away from him, another defence. He wanted her so much, so terrifyingly much. He'd never known it was possible to *need* this way.

'Marcus...'

He bent to kiss her, almost afraid. His hand slid down, back to the waiting damp heat between her legs. Her tongue touched his and retreated as she arched into the slide of his fingers against her clitoris. Her nails pressed into his back.

'I want you so much, so much...' Her voice was barely there, it echoed in her chest and he caught it against his mouth and then bent to finally brush his lips over her beautiful breasts. Her nipple was hard, waiting. She writhed as he flicked it with his tongue, licked it harder even as his fingers teased and stroked her.

Her legs spread and strained under him, her hands shifting in his hair, over his back, reaching. He saw the moment she tried to pull back. Her eyes opened, searching his.

'Don't you want...?'

'Trust me,' he answered, kissing her long and hard and then softening, suckling her soft lower lip as he coaxed her higher. Then he slid down, his mouth mapping a trail of beauty and pleasure and love as he slipped his hands under her buttocks, raising her for him.

'No, Marcus...'

'Trust me,' he whispered against her heat and her head arched back in a moan, her hands scraping against the linen, gathering it into fists. She tasted of life and earth and something deep inside him unravelled at this possession. His. Only his.

His hand caressed her breast, its sensitive peak, mirroring his tongue teasing and suckling. He felt it when she gave in, stopped thinking, worrying… Trusted him… Her cries were still deep inside, as if coming from some inner cavern, but she spoke his name, her need. She came with a long, agonised moan, her body bucking under him, her hands grabbing at his hair, scraping his shoulders.

He held her as she shivered through her climax. He'd never felt so content in his life. His body was at a peak of lust, but he didn't want to take his own pleasure right now. Not yet. He wanted this moment to last and last—to watch every tiny stage of her joy, that slow sinking down, the flush of contentment, the warm floating.

Lily being content and safe and here. With him. Nothing else mattered.

She drew a breath and held it for a moment before letting it out. 'I didn't wait for you. I'm sorry.'

He shook his head. 'I'm not. I didn't want anything distracting me from watching you. You're so beautiful.'

She squeezed her eyes shut, her arms moving to cover her breasts. He shifted over her, his erection hard against her thigh, and captured her wrists, pressing them into the pillow by her head, baring her body to him.

'Beautiful. Look at me.'

She looked. After a moment her mouth softened into a smile. 'I don't want to argue with you, not now, not about this.'

'Good. What do you want to do?'

Her legs shifted under him, one of them hooking about his thighs, pulling him closer. 'I want to unravel you. I want to touch you and kiss you and taste you until you beg for release...'

His breathing was already unravelling, his blood thumping hot and hard through his veins. She untangled one hand from his hold, scraping her nails very lightly down his chest as her voice sank lower and lower as well.

'I want to keep you hanging on the edge of that cliff, just as you kept me there, until you can't bear it...'

'I'm already there,' he said, his voice hoarse.

She shook her head, her palm just brushing over his erection, as light as silk. 'Oh, no. Not yet. Not even close.' Her eyelashes lowered, but she held his gaze as her hand stroked back over his abdomen and down again, slipping gently between his thighs and up with the same feathery touch.

'Now, I want you on your back, Marcus Wolfram.' The words, a mix between sultry and schoolmistress, were a kick in the gut. He did as he was told and she raised herself on her elbow, her lips parted in a satisfied smile as she continued her exploration.

He held himself there, on the edge of that cliff, in blissful agony, as she stroked and kissed and murmured her spells, piercing him again and again with spears of pleasure.

He'd never felt so exposed or so right in his life, giving himself over to her touch, her care. He didn't want this to end any more than he'd wanted her pleasure to end.

'Do you like it when I touch you, Marcus?' she whispered, raising herself to straddle his thighs, her hands sweeping down his chest and closing on his erection.

'Yes,' he gasped, his hands closing tight on her hips.

'Good. Because I love touching you.'

That word shot a different kind of spear through his heart. He knew she'd used the word lightly, but it still added a subterranean longing to the explosive mix churning through him. He could feel her damp heat against his thighs, the subtle motion of her hips against him. He drew her forward, cupping her breasts in his palms. They were cool against his heated flesh, but her nipples tightened at his touch and her lashes dipped, sheltering her gaze again.

She licked her lower lip, drawing it in between her teeth as she had after her climax, as if tasting herself. Slowly he drew her down and kissed her as his fingers slid between her curls again. She shivered and twisted.

'Shall I stop?' he asked against her mouth and she made a strange sound in her throat.

'No. That... But I've never...never peaked twice. Is it possible?'

'Sometimes. We can try.'

She shivered as he brushed his thumb over her clitoris, her hand closing almost painfully on his erection. He loved it. He would love it even more if he were inside her right now.

'I want you inside me first, Marcus.'

He locked his jaw, tensing against the need to tighten his hand around hers and finish it right now. 'Then we need protection. That box.'

Her eyes widened. He hated bringing guilt and fear into this moment, but he'd promised her and himself. There were advantages to widows, indeed. She clearly knew how to use the French gloves.

He brought her down on him slowly, using every ounce of his remaining control to let her adjust and settle and to stop his hands from biting into her hips. She rested her hands on his chest, brushing gently over his sensitised nipples. He splayed one hand on her thigh, his thumb pressing against the core of her pleasure.

'I like having you inside me, Marcus, all hot and hard and pulsing. I like the way you fill me.'

'If you keep talking like this, I'll be done before you can count to ten.' His voice was ragged and she laughed and shifted, her own breath catching as she moved against his thumb.

'I might… I might be as well,' she said in a rush, shifting again. 'It feels…close.'

He didn't answer, couldn't. Her hips rocked against him, shifting up and down, her nails sinking into his chest, her palms scraping against his nipples. He gave up thinking and planning, his body grabbing the reins.

He had no idea if they made it to ten. She came first, tensing and bucking on a long breathy cry, her body clenching about him and shoving him that last inch off the cliff. He caught her hips, moving her against him, driving into her again and again until he burst into joy and sailed into blissful oblivion. She sank down against him and he held her, their bodies clinging, slick and hot.

A flurry of summer rain struck the window and left glistening streaks as it continued on its way with a faint grumble of thunder.

'You most definitely can't blame that on me,' she murmured. 'Because the very last thing I am now is sulky.'

'What are you then?' he asked lazily, tracing the line of her arm. He felt absurdly content and lethargic, but he didn't want to sleep. He wanted to register every moment of their new, joint world.

'Happy. Very happy, Marcus St John Wolfram Septimus Magic Hands Endicott.'

Chapter Twenty-Five

Ombra noticed him first.

The wolfhound raised his dark head from Lily's knee, ears perked. With his red India rubber ball between his teeth on one side and his tongue lolling out the other he looked adorable. Lily ruffled the shaggy head and watched Lord Wrexham cross the lawn towards them.

She ought to be disconcerted to be discovered here but she wasn't. She trusted Marcus and he seemed to trust this unpredictable man.

'Hello, beauty by the willows.'

'Hello, Lord Wrexham. Is Marcus with you?'

'Unfortunately not, though I have little doubt he shall be here soon. I was wondering why he was spending most of this time here this past fortnight. Now I know why.'

Lily was saved from answering by Ombra who gave a woof and the ball he'd been chewing on shot out and bounced on the grass. Lord Wrexham caught it nimbly and dangled it above Ombra's head before tossing it across the lawn. Off went Ombra in pursuit.

'Now I've sealed my fate for the next half-hour. Damn, he's still fast, the old boy. May I?' He indicated the empty armchair.

'Of course. I'm surprised Juan let you in.'

'He didn't. I know how to unlock the gates without a key. I'm useful that way. I'm also in a bit of a hurry and it is important I see Marcus before I'm off, otherwise I wouldn't have intruded. Hopefully he'll forgive me for trespassing.'

'Off?'

'On my travels. Venice. A trifle hot in summer, but full of distractions. I sail tonight. You look very at home here. I like it.'

'You do?'

'Very much. Don't be offended, but I wasn't too happy about your sister. Marriages of convenience are all well and good. I dare say I'll find myself in one eventually. But Marcus is too warm-hearted for such a bloodless arrangement. I was becoming worried he'd dry up like those herbs they hang upside down in the pantry.' He grinned. 'That's what you did, plucked him off, turned him over and planted him the ground again. I haven't seen much of him recently, but when I do it's clear the bastard's thriving. I thought it was due to being released from his engagement, but now I see there's much more to it than that.'

His words warmed her, but this intrusion into her and Marcus's world was frightening her. She felt like a child clinging to the dissipating tail of a beautiful dream, fighting back the sounds of the intruding day. She picked up the slimy ball Ombra dropped by her feet and handed it to Wrexham.

'You throw it further than I. I'm glad you think it wasn't a mistake. Not marrying Annie, that is. I dare say most people think it was.'

'Well, most people are fools. That's why the world looks the way it does. *We* know better. Not being fools.'

She couldn't help laughing. 'Thank you, Lord Wrexham.'

'Dominic. I like your laugh. I noticed that right at the start.'

'I think you noticed quite a bit.'

'Not hard to. I've known Marc more than half my life. It helped to have a big burly fellow like him to protect me at Eton while I was still a weedy ten-year-old. School would have been a nightmare without him.'

His tone spoke of something deeper than gratitude for protection from bullies. Perhaps even deeper than friendship. She thought of what Marcus had told her of Wrexham's childhood. Colder even than hers. She at least had had Annie and Piers.

Perhaps she and Wrexham were alike: all bundled up and wrapped away until someone like Marcus came along and let them…be. She held out her hand. 'We are lucky.'

He gave a faint laugh and took her hand. 'I suppose we are, though it does not always feel like it. And so is he lucky. Try not to hurt him.'

She shook her head, not in denial, but because that went a little too far into painful territory. It was far more likely to be the other way around. 'Do you always admonish his mistresses thus, Lord Wrexham?'

Ombra returned with the ball and Wrexham extended his hand to take it, but this time the wolfhound plopped on to the grass beside them, panting, his brows twitching as he looked from one to the other as if waiting for the answer.

Wrexham sighed. 'No, but this is hardly the same.'

She wanted to ask how, but Ombra jumped to his feet with another woof altogether and she knew what that meant. Marcus was here.

And rather annoyed, by the pace with which he crossed the lawn towards them. He threw a worried look at Lily, but she smiled and held out her hand. He took it, but the frown he directed at

Wrexham was still uncompromising. 'You weren't invited.'

'I know, Marc, but I couldn't find you anywhere and Blunt said you were on your way here. I wouldn't have come here if it wasn't important. I need a quick word with you. I've been summoned and will be off on the evening tide.'

'Venice? I thought that wasn't until the end of the month.'

'Apparently there have been…complications. I'm to sail on the first ship and I'll need a letter of introduction to your cousin. In case.'

Marcus tucked Lily's hand under his arm, holding it to his side. She thought he didn't even notice he was doing it.

'Of course. Give me a moment here and I'll join you in the study.'

Wrexham nodded and bowed to Lily. 'Adieu, fair sprite. Take good care of the lug.'

She smiled and held out her free hand. 'I shall try. Safe voyage, Dominic.'

When they were alone Marcus turned to her. 'I'm sorry, Lily. I promised you privacy here…'

'Don't be silly. I know he would not have come if it weren't important. And he is in a different category, like Juan and Blunt.'

'Yes.' He smiled his relief. 'Wait for me here?'

'Of course.'

He hesitated, then pulled her into an embrace

that reminded her of the first few days she'd been here and he'd arrive from London, gathering her up as if relieved she was still here and had not taken the little blue rowboat from the boathouse and sailed away.

'I missed you.'

Everything inside her squeezed into the size of a pea and then burst in a cascade of warmth and love. She fought against the need to say something light and dismissive, like 'you've only been gone a few hours'. Honesty wasn't easy, but she owed him as much as she could manage.

'I missed you, too. Now, go and help your friend. I'm here.'

'I'm debating whether to be offended you kept me in the dark, Marc. Here I was, wondering why you'd let her return to Birmingham, and wondering if this was merely you biding your time, when she was here all along. So, what is afoot?'

'None of your business. What did you mean by complications in Venice?'

Dom smiled. 'Fine, we won't discuss your lovely Lily. Just know I'm very pleased. As for the Venetian complications, Bodley has disappeared. Not reported back. They're worried.'

'Hell.'

'It is highly likely that is precisely where he is. I was never particularly fond of the fellow, though if he fell into Haas's hands, I do feel sorry for him and even more sorry for us. Because if he did, he might have compromised our other chap there. Which was why they want me to toddle over. Apparently my rakish reputation suits Venice well. What better tale than a profligate, penniless wastrel with Italian relations there to enjoy the thriving casinos and bordellos? They are setting about rumours here that I'm being dunned out of London. Charming of them. That is sure to delight my father and dear Robert. No doubt they would be even more delighted if I found my way to the bottom of a canal.'

Marcus nodded and went to his desk. 'I'll give you a coded letter for the Montillios. They can see you safe if necessary. Be careful there. Haas is a smooth bastard and he has the force of an empire behind him. Venice is the new jewel in Austria's crown and they won't take kindly to it being tarnished.'

'I shall tread as lightly as a dandelion.'

Silence fell until Marcus sealed the letter and held it out. He couldn't help repeating himself. 'Be careful, Dom.'

'Always. I value myself too highly to damage the goods. Besides, I now have the added incentive of being a godfather.'

Marcus frowned. 'To whom?'

'To your firstborn, of course.'

Hope and fear and need and more fear all crashed into each other and Marcus flushed as hot as a maiden at her first ball. 'That…that isn't at all certain, Dom. You didn't say any such thing to her?'

'I'm not an idiot. I told you, I tread lightly. But I live in hope. She is right for you.'

'I know that. She doesn't. I am, to use your phrase, treading as lightly as I can manage. This may take a while.'

'I have faith in you, Marc. You always had patience.'

'I don't feel very patient.'

'Excellent. And when your children are old enough to humour their honorary bachelor uncle I shall inform them that I knew before you did that you were in love with their mother. Now I'm off before you toss me into the river. I'll even forgive you if you feel you must marry before I return from Venice. Adieu, lug.'

'Will he be all right?' Lily asked when Marcus joined her on the sofa under the tree. He took her hand and laid his over it lightly, soaking in her warmth. There was so much pleasure in that it was his right to do this. So much pleasure in returning here each day. Even pleasure in the resistance he felt when he forced himself to return to London so as to give her time to absorb what he hoped was growing between them.

He felt no jealousy at her concern for Dom, nothing like the bitter acid that had struck him when his friend had tried to kiss her in London.

A good sign. He smiled and kissed her hand lightly.

'Dom will likely survive the second coming. He is resilience personified. Unfortunately, it comes with having very little to lose.'

'That is rather sad.'

'I know. Hopefully that will change one day. But to give him credit, though he often appears frivolous, he rarely makes mistakes where it matters.'

'Good. But you are still worried.'

He leaned back with a sigh, threading his fingers through hers. He had told her as much as he could about his old activities for the War Office and his tamer work for the Foreign Office, but he couldn't begin to explain how her presence in his life had changed his relations with what had been the central part of his life for over a dozen years.

'Yes. I was far less prone to imagining the worst in the past.'

'What happened to change that?' She sounded a little worried herself and he smiled.

'Realising I was not the centre of the universe. That I depended on others as much as they depended upon me. It was quite a blow to my poor vanity.'

She leaned her head against his shoulder. 'It appears to have survived intact. And you always struck me as very much at the centre of the webs you wove. But what brought about that realisation?'

'Are you likening me to a spider?'

'A very handsome one who is currently trying to distract me and scuttle away without answering. Tell me how it came about.'

He sighed. It was too soon to tell her she was to blame. She had realigned inner constellations and placed herself at his core just as Copernicus had rearranged the universe to place the sun at its heliocentric core. He smiled. He supposed that now made him Lily-centric.

'What is so amusing?' she asked and he shook his head. He doubted she would appreciate the burden of being his sun quite yet. If ever.

'It just happened. The wisdom of age.'

She stroked his cheek. 'My Methuselah. I think Dominic very lucky to have you as his friend. It is one of the things I adore about you.'

He pulled her on to his lap. The words were burning inside him, but he pressed the lid down hard.

Patience. Patience. He didn't want her tugged

this way or that. He wanted what he felt inside her to bloom at its own pace. Or not.

It had to. He couldn't bear it if it didn't. That would be too great a blow.

'You're exaggerating,' he managed to say. She shook her head and snuggled closer, tucking her head into the curve of his shoulder and neck, her mouth warm against his skin, bringing something far more basic into bloom. He felt her smile against him as she shifted against his hardening erection.

'No, I'm not. And don't belittle it. I think you are marvellous to care so for people.' Her voice was rough and muffled against him.

'For very, very few,' he corrected, even more roughly. She didn't answer, concentrating on unfastening his waistcoat, slipping his shirt from his breeches, finding the taut muscles beneath with a sigh of satisfaction and yearning that dragged an answering groan from him. He loved her touch. Loved it.

There were too many things he would have to struggle to live without now if she chose to walk away. The list kept growing. A list which had been near empty only a few short months ago. It made no sense, but it was undeniable.

Being in love was a damnable state.

Chapter Twenty-Six

It was a bad sign that she hated it when Marcus dressed to leave.

It was still early afternoon; the willows were only just beginning to scratch the sun's underbelly. She never asked where he went or what he did when he left their haven though she knew he was busy with meetings ahead of the Congress.

They often talked of the less sensitive issues surrounding the upcoming meetings. She loved those talks and could well understand why he was so useful for the politicians and generals. He had the capacity to hold so much together in one complex image, turning it this way and that to make sense of it, making adjustments here and there as he did.

She loved learning how his mind worked. So much so that quite a few of those discussions led to the bedroom, or the sofa, or—as they'd just concluded now—a more creative use of his desk than reviewing documents.

'Do you know, Lily-fox,' he said as he slipped his shirt back on, 'that you are the only woman I know who becomes all hot and bothered when I discuss treaty clauses.'

She slipped off the desk and arranged the skirts of her morning dress. They were a little smudged with ink, but at least they'd done a good job polishing the wood.

'I think you could make women hot and bothered reading the Naval Lists backwards.'

'Bothered, certainly.' He grinned, but then his expression turned serious. 'Do you know it has been precisely a fortnight since our agreement on Midsummer's Day?'

'Yes.' She knew. She counted the days. Like his three kisses, she wished she could somehow stop the clock right here, at the midpoint. Just as they were.

They had talked about a great deal. She'd even shared some of her fears, though not her fears about him. She'd never asked what he was planning, whether he had changed his mind. Whether what they had would be enough if that was all she could give.

She knew the answer to that, though. Whatever he said, she knew the answer was no. He wanted more and he deserved more. She wanted to give it to him, that opportunity to be the wonderful father she knew he could be. She wanted to give that to herself, but…

She no longer even knew what followed that 'but'. Fear, mostly. The big thudding monster waiting to devour what she loved. For all she knew, if she loved Marcus openly it might devour him as well.

She touched her throat, trying to stop the climb of that swampy, swamping beast.

'Lily?' She saw his concern and held out her hand, palm out, stopping him. She didn't want comfort now, she needed answers.

She pushed the words out before they could rebel. They tried, grabbing on to the door frame, but they lost the shoving match and came out a little too loud.

'What…what will you do if I say I don't wish to marry? Do you have someone else in mind already?'

He went quite still, his eyes hard and intent.

He was weighing his answer; she could almost feel him think, though she had no idea what the components of those thoughts were.

'No.'

Waves of relief shimmered up from her feet and down from her tingling scalp, meeting somewhere in the middle. 'You aren't leaving yourself much time, if you plan to honour your mother's wishes.'

'Is that your answer, then, Lily? That you don't wish to marry?' She hadn't heard that tone in a while, each word carved out of ice.

'I didn't say that.' This time the words flung themselves out and landed between them, a little breathless. 'I merely wondered…'

'Perhaps it is time to make something clear, Lily. In the event you decide not to marry me, I plan to postpone the whole notion of marriage until after the Congress.'

She was very grateful for the desk behind her. It pressed into her buttocks and was cool under her burning palms. 'Oh. I see. What of your word to your mother?'

'My mother was an eminently sensible person. Had she known how badly I would botch her wishes she would never have made me give my word. She wanted me to be happy.'

'You are very lucky to have had such a wonderful mother. I'm very jealous.' She tried to smile. She wanted him to come to her and comfort her as he did when she started decomposing, but he merely stood there. She gathered her courage and continued, 'So doesn't that mean you wish to withdraw your offer? I have told you that you are always free to do so.'

'I know I am free to do so, Lily. However, my offer stands.'

She drew a deep breath. She had best put all

her thoughts on the table and have done with it. Carrying them around inside her wasn't doing either of them any good. This must be settled, once and for all.

'I know these two weeks have proven we are most definitely compatible in terms of body and... and of mind, Marcus. However, if there is no longer any imperative for you to wed, it would be sensible of you to reconsider. You never would have offered for me if you had not found yourself in such a unique predicament. I think it is best we face the truth.'

'I see. And what is that truth, according to you?' Still cool and calm, damn him. She smoothed out her wrinkled skirts, plucking at the pattern. She was still wearing Anne's repurposed gowns.

'Very well. The truth, as I see it. I think you came to regret your engagement to Anne. I know you meant well and had every intention of honouring your commitment to her, but as the truth began to sink in, that you would have to spend your life with a woman with whom you had very little in common, you rebelled. Or at least part of you did. And that part of you sought some way to make this enforced arrangement as repellent as possible so you might find a way out. And what better way to make it feel impossible than to be attracted to Anne's sister.'

'I see. So this attraction between us is merely

the diabolical plot of some internal *eminence grise*?'

He was still taking this very calmly, she thought, uncertain if she was pleased or not.

No, she wasn't.

'Is that how you see your attraction as well?' he asked in the same curious voice. 'Some utilitarian attempt to ensure Anne is free to pursue her romantic dreams? What obedient libidos we both have.'

'You're making fun of me.'

'You ought to be grateful I am. The option isn't pretty. I have a temper, too, you know.'

A little knot inside her unravelled. She had to remember he had trained himself to appear calm. 'You think my interpretation is wrong?'

'I think you're talking a load of bollocks.'

Another knot unravelled at his vulgarity. 'If Anne hadn't heard from John and I hadn't come that morning to your study, you would have wed her.'

His jaw was clenched so tight. She wanted to touch him just to reassure herself there was still Marcus beyond that hard shell. No, she knew there was. She didn't know why she was prodding at him like this. Out of fear and need, and more fear. Foolish.

'Marcus—'

'You're right,' he interrupted. 'I might have

wed her in the end. Choices have consequences and I would have accepted mine, however painful. Sometimes actions must be separated from thoughts and feelings. And wishes.'

'Marcus, please stop, I didn't mean it. I'm a fool and scared, and I keep hurting you. Don't listen to me. It's just sometimes I think it is best I remain alone.'

'I know you *think* that,' he said, clearly fighting to keep his voice level, 'but do you *wish* it?'

'No.' It was a little on the hesitant side and she waited for another burst of that icy anger, but his voice had softened again when he spoke.

'If you throw your lot in with mine, you won't be alone any longer.'

She was never prepared for these blows—the burst of warmth and need and *hope*. He kept tossing embers into the dry sticks and twigs that she'd become.

You won't be alone any longer.

She tried to smile. 'Being with someone does not always mean not feeling lonely.'

'Were you lonely with your husband?'

'Yes. Eventually. He was so outgoing. Everyone loved him and he loved everyone. At first it went well, but after Emma... I wanted to talk about her, to keep her with us, somehow. He didn't. We stopped talking, stopped everything. When he was killed we hadn't spoken to each other in over a fortnight. Not a word.' She knuckled her eyes, pressing back at the tears.

Two firm arms came around her, pulling her against the warmth of his linen shirt. She didn't understand why he bothered to be so nice to her when she was so nasty and useless and broken. Eventually he would tire of her indecisiveness and maudlin tears. He would come to regret he hadn't found someone like Anne after all. No one could possibly prefer *her*.

She pushed him away. 'You're like him. Everyone…' She couldn't say love. It felt…naked '…dotes on you.'

He shifted away as well. 'Don't label me simply to satisfy your need to keep people at bay.'

They both leaned in silence against the desk, two hands apart. Slowly her darkness fell apart, like fog clearing.

'No, you're not. I'm sorry, Marcus. That was cruel of me.'

He shrugged.

Don't be angry. She almost said the words aloud, but they were childish even in her mind's echo chamber.

This was a mistake.

She'd been hopeful, but she couldn't seem to be what she ought to be. Perhaps it was a mistake to spend this month with him. Perhaps it was best to allow him time to consider while she was far away. While she was here, while they shared a bed, his conscience would never allow him to realise he must be a little mad and quite a lot guilty to consider tying himself to such damaged goods.

'Perhaps it is best I return to Birmingham for a while. So we can both think clearly.'

'Do you wish to?'

She shook her head and reached across to touch the back of his hand.

He moved away as if he'd sat on a bee and she had barely a moment to breathe in when her bottom landed on the desk, his hand in her tangled hair. His eyes were shards of gold, like those scudding along the stream as the sun lowered itself between the willows.

'How the devil do you find all my weak points and take a sledgehammer to them, Lily?'

'I didn't mean…'

'I know that, damn it. You don't mean a million things and yet you do them anyway. It only makes it worse. I am not Tim and I don't run away when I find myself in a pit and I am not your mother who was too afraid to love what threatened her.'

'I know, I know. You are nothing like them.' Her voice was hoarse and hurried.

'Don't patronise me, Lily. At least be honest in your contempt.'

He let go of her and pushed away and before

she could take another breath he was out through the door and gone.

She stared at the door. She was still on the edge of the desk when she heard the front door close and the clop of hooves drawing away.

Chapter Twenty-Seven

Marcus pulled on the reins and the bay gelding trotted to a stop just before the gates. It was cowardly to run. It was also cowardly of her to push back every time he came close.

Perhaps she was right. Perhaps she could never care for him the way he hoped she might. Never risk herself. She had never said she loved him.

Well, neither did you, said the voice of reason that had finally managed to catch up with the rest of him.

I don't want to frighten her any more than she is. Huh. Who's the coward now?

A sprinkling of rain blew against his face and the gelding shook its mane, scattering the droplets before they settled. There were just a few grumpy clouds passing by and beyond them the sky was turning lavender as the sun slipped into the willows. He sighed and turned his horse around. He didn't want to return to London and worry and sulk. He'd rather do that here.

Blunt met him by the stables, his brow wrinkled in confusion.

'Back, sir? And I was just harnessing the horses to the carriage, sir.'

Marcus swung off the horse. 'Why? What has happened?'

'Nothing I know of, sir. Mrs Lily asked me to ready the carriage.'

'Belay that order. Here, stable Mercury.'

He was halfway across the lawn when the back door opened and Lily stepped out, her bonnet dangling from her arm and bouncing as she struggled with a stubborn button on her pelisse.

'Where are you going?' he demanded, and she looked up and stopped.

'Marcus. You left.'

'I came back. Where are you going?'

'To you.'

Anger and Fear clung together as Hope gave them a shove towards the cliff's edge.

'You could have sent Blunt with a message. He would have reached me faster on horseback.'

She let the button go and the pelisse popped open. She was still wearing the same dress she'd worn since he'd arrived this morning, ink stains and all.

'I know. But I'm not as good as you with messages. "Come back" could be misconstrued.'

He shook his head. 'No.'

She held out her hand and he took it and they walked towards the stream. The grass was wet from the shower and pliant underfoot. It was cooler in the shade of the willows and the water slipped by, a darker green, little fish glimmering for a moment at the surface. She was right, it was an idyllic place, but that didn't make it any less real. Just as pain and fear didn't make love any less real.

He heard her draw breath and hold it for a moment before she plunged in.

'I keep testing you, Marcus. I'm so sorry.'

'Lily...'

'Wait, please, let me say it. It is hard for me to trust. To really trust. In my mind, in my heart, I *do* trust you, but there are other voices hiding in all kinds of dark corners that are still afraid. They tell me that there is a reason why my mother hated me and why I was relieved when I was free from Tim even though he wasn't really to blame. That there is something wrong with me and that is why Emma died.

'When I'm alone and in my safe little world it is easy for me not to listen to them, but since I came to London they all creeped out of their holes, and sometimes I cannot silence them. I hate that I hurt you. None of this is your fault.'

He listened in silence, letting the rushed words

flow out of her. When she fell silent he took the bonnet she was crushing between her hands and hung it from a branch and took her hands. They were as cold as when she was deep in her memories. He pressed them between his.

'It isn't your *fault* either, Lily. This is who we are. But there is something I insist you try to accept. I hope we live a long life together and that means bad things are likely to happen at some point. But if something so terrible as what you have lived through were to happen to us, it would happen to *us*, not only to you. It might hit us differently, but it would still be ours. If we never have a child or if we have a dozen, we would be there together.'

She leaned her hands against his chest and then rested her forehead against it as well. He could feel his heart beat fast and hard against the gentle pressure and he wondered if she could even fathom how much she hurt him. How much she yet could.

He brushed his mouth over her silky hair, breathing her in. He spoke more softly this time.

'I am not Tim and I won't run away when I find myself in a pit. I will do my damnedest to climb out and for the first time in my life I want to share my pits and peaks with someone else. *When* we marry you shall have to accept that. You may choose to slink into your hole, but I won't let you shut me out of it. I'm coming after you, Lily-fox.'

'You're rather large to squeeze into my hole.'

The words were mumbled against him and though he didn't want her slipping into humour just yet, he couldn't stop a smile of relief.

'Trying to distract me with euphemisms?'

'You started. All this talk of holes and peaks.'

'Why don't you just apologise nicely and say you were completely wrong about me and you won't misjudge me again?'

'I don't think I was *completely* wrong about you. I knew from the very beginning that you were very special.'

'And I knew that you were…' His voice cracked. He wanted to shake the words out of her. *Tell me you love me, damn it.*

Steady on. Patience.

No, his patience was worn thin. He *needed* to know.

He needed to tell her.

'You were utterly wrong, Lily. That nonsense about my fixing on you because of wanting to shake free of Anne. What I felt for you had nothing to do with anything but who you are. You have no idea how much that month was an exercise in misery. I would wake up every morning to the sound of my heart breaking and would agonise for hours trying to think of ways I could escape my fate without harming your sister and yet somehow still…still keep you close.'

Her eyes widened and she finally moved, her arms closing about him, her cheek pressed hard against his shoulder. He could hear her breath, feel it, shallow and forced.

'Marcus—'

'No.' He cut her off, his tone as sharp as a blade, and she fell silent. All those forces he kept at bay were shimmering inside him, he could feel them churn and collide as his words kept coming.

'I've been walking on eggshells around you from the beginning, Lily. Do you think I don't know how terrified you are? What it means to you to contemplate opening yourself to pain again? Why the hell do you think I've allowed you to set all the boundaries? But I'm damned if I will let you dictate to me what I felt or what I feel and I am sure as hell not about to let you belittle it.'

He stopped as anger dragged itself up from the abyss again, fear clinging to its back. He took a deep breath. She might as well hear it all.

'I was in agony. I had no idea I had such depths in me and it was damned terrifying to discover them when I could no longer do anything about it. I might be a devious bastard at times, but I had to draw the line at dishonouring a young woman by jilting her. When you came to my study that day it felt like a miracle. If Ombra hadn't been snoring on my foot, I could as easily have imagined this was just a continuation of the dreams you'd been plaguing me with for the past few weeks. I didn't deserve such luck.'

'Marcus…' His name was barely a whisper on her lips.

'I've shocked you.'

'You… Yes, you have. I… Why didn't you say anything when I came to bargain with you?'

'What could I say? I'd never been so shocked in my life. There I was, stewing in misery, and you walked into my study like a damned fairy godmother and offered me a solution to all my problems on a silver platter. It's a wonder I didn't faint at your feet in relief.'

'I thought you would kick me out on my behind.'

He slipped a hand over her posterior, giving it a gentle squeeze.

'I would never do anything to damage this work of art, Lily-mine.'

She wrapped her arms around him again, squeezing hard. 'I never guessed any of this, not even a smidgen.'

'I told you that you weren't as clever as you think you are.' He couldn't hide the touch of satisfaction and she laughed, rubbing her cheek against his chest. She hadn't spoken the words yet but somehow he felt them.

In time. They were there.

'I was clever enough to extract you from your betrothal, Marcus Wolfram.'

'For which I shall be eternally grateful. And even more for the speed with which you agreed to my outrageous proposal. I will only admit now that I was preparing for a far longer campaign.'

'Are you saying I am easy?'

'I am saying you are the most precious thing in my world and I will do anything and everything in my power to make you happy.'

'Oh, damn you, Marcus.' She shoved her face into his shoulder again. 'Stop making me cry.'

'I'm developing a fondness for your tears, Leaky-Lily.' He drew her towards the chairs. They were a little damp from the rain shower, but he pulled her on to his lap and handed her his handkerchief.

'Leaky-Lily is an awful name,' she mumbled into the soap-scented linen.

'Is Lily-love better?'

She shivered, tension thrumming through her. In time. 'Better, but I prefer Lily-fox.'

'Lily-fox is my favourite, too. My sweet-hearted little vixen.' His words were a warm caress against her temple. He took a deep breath and it felt rather like he was letting himself fall. 'I love you, Lily-fox.'

Don't believe him… Don't…
Don't…
Don't fight.
You know it is true.

You know it in every cell, every tense breath, every thudding heartbeat.

It is in his eyes and has been there for so long.

She touched his cheek.

You make your luck.

Somehow life had given her this wondrous gift and she must be brave enough to take it.

'I love you, too, Marcus,' she answered, her voice tight and rough, and added, 'I rather think that *"My heart unto yours is knit."*'

He drew her head into the curve of his neck, holding her there, tension thrumming through him. She waited in silence until it seemed to peak and settle and finally his laugh whispered over her ear, sending shivers of fire through her nerves.

'I thought you hated that play.'

She nuzzled into the curve of his neck, breathing in his wondrous scent. She brushed her lips against the warm flesh and a shudder ran through his body. She loved that she could do that to him. He was hers now, she thought with savage pleasure. Truly *hers*.

'I read it again because of you while I waited for you here.' She closed her teeth very gently on the lobe of his ear, tracing it with her tongue and winning both a shudder and a groan. 'All this talk of midsummer madness…'

'I don't feel mad,' he said, his voice hoarse. 'I feel blazingly clear-headed since you turned my world upside down, Lily-fox. And that quote won't do. It states clearly that love is blind to faults, but you seem to be all too aware of mine,' he grumbled, but his hand was sending very different messages as he slipped her sleeve from her shoulder with the deftness of a lady's maid.

The strap of her chemise followed and she found one arm was now completely bare, her morning dress transformed into a toga and her skin tingling from the cool breeze and his featherlight touch.

Instead of objecting to this sleight of hand, she shifted and shrugged off her other sleeve with a happy sigh. This was utterly improper and mad and she didn't care. She was in heaven.

'I adore your faults, Marcus St John Wolfram Septimus… I can't remember any more of your multitude of names.'

'Good. I never should have told you any of them, though I dare say you would have to find out when we marry.'

She stilled and shivered a little, pressing against him. 'If you have accepted that you needn't marry at all, then we don't have to marry, Marcus. As long as we are discreet…'

He leaned back abruptly, his hand frozen inches away from her breast.

Oh, dear, she hadn't meant to wake the serious Lord Sherbourne. He really could look quite ruthlessly disapproving. She smiled and touched his cheek.

'I said you don't have to and I mean it, Marcus. But I admit I would prefer it. I think I would find it very hard to hide how much I adore you. I shall likely grow bitter and sullen having to wait here for notes and kisses when you have time. You're quite right; I can be a shrew.'

'I distinctly remember saying vixen, not shrew. As a naturalist, I wouldn't make that mistake.'

'A fake naturalist.'

'A very good fake naturalist. Who you will be marrying as soon as that idiot John Smithson is secured in matrimony for your sister. I'll wait that long and not a day longer. Understood?'

'Understood.' She nodded meekly and his frown fled.

'Damn, I love you, Lily. So does this mean I pass the breakfast test?'

'Didn't you once tell me you prefer to breakfast alone, Lord Sherbourne?'

'It depends on the company. And on what I am feasting on, Lily-fox, soon-to-be Lady Sherbourne. I hope you don't mind being woken up early every morning. And vigorously.'

'I think I require some more examples of your…ah…rousing methods before I answer that question.'

She gave a whoop of surprise as he swept her

into his arms with a grunt, barely managing to pull her bodice back up over her almost wholly exposed breasts. His eyes narrowed, taking on a decidedly wicked glint.

'It will be my pleasure to supply as many of those examples as you wish, Lily-fox. As a budding naturalist you should always choose to observe animal behaviour in its natural habitat. In this case, that habitat can be found upstairs, second door on the right. Shall we?'

Lily woke to a setting sun gleaming pink and orange through her window. To a hard, warm body cocooning her from behind, to a shimmer of silver on the pillow beside her...

She raised herself carefully on her elbow. He'd arranged the silver chain in a heart-shaped frame about the locket.

She touched her finger to the little amethyst at the centre of the pearls. A little gleaming purple-crimson heart, glistening in the sunset. Her own heart was thumping so hard it hurt.

She felt him raise himself as well behind her, his voice low.

'My life since I met you is a series of some very strange moments, Lily. That day in Cheapside, in the coach when you held the locket... I'm not a superstitious fellow, but at that moment I wished I hadn't shown it to you. You seemed to glow together, as if you'd found each other. Perhaps part of me knew even then.'

She wanted to object, to tell him she couldn't bear this burden, to say, *What if I can never fill this gift with the life and laughter and children you deserve?*

But she didn't say any of that. He was so brave, in his way, and she would try to be as well.

What do you want, Lily?

I want this. I want him. I want us. I want to live, fully, deeply...even painfully.

I want what I had with Emma even if I shall never have Emma.

I want to love.

She took the locket and sat up, holding it out. He sat as well, the sunset warming his bare chest and raising his tiger eyes to pure gold. Wary gold. She didn't want him to worry every time he opened his heart to her. She smiled.

'I'm terrible with clasps. Could you put it on for me?'

He gave one short nod, still very serious, and she turned a little as he secured the locket. The sun or his hands had warmed it because it was not as cool as she'd expected as it lay just at the tip of the valley between her breasts. It felt right.

She touched it. 'I want to fill this with love, Marcus.'

He breathed in and out slowly and nodded again.

She continued, 'And I don't want you to worry about telling me what you feel. If I'm an idiot about it, just tell me so.'

He smiled a little. 'Oh, I will.'

'Good. I love you beyond anything. Beyond anything, Marcus. I pledge to work as hard as I can to stop being an idiot so that I can love you as you deserve.'

He clasped her face in his hands. 'As *you* deserve. You are not doing this for me, Lily. *You* deserve to love and be loved. We both do. I already feel your love in everything you do. In the way you make love to me, in the way you greet me, in the way you are with my friends, in the way you struggle with yourself. That is probably why I haven't been more terrified than I could have been waiting for you to come to me. You don't have to *prove* anything.'

She pressed her hands over his and sniffed. 'I don't see why we must wait on Anne and John to be wed. We are older, after all.'

'That is undeniably true. Practically doddering.'

'And it would be nice to have some time for you to acquaint me with my new home before you must run off to the Continent and leave me to my devices.'

'I'm tempted to agree to that as well if it convinces you to wed me as swiftly as possible, but I'm afraid you are labouring under a misapprehension.'

'I am?'

'You are. I have no intention of leaving you to your devices. You are coming with me.'

'To Aix? But surely they shall object.'

'I would rather they object to your presence than suffer because of your absence. I won't have it said I endangered the discussions on the withdrawal of the allied powers from France because I was pining away for my wife.'

She nudged him back and curled up against his chest. 'You wouldn't pine. You would be far too busy.'

'Pine. Long. Yearn… Every maudlin verb you could imagine. It would be very embarrassing. We are trying to present a resolute front to the other powers, you know. Languishing might compromise the well-being of the Continent. Do you want that on your conscience?'

She kissed his chest, her fingers following the arrow of dark hair downwards.

'I never knew I had the power to threaten the stability of nations.'

'Well, now you do. So will you wed me in order to prevent the Continent from descending once again into chaos and misery?'

'No. But I shall wed you to keep my heart from descending into chaos and misery. Will that do?'

He nodded, his jaw tense. She smiled. Right now, at this moment, she had no doubts and her fears seemed very far away. They might yet return. They probably would, but she felt there would be more and more moments free of them. More room in her world to be herself. To love. He'd opened that door to her and she had walked through it. She would never turn back.

Her fingers closed gently on the pulsing heat of his erection and he sucked in his breath. She smiled and watched the colour of his eyes shift as she softly stroked him. She loved loving him.

'I want a son with your eyes, Marcus Wolfram. He'll play on the grass with Ombra and ruin our walls with his wonderful scribbles.'

He stopped breathing for a moment, tension holding him taut. Then she found herself flat on her back, his leg heavy between hers.

'I want a daughter with your eyes and tumbling hair, and freckles, who sits on the edge of her seat when she's excited... I want... Hell, I want you, Lily. I've never wanted anything so much in my life. What the devil have you done to me?'

She laughed, brushing the dark hair falling over his brow. 'I did warn you about all those pacts you made on Midsummer's Day, didn't I?'

'You needed no magic to make me fall in love with you, Lily. You did that all on your own.'

Lily closed her eyes and wrapped her arms around his nape, pulling him to her. 'How can I seduce you properly if you keep making me cry, Marcus?'

His laugh was warm against her mouth. 'You could try seducing me improperly, Lily-love.'

'With great pleasure. Now, kiss me, Marcus St John Wolfram Septimus Endicott Something-Something.'

Epilogue

Asturias, Spain—Midsummer's Day 1819

The distant mountain peaks were sharp against a perfectly blue sky. She could see why the villagers believed you could step straight into heaven from them.

She wished *she* believed in heaven. That when she died she would find Emma living joyously somewhere. But she didn't. Emma was gone. She'd been loved so much, but was gone. There was only now to be lived and the man by her side who brought joy to her life.

She knelt by the lone olive tree tucked between the old oaks and ash and elderberry. No one in the village knew where it had come from, but it seemed content to be a stranger here in this place of beauty. Lily had chosen to lay Emma to rest among its roots rather than in the makeshift graveyards of the soldiers or to have her small body sent back to England to families that had never wanted her.

The grey cracked bark was rough and solid against her hand, almost the same colour as the gravestone nestled between its protruding roots. Olive trees lived hundreds of years and this would be here sheltering Emma long after she and Marcus died.

She touched her locket. It was no longer empty. While they'd been in Aix-la-Chapelle Marcus had coaxed her into describing Emma and after a few painful iterations he'd produced a tiny, delicate likeness of her daughter, eyes wide and smiling. It was a gift almost as great as the child growing inside her. They had not planned it thus, but it felt right that they had come here on Midsummer's Day, linking Emma even more firmly into their lives.

Marcus had wanted to come sooner, in the cool of early spring, but Lily had not wanted to interrupt her work at Hope House in London so soon after beginning. She missed Eleanor and the Birmingham school, but she'd already come to love her new pupils and the buzzing excitement of London. As she knelt there she told Emma everything that had happened that year, good and bad.

'So, you see, your mama is a very happy woman, Emma dear.' Lily touched the flat stone set between the roots. A shadow settled on it as

Marcus crouched down beside her and Lily laid her other hand on his knee. 'And this fellow is mostly responsible for that.'

'Only partly responsible,' Marcus amended. 'Your mother has done most of the hard work, Emma.'

Lily shook her head, her throat closing. 'He's usually not this modest, but I love him dearly and I wish you could have met him. I know you would adore him. And Ombra… I miss you so much…'

They fell silent for a moment and then Marcus took the little ink-stained paper bird she'd cherished all those months ago from his pocket and laid it in the cracks of the ancient tree.

'I was thinking of suggesting we bring Emma with us to Sherbourne when we return, Lily-fox, but you have found her one of the most beautiful places on earth. I leave it to you. It can be done if you wish.'

She wrapped her arms around him and pressed her wet face to his chest.

'I don't know. This is where I always think of her. I imagine her sleeping here, all warm and touched with sunlight like when she slept curled up on a blanket like a contented puppy on the cart between barracks. When I talk to her, this is where I see her. I'm afraid to lose that.'

'I understand. You don't have to decide now. Or tomorrow. Just know that it is possible.'

Her breath managed to get past the obstacle course of lumps. 'Thank you, Marcus. If I did believe in heaven, I'd believe that she pulled all the midsummer magic strings to make you care for me. Perhaps that is why you knew how to draw her so well.'

He laughed and kissed her cheek. 'The only strings pulled were by you. I might have used subterfuge to snare you, Lily-fox, but I didn't need any magic to be snared.'

'Neither did I,' she objected.

'You wouldn't have married me if I hadn't trapped you with my brilliant scheme.'

'If it pleases you to think yourself so clever, Marcus St John Wolfram Septimus Bighead Endicott…'

'Ouch. At least my head isn't the only big thing about me… Oh, sorry, not in front of Emma.'

For a second her heart stuttered as laughter and pain collided. Laughter won. 'I'm glad you have *some* scruples.'

'No more than one a week and that was it, so we'd best head back to the village for our afternoon siesta. We'll return tomorrow.'

She smiled at the headstone engraved with Emma's name below the olive tree and tucked her hand through his arm as they descended the path.

'I don't think you quite comprehend how siestas work, Marcus. One is meant to sleep,' she said primly, but her body's imagination was already happily rushing down the path to their bedroom with its wide bed and balcony with a view over the stream cascading down into the valley.

'And you believed that fairy tale?' Marcus scoffed. 'That is what they tell the children. *Don't you dare barge into our room during siesta hours. Mama and Papa are sleeping.* Very believable. Everyone has their own methods. Why do you think the English invented the nanny? My mother told me the truth.'

Lily giggled. 'I wish I'd met your mother. Then I could tell her what a monster she begat…'

She gave a whoop of surprise as he swept her into his arms.

'Monster, eh?'

'I'm sorry, Marcus! I didn't mean…'

'I wish you'd met her, too.' He stopped and nuzzled her ear, his arms tightening around her. 'She would have absolutely adored you. And you're right about the monster, but that's your fault, not hers.'

He let her go very slowly, her body sliding down his, holding her for a moment against him.

'You're the one who keeps waking the monster, sweetheart. So what are you going to do about my big…head?'

She slid her hand from his nape, down his chest, her fingers pausing on the tense muscles of his abdomen.

'I'm going to tame it, but not too much. Just enough so it keeps coming…back.' She slid her hand lower, rubbing the hard length of his erection, watching the tension deepen the grooves beside his beautiful mouth. It felt wonderful to shamelessly enjoy her power over him.

'There's that pretty little clearing we saw between the oak trees on the way up, remember?' she murmured, clasping her other hand about his tense fist, leading him between the trees.

'You want…? Here?'

She knew what he meant. This place was Emma's, after all.

'Yes. Here. *Everywhere.* You're part of everything that is beautiful and painful and wonderful and horrid in me. Unless you're too old for… Oomph! Careful! You shall hurt your back doing that one of these days.'

He shifted her higher against him and strode through the trees. 'I'm not that old, vixen. And I have to practise. You'll only be getting heavier.'

She laughed. 'Not for a while yet. It's only been two months, I think.'

They came through the trees to a little natural clearing beside a narrow stream coming down from the gorges. Warblers and nightingales sang in the old oak and beech trees and the clearing was crowded with wood sorrel and primroses and dog violets.

He set her down and they stood for a moment absorbing this little pocket of beauty.

'Perhaps we should wait until we're back in our rooms,' Marcus said. 'I don't want…'

Lily smiled at the reappearance of the mother-hen side of his character. Since they'd discovered she was with child it was making regular visits and she had to admit she didn't mind it that much. Just not *now*.

'Take your coat off.'

'Are you cold?'

She rolled her eyes. They were both perspiring from the climb and the Spanish sun in June was anything but gentle. She sat down on a boulder and untied her bonnet.

'Take off your coat and spread it out. Or better yet, roll it up and use it as a pillow, for you.'

He planted his hands on his hips and tried to look disapproving. 'How come the monster is on the bottom? Isn't he supposed to be the one doing the ravishing?'

'Not when there's an even bigger monster about. And you love it when I'm on top. And I want your shirt off as well. Please.'

'At least you haven't forgotten *all* your manners.'

She watched as he began unbuttoning, her insides straining to hold in all the love she felt for him.

Her Marcus.

'Do you know how much joy you bring me every day, Marcus? How grateful I am to have you right at the centre of my universe?'

He paused, his coat half off, the laughter fading, leaving his face taut and raw. He dropped the coat and sank down on one knee by her boulder, his hand cupping her cheek.

'Lily.'

'You look as though I've said something terrible.'

'Terrifying, not terrible. I've never been so scared in my life of losing something. This feeling keeps…growing and sometimes I can't breathe past it. You've tangled me in so many knots I can't make sense of myself some days.' His voice was as raw as the stone path. She turned her head and kissed his palm.

'That's awful of me.'

'It is. You're pitiless. I love you so damned much, Lily-fox. You must stop making me love you more.'

'Oh, very well. Now, take off your shirt and lie down. This midsummer monster is ready to do some ravishing.'

* * * * *

COMING SOON!

We really hope you enjoyed reading this book. If you're looking for more romance, be sure to head to the shops when new books are available on

Thursday 26th May

To see which titles are coming soon, please visit

millsandboon.co.uk/nextmonth

MILLS & BOON®

Coming next month

HOW TO CATCH A VISCOUNT
Annie Burrows

"You and I must part here," Betsy informed him.

"No. I mean, I am sure I can get Socks, that is, my mare, across this wall."

"That is not it. This is the boundary to my father's land. Once I am on the other side of it, I will be, more or less, home."

His face fell. Then brightened. "You know, if your father really is as knowledgeable about the feelings of the folk in these parts, and so influential, I really ought to visit him and make myself known to him."

"No! I mean, not today, anyway. Or at least, not with me. Not like this! Please!"

He tilted his head to one side. "You really don't want anyone to know we have been alone out here, do you?"

"No!" Her reputation was in a precarious enough state as it was. "You are bound to meet him at church on Sunday. Can you not wait until then? And meet him in a perfectly natural fashion? Everyone is bound to want to know who you are, and once Father learns why you have come here he is bound to want to further your acquaintance, since the state of the Earl's holdings had been vexing him for years."

"If that is the case, could I not simply call on him and pay my respects?"

She turned her back on him and began to scramble over the wall. Even though she could manage perfectly well, and had done on many occasions, he seemed to think he needed to place his hands at her waist to steady her, lest she take a tumble.

It was all she could do to turn and face him once she was safely on the other side. Her body still burned where his hands had been, as if he had left a fiery imprint. And warm tingles were spreading to the rest of her body. She'd never experienced anything like it. Men had touched her before, when helping her alight from a carriage, or during the measures of a dance. But none of their hands had felt as if they'd seared their way through every single layer of clothing she wore.

"P...please don't," she found herself begging him. In regard to what he'd said, rather than what he'd done. "If you were to turn up at the house, I would be sure to give away the fact that I already knew you, by blushing, or being unable to meet your eye, or something of the sort. And Mother, who is a veritable bloodhound when it comes to that sort of thing, would be bound to sniff out the truth, somehow."

"Then, to spare your blushes," he said, giving her that mischievous smile once more, "I shall wait to present myself to your father until Sunday."

"Thank you," she breathed.

"I shall be counting the days," he said.

"I...I..." She would be too, she realised. Not that she could tell him so. Or even let him guess she might be thinking such a thing.

Her head in a whirl, her body tingling, and her heart pounding, Betsy turned away from him, and pelted down the hillside.

Continue reading
HOW TO CATCH A VISCOUNT
Annie Burrows

Available next month
www.millsandboon.co.uk

MILLS & BOON

THE HEART OF ROMANCE

A ROMANCE FOR EVERY READER

MODERN — Prepare to be swept off your feet by sophisticated, sexy and seductive heroes, in some of the world's most glamourous and romantic locations, where power and passion collide.

HISTORICAL — Escape with historical heroes from time gone by. Whether your passion is for wicked Regency Rakes, muscled Vikings or rugged Highlanders, awaken the romance of the past.

MEDICAL — Set your pulse racing with dedicated, delectable doctors in the high-pressure world of medicine, where emotions run high and passion, comfort and love are the best medicine.

True Love — Celebrate true love with tender stories of heartfelt romance, from the rush of falling in love to the joy a new baby brings, and a focus on the emotional heart of a relationship.

Desire — Indulge in secrets and scandal, intense drama and plenty of sizzling hot action with powerful and passionate heroes who have it all: wealth, status, good looks…everything but the right woman.

HEROES — Experience all the excitement of a gripping thriller, with an intense romance at its heart. Resourceful, true-to-life women and strong, fearless men face danger and desire - a killer combination!

To see which titles are coming soon, please visit

millsandboon.co.uk/nextmonth